YOU WHO ENTER HERE

SUNY SERIES, NATIVE TRACES

Jace Weaver and Scott Richard Lyons, editors

You Who Enter Here

ERIKA T. WURTH

EXCELSIOR EDITIONS

AN IMPRINT OF STATE UNIVERSITY OF NEW YORK PRESS

Cover art, Douglas Miles
Book design, Aimee Harrison

Published by State University of New York Press, Albany

© 2019 Erika T. Wurth

Printed in the United States of America

Excelsior Editions is an imprint of State University of New York Press

For information, contact State University of New York Press, Albany, NY
www.sunypress.edu

Library of Congress Cataloging-in-Publication Data

Names: Wurth, Erika T., author.
Title: You who enter here / Erika T. Wurth.
Description: Albany : Excelsior Editions / State University of New York Press,
    [2019] | Series: Suny series, native traces
Identifiers: LCCN 2018015534| ISBN 9781438473161 (paperback : alk. paper) |
    ISBN 9781438473178 (e-book)
Classification: LCC PS3623.U78 Y68 2019 | DDC 813/.6—dc23 LC record
    available at https://lccn.loc.gov/2018015534

10 9 8 7 6 5 4 3 2 1

Abandon all hope,
Ye who enter here.

—Dante Alighieri

ONE

"YOU EVER HELD A GUN BEFORE?"

Matthew glanced down at the slick, silver gun in Chris's stocky brown hand. A sharp, electric feeling coursed through him, and he held his hand out for the gun.

"You wanna hold it?"

"Sure," he said, moving his hand farther out. Chris placed it in Matthew's palm, and he closed his fingers around it, hard.

"Don't worry bro, the safety's on."

"Ha. That's what she said."

"Aw, shit, lame," Chris said. "Lame bro."

"OK," Matthew said, holding it facedown in his long, thin hand.

"You like the feel of that? It's a .22. It's perfect because you can put it here," and with this Chris plucked it expertly out of Matthew's hand and, making sure the safety was on again, tucked it neatly into the back of his oversized khakis, behind his tightly buckled belt. He turned all the way around, his small black eyes beaming with pride, and then pulled it out and handed it back to Matthew. Matthew smiled back. Matthew loved him. He loved him so much.

Chris had cleaned him up. As long as Matthew could remember, he drank, and he wanted to drink, and to drown himself. The urge for it was stronger than the urge for anything. In Farmington, in the apartment he'd grown up in, his mother had started bringing men around, and she would drink, and the men would drink, and some of them would hit Matthew, and some of them would touch him at

1

night while his mother was passed out. "Ishkeh," Chris would always say, "don't take shit from *anyone*, white or Indian. Including me," and Matthew would nod, thinking that he would take any shit from Chris, that he'd do anything for him.

"I like the feel of it a lot," Matthew said, though to be honest, he was feeling more fear than excitement. It was like the gun was a big, angry silver snake that had somehow found its way into Matthew's hand. A snake that was going to bite him long before it bit anyone else.

"We're gonna have to work on getting you your own gun, and that'll take some time."

"You're gonna get me my own gun?" Matthew asked. They were about twenty miles outside of Albuquerque, at the base of the mountains, in a spot the guys used for gun practice. Or just to fuck around, get drunk, and shoot shit for fun. Or sometimes where they took people. A bunch of cans were lined up on old stumps, abandoned car parts, old furniture. Chris laughed.

Matthew could feel the dry, desert wind on his face, the heat winding off the beige and green landscape in waves.

"Of course," he said, patting Matthew on the back. Matthew looked down at the gun suspiciously, like it had a mind of its own, one that Matthew couldn't control. But Matthew was used to feeling like that, like so much was out of his control. Most of the time, he found ways to crawl inside himself, to not be.

"It's not gonna be perfect, but you wanna practice, Ishkeh?"

"Sure," Matthew said.

"Will anyone hear?"

"Not this far out, man."

"OK," Matthew said uneasily, lifting the gun close to his eye.

"Whoa! Wait a minute!" Chris said, clapping his hands on either side of the gun and pointing it quickly, but carefully down at the dusty ground rich with sagebrush. Don't hold it that close to your eye—when it kicks back, and it will, you're gonna do some serious damage to your eye, bro. We need your eye."

"Sorry," Matthew mumbled, embarrassed.

"Don't be sorry. Though damn, kinda funny to think of an Apache who ain't never learned to shoot a gun," Chris said. "You guys were the OG Indian gunslingers, like giving those fucking government cowboys the slip all over the place."

"We're pretty wily," Matthew said, arching an eyebrow.

"Wily my ass, you skinny shit. Just—" and Chris helped Matthew position it in his hands.

"OK," Matthew said, afraid that the way his hands were sweating, he was going to drop the gun and shoot either himself or Chris in the balls. There was something cartoonishly funny about that, and Matthew giggled.

"What you laughing like a six-year-old girl for? Someone be tickling you? Yo, just relax. Don't shoot yet, Ishkeh. Think about— you ever play basketball?"

"Yes," Matthew said. That had been the one sport he hadn't completely sucked at, the one sport that when the ball came toward him, he didn't close his eyes and let it bounce off his head. He had liked the *ping* noise it always made when he dribbled, the rubbery smell the ball had when he lifted it up to his nose. He had gotten pretty good when he was still going to school, before he had completely given up on that, gone to the streets to drink full-time.

"OK, well bro, like think of this the same way," Chris said, running his hand over his shaved head. "Like this shit's fun. And you gotta get in the zone, you know, you can't overthink it."

"Oh, *fuuuuun*," Matthew squealed in a teenage girl's voice.

"Shut the fuck up, Ishkeh, and shoot."

Matthew sighed and tried to relax. He looked at the faded can of Pepsi a few feet away and squeezed the trigger. It kicked back, and he yelled happily, and he could hear Chris laughing and shouting.

"Not bad for your first shot! You hit the TV, man."

Matthew looked at the old television that the coke can was sitting on and saw that there was a new hole.

"You a regular fucking *gangsta*," Chris said, and they both laughed. Chris patted Matthew's shoulder affectionately, and Matthew felt good.

"Don't get cocky on me now," Chris said, and Matthew laughed. "Man, I been raised in this shit, like, Pee-Wee to OG," Chris said, running his short, callused hands over his shaved head. "But I think we can get you up to par. You gotta be ready to heart-check though yo."

"Heart check?" Matthew asked, frowning.

"Yeah, I mean, it's no biggie, just shit the guys are gonna want to see you do, like you know, in front of God, just to make sure you're in it to win it. You know, to make sure you're down."

"I'm down," Matthew said seriously, and Chris laughed, hard.

"Bro, I know you down. You down as hell, but you know how it is, it's tough this shit, this slanging drugs and shit, and dudes gotta make sure other dudes have each other's backs or shit gets fucked fast."

Matthew was silent for a while and then nodded. "Can I try again?" he asked.

"Hell, yeah. That's what I brought you here for."

"Cool," Matthew said, and held the gun back up.

"OK, remember, don't hold it too close to your eye, and remember everything else I told you on the way up."

"OK," Matthew said, and took another breath. He shot, and this time he missed even the television. It spun somewhere deep into the cracked, brown desert.

"That's OK, that's OK, just keep practicing."

"OK," Matthew said, and held the gun up again. They were there for a few hours, Chris getting some shots in as well, and by the end of the day, Matthew had hit the can twice.

"OK, rock star, let's go the fuck out on the town to celebrate. I wanna give some bitches some dolla dolla bills y'all."

"Like just hand them some dolla dolla bills or what?" Matthew asked playfully, following Chris back to the SUV.

"Nah, son. You know I make them work for it."

"Like as in hire them to move furniture?"

4

"Very funny playa," Chris said, and Matthew got into the driver's side and sunk back into the seat.

"What about . . . about Maria?" Matthew asked tentatively.

Chris frowned. "Yo, *fuck* that bitch. I don't wanna hear another word about that cunt today."

"OK," Matthew said, feeling bad. He scratched awkwardly at the side of his wide, brown face.

"Wanna Bud?" Chris asked. They had brought a cooler, one of those cheap foam coolers that you could buy at Smith's for a couple of dollars.

"Sure," Matthew said. He reached back and got one for both of them, his arm thrusting deep into the ice. Matthew cracked the beer open, the sound of it beautiful, the taste of the foamy, tart beer trailing down his throat something he tried not to enjoy too much. That was the thing. As soon as he got the taste of one beer in his mouth, he wanted another. And another. But he was getting better about that.

When Matthew allowed himself to think about why he drank, which wasn't very often, he thought about running up to his mother when he was very little, hoping she'd hold him, let him sit on his lap. She smelled of lavender soap and beer. But there was always a man there, and if he didn't slap him away like he was some sort of stray cat, his mother would. He would go to the white-walled bedroom he shared with his sister and curl into the dirty sheets and cry, the sound of his mother's laugher echoing throughout the tiny apartment. That was the thing with Maria. She was tough, like his mom. But she also knew how to be sweet. Sweet in a way that got to him.

Chris turned the Tupac up. "California" echoed throughout the gray pleather interior of the SUV.

"Yo this song is *the shit* son," Chris said, turning the radio up and rolling the window down.

"It is so much shit," Matthew said, and Chris hit him in the arm, both of them giggling like little girls, rolling his window down too. Matthew's thing had always been classic rock and heavy metal. Especially death metal. But Chris loved hip-hop, especially Tupac.

Chris took a swig of his Bud and wiped at his mouth, looking over at Matthew and smiling.

"You know what? When we hit it big time, this is gonna be a big black Escalade. And we'll be drinking nothing but Cristal, son. *Shiiiiit.*"

"What's that?" Matthew said, and Chris laughed.

"You ain't never seen that shit in a rap video?" Chris asked incredulously, while Matthew threw his arms around himself in exaggerated gang posture, his lips poking out.

"*Yeeahhhh giiiirll*," he said, and Chris told him to shut the fuck up.

Chris swallowed nearly his entire beer in a couple of long gulps and then tossed the empty can into the back. "It's champagne. The best fucking champagne in the world, *mothafucka*, that's why gangsters and rappers and rich white fuckers drink it. And soon we'll be doing nothing but celebrating with Cristal like glued to our *fucking hands.* You'll see."

"Sounds good," Matthew said. "Scary, 'cause once superglue gets on you, it's like, really hard to take off. But still good."

"Hell, yeah, it sounds good—it sounds great. Hand me another Bud," Chris said, and Matthew reached in the back again, pulled another Bud out of the cooler, pulled the tab back and handed it to Chris.

"Thanks bro," Chris said.

"Sure," Matthew said.

After a few minutes of singing along with Tupac, Chris turned the music down and said, "I'm serious. You and me and the rest of the 505s. We gonna be living the high life. I've heard shit about guys who've worked their way up and got mansions on the edge of their reservations."

"Really?" Matthew said, but he'd only spent a few days at a time on his mother's reservation where she had lived until she was a teenager until her father had gotten a job in Farmington through a relocation program.

"Yeah, man, I mean, like I'm an urban Skin, but I know where I come from, you know what I mean?" Chris said, and took a long drink.

"Yeah," Matthew said.

"You know son, suddenly I don't feel like fooling with those goldiggin bitches up at the strip joint. What you say we head home and just have a few beers, kick back, and get mothafuckin high as hell."

"Sounds good to me," Matthew said, and Chris worked his mouth into an uneasy, crooked smile.

Matthew knew what was up. Chris was worried about Maria. But he didn't want to admit it. Didn't want to seem weak, call her.

Matthew thought about Maria and sighed, heavily. They weren't far from home. Maybe when they got there, her car would be in the drive, and she would be sitting on the couch, a cigarette in one long brown hand, and an old paperback in the other. He looked out the window at the sagebrush, the red red earth, the beige mountains blurring past him as they sped home to the house they shared with the rest of the 505s.

But Maria wasn't there. And though Chris tried not to show it, he was disappointed, hurt. Angry. And to be honest, though it made him feel strange, so was Matthew. Matthew had plopped down on one of their ratty couches, Chris on the other, adjacent to the one Matthew was sitting on. They were passing a joint back and forth. Matthew liked weed, though not nearly as much as Chris did. Chris liked to go on and on about all of the things it cured, including HIV and cancer, which Matthew highly doubted but said nothing to contradict. But along with the companionship he got from the guys, weed nearly killed Matthew's usually insatiable desire for alcohol. That much it did cure.

"You remember your father?"

Matthew was silent for a while. Then, "A little. Yeah. I visited him once."

"What was he like?"

"Well," Matthew said, handing the joint back to Chris and lighting a cigarette, "I remember that him and my mom argued a lot, though he was gone by the time I was ... I don't know ... I don't remember. I was so young. But I know I look like him. He's also got that *greeeasssy* black hair."

"That's for the ladies," Chris said, and Matthew nodded.

"He's Apache. Mescalero and Chiricahua. He lives here, actually, in Albuquerque." Matthew exhaled and was silent for a moment. Then, "Well, he did live here. I guess he might still."

Matthew had sought him out once. His father had grown up in Farmington, and as far as Matthew knew, had no interest in going back to his father's reservation, the Mescalero reservation. He had been living in a tiny, shitty apartment in Albuquerque, his television his only company. They had sat there watching it, and drinking, until Matthew had left.

"I thought you were Nav, bro," Chris said, taking another toke and gesturing with it toward Matthew, who shook his head no, as he was beginning to feel really, really high. Chris, he was never high enough.

"My mom's Navajo. Though both of my parents are part white too," he said.

"Ain't no shame in that game," Chris said. "Nah. No shame, no shame at all."

"No. I guess not," Mathew said, not really understanding why Chris was saying that. "And he was like me ... kind of quiet. So maybe that's why my mom always hated me."

"Hmmmm..."

Chris shifted on the couch, and looked at Matthew for a moment before responding. Matthew could tell he was getting to that point in his high where he might start rambling.

"Yeah. My mom was a bitch," Chris said.

"Really?" Matthew said, feeling his stomach twist. He hated his mother too, but it always bothered him when Chris talked about his mother or Maria this way. Especially Maria.

"Yeah. She drank too, and I never even met my dad. He was Mexican. But I always wished he would come back and we could run away together, to some city like New York. I mean, I visited my mother's people and there's nothing to do on the reservation but herd sheep and work for Peabody coal and shit. And I ain't into that. No way."

Matthew laughed. "Yeah. I can't picture you herding sheep."

"Ya'ta'eehhhhhh little cousin," Chris said, sounding like one of those sweet old Diné guys you'd see in town doing errands with their wives sometimes.

"Yeah, man, like, with a cane and shit."

"Here little sheepie," Matthew said.

They both started laughing hysterically, Chris's laugh ending in a long, harsh cough.

"Oh shit, oh, shit," Chris said.

Once they'd both stopped laughing, Chris took another toke, gestured again to Matthew who again shook his head no and said, "Speaking of bitches, I'ma call mine."

"Oh," Matthew said, feeling his stomach twist again. He had hoped Chris had let it go. Matthew grew silent, and Chris took yet another toke, then set the joint down. Maria had grown up in a foster home in Albuquerque. She had met Chris at a party when they were twelve and they had been together, relatively speaking, ever since. She was tough. She carried Chris's gun for him in her giant purse. She carried a short, wide knife in there too—but that was for her.

"I'ma call that bitch," Chris said, repeating himself, and Matthew sighed, heavily.

Chris dug his phone out of the pocket of his oversized khakis, and sat with it to his ear. Finally, Maria picked up.

"Where you at?" Then, "So, get out of it. You told me you was going to be here. So? Get the fuck over here!" Chris's expression turned from one of frustration to pure rage. "Fuck you? Fuck you too, bitch!" He threw the phone across the room. It hit the yellowing wall and landed a few feet from Matthew.

"Stupid bitch!"

"Maybe . . . maybe she's just high," Matthew offered, tentatively.

Chris looked at him with fire in his eyes. "Ishkeh, don't *ever* tell me about my woman!"

Matthew nodded but felt something like anger, though he pushed it down, away.

"She's always fucking high! She can't control herself! What the fuck is wrong with her? I went through shit! Terrible shit! And I still got control. I told her to get off the fucking H! That shit is nothing but death, and that's something we sell to other people, weak mother-fuckers. There's one thing I can't respect and that is, man or woman, a bitch with no control." Chris lifted the joint and sucked violently, looking so much like a baby with a bottle that Matthew had to refrain from laughing. After a few minutes, Chris seemed to calm down. His phone rang from across the room, the ring tone "Gold Digger." Chris walked over, scooped it up from the old, gray carpet, answered and said nothing, his expression petulant, sullen. Matthew could hear Maria on the other side, the silvery phone large in Chris's short, wide hand.

"So are you coming?"

Matthew watched him, Chris's expression one of anxiousness.

"Cool," he said, and hung up. "She's coming," he said, and as hardcore as he wanted to look, he seemed relieved. Matthew knew everything about this routine. He remembered it from his childhood. His mom had played it out with man after man.

Chris sat down and hung his head between his knees, the way you're supposed to do on a plane in the event of a crash. He ran his short, brown hand over his shaved head and took another hit from his pipe—the dank green smell filling the room like a fog.

"Crazy bitch," he said, but Matthew could hear how happy he was.

"You like crazy bitches," Matthew said, offering a kind of apology.

"Yeah, I do. I really do. If they ain't crazy, they ain't no fun."

Matthew sighed. Chris was sucking on his joint again, and as Matthew stared at his wide, childlike face, the hate began to boil up, just a bit. He closed his eyes. With Chris he felt for the first time in his life that he had a home, a family, that he belonged. He had gotten his first tat with Chris, looking up while the silver needle drove into his skin and smiled, thinking of all of the times Chris would try and wrestle with him the way a dad might've, or an older brother, his short muscular arms pulling Matthew's tall skinny frame into a headlock. Matthew would laugh, and struggle, and tell him to fuck the fuck off, but he loved it.

He opened his eyes and reached for the joint. He wondered how this night would turn out. Probably not well.

TWO

"MARIA! GET THE FUCKING GUN OUT YOUR PURSE, BITCH! *Goddamnit* you dumb fucking cunt, hurry!"

Chris was angry again, really angry. They were in the middle of a smash and grab and someone was coming around the corner and yelling, and his boys were panicking. Maria was just sitting there in the backseat staring at her phone instead of doing what she should be doing, which was handing Chris the gun she had in her fake leather, fringe purse. She liked to ride along during the smash and grabs, during the drive-bys—she liked the drama, the blood. But right now she was staring at her phone slack-jawed, ignoring Chris either on purpose or because she was about to nod off. Matthew had watched her as she had gotten in the car, that sleepy, dopey expression in her eyes, that loose way her legs swung with each step.

For about a week, they had scoped out a little corner store on the west side of Albuquerque, the territory of a rival gang. It was small, shitty, smelly, and Chris was sure that the security would be minimal. They had waited until about two in the morning to back Chris's big, black Ford SUV into the side of the faded adobe building with the most window.

This, Chris told Matthew, would mean something. The OGs were going to see this and they were going to look good, get more opportunities. The key, Chris said, was to show them that they were willing to do anything, and that included going to jail if they had to. Matthew had spent some time in detox, and he figured

13

proper jail couldn't be much worse. He didn't mind. He loved Chris, and he was willing to do what he had to, what Chris told him was good.

When they had backed the old, solid SUV into the windows, one of the windows smashed up but hadn't come down, and the other one just cracked—one long crack from the point of impact and up a few inches. And the alarm had gone off. And it was loud. Matthew knew that it meant the cops would be coming, and soon.

"Do it again!" Chris yelled. Matthew was driving.

Matthew had thrown the SUV into drive, the car screeching forward. He put on the brakes and threw the car back into reverse, hard. This time both windows were smashed up good. Chris and the other guys had scrambled out of the car and were busily stuffing cash from the register into their pockets when they had heard yelling outside.

Matthew's job was to stand watch. He had seen the guy come around the corner, and he knew it would be trouble. He was an older Mexican guy, and he was yelling at them in Spanish, about how they needed to leave, to get lost, to behave. Matthew stared at him, and something about the man reminded him of one of the men his mother had taken up with. That man had come into their lives right when Matthew had thought he had finally gotten his mother all to himself. That man was the first to touch Matthew.

Matthew whipped the .22 out of the back of his jeans and without thinking shot the man, three times. He and Chris had been practicing a lot, and he had gotten good. He had always been somewhat of a natural. The man looked surprised, like it was his own nephew who had turned on him, and in fact, he did look a little like Matthew, tall and skinny and brown. As the man fell, the boys went silent, still.

"Shit! Oh, damn, bro! You went all Kamikaze bro!" Chris said, running up to him and slapping him on the back. Matthew looked over at Chris and then down at the man. He was not the man who had touched him. He was just a man from this neighborhood. Matthew

14

watched the blood pool around him, the light going out of the man's eyes. Matthew turned to Chris and smiled weakly. "Did I do good?"

Chris laughed hard. "Shit yeah!" Then Chris turned to the guys who were staring at Chris and Matthew. Matthew, who until that moment had just been Chris's strange, quiet project. "You stupid fucking ... get the fuck moving before the cops come! We gotta 'nother smash and grab at a pawn shop to do before the sun comes up you stupid fuckers, so let's go!"

The guys in the store, one of them fourteen years old, a short, stocky Pueblo boy, a neighborhood kid who had been nothing but a Pee-Wee a number of years ago until Chris finally moved him into the house, stopped staring and continued to shove the rest of the cash into their pockets. Two of them started scrambling out of the window and running toward the SUV.

The other guy was Mexican and Navajo, and maybe sixteen. His name was Damien. He had popped his head up when he'd heard the shots, and then got back to smashing at a safe under the register with a hammer. The whole drive there, he had been saying, "Yeah, fuck, I brought this hammer, see? 'Cause I know these fuckers gotta have a safe for the big bills under the register. And when I bring back them Benjamins, those OGs, they gotta take notice, you know what I'm saying?"

Chris had just nodded while Matthew teased him saying, "Yeah bro, we got it. Your *Benjamins*," while the other guys laughed. Matthew had known what Chris had been thinking. That it was not going to work, that the kid would be hammering away at the safe when the cops came—a nice distraction for the rest of them, that he could be someone who could take the blame.

"Ya'll are minors, so don't worry," Chris had said, staring intently at the road as they drove. "If you get caught, it ain't no thang."

"Nothin but a G-thang, bay-bay," Matthew had starting singing in a high-pitched, female voice until Chris told him to shut up.

"Just a stint in juvie, which ain't nothing compared to real jail. Unless you up and murder some poor fucker. In which case you'll be a

God," he had said, and laughed. Matthew remembered feeling angry at Chris again for this. He tried to push it down, but he didn't like it.

"Go," Chris said softly, after the first two kids, who'd stuffed all the cash into the pockets of their oversized jeans had jumped into the backseat next to Maria, who looked like she had just woken up from a nap in a Lay-Z-Boy because something interesting had happened on TV. Matthew had hit the pedal.

"What about Da..." one of the kids said from the back, and Chris had stared at him in the rearview mirror until he shut up.

"He's getting his Benjamins *now*," the other kid said, shaking his head, and Matthew suddenly very felt sorry for Damien.

Chris turned around and looked at Maria who stared back at him. "What," she finally said listlessly, looking back down at her phone as Chris's hand came around.

"You stupid bitch!" he said and slapped her, hard.

"Chris—" Matthew said, and Chris had time to give Matthew a look of pure rage before Maria looked up sharply from her phone, her long, black hair swinging as she did. "You cunt! You fucking—! How dare you!" she said, pulling her skinny, scarred arm up and rearing back.

"You dumb bitch, can't even count on you for the gun! That's all you gotta do you *stupid junkie whore*. I should dump you out right here!" Chris said, holding her fist. She wrestled to grab it out of his hand, hitting him on the face over and over while the kids in the back pulled themselves as far away from their fight as possible. It was almost funny, because Maria was so strong that half the time she nearly won, and Chris, a dude who'd killed men, would flinch with every blow.

Matthew just kept his eyes on the road, but it took everything inside him to not try to stop this, to hate Chris, just a little bit. More than a little.

"I *want out* you stupid fucker! Puta! Let me *out*," she screamed, pulling her hand out of Chris's grip. "Matthew pull over! Now!"

Matthew cut his eyes over to Chris.

"Yeah! Fine bitch. Get the fuck out. That way I don't have to stare at your useless, slutty face anymore," Chris said, and turned around and sat back in his seat.

Matthew pulled over, and Maria opened the door and practically leapt out of the car, slamming the door as hard as she could behind her, lifting her phone quickly to her ear. Matthew could see Chris watching her in the rearview mirror as the car pulled away.

"We ... got enough people for the next smash and grab?" Matthew asked quietly, the rage inside him still quietly boiling.

"Fuck yeah. We got who counts. Fuck that bitch." Chris went silent and took his phone out of his back pocket and stared at it. "Oh, fuuuuck," he said, sighing and rubbing his head.

"What?" Matthew asked, thinking maybe Chris might express some regret. He felt a little better.

"Dumb bitch'll sell the gun for drug money. Fuck ... just ... go back so I can get it from her."

Matthew sighed, turned around and drove back the way they'd come. Maria was nowhere in sight.

"Fuck!" Chris yelled, hitting the dash hard with both of his thick, short hands. He was silent for a minute, and then he said, "You know what, fuck it. That's one gun. If we can get a bunch of guns, shit, it'll all be worth it. Let's go. Hit it."

Matthew did. The pawn shop they were going to hit was on the East side, and they had been scoping it out too. Better security. Bigger risk. But even bigger show of power if they succeeded.

Matthew wondered where Maria went. If she had hooked up with some of her junkie friends. She and Chris fought like this all the time and it was something Matthew found both comfortably familiar and disturbing at the same time. Whenever they'd fight like this, Chris would get really impatient and short-tempered, pace the long yellow hallway of their apartment, start fights with younger guys living in the house. Matthew knew to stay away when he was like that. After a few days, he would stand over Matthew on the couch, and Matthew would look up and just know. Chris had been calling around. He had a lead on where Maria was. Matthew would get up, put his phone in his pocket, get his .22 and they'd hop in the SUV. Sometimes they'd get her on the first try. The place that Maria liked to hole up was in the valley, in this big abandoned house that the junkies had taken over. Usually, they would go there first, and they'd go through the whole collapsing, stinking building until they found her. She was generally passed out in a corner—dirty, skinnier than ever. Chris would pull her up, tell her that he was taking her home, tell her that he was going to get her a bath and some food, that she needed to stop. "I will baby," she would say sometimes, or "You know I can't." Chris would pick her up either way, and though there were times she would try to fight him, she was too weak to really resist and they'd throw her in the back of the SUV like a sack of potatoes. She would cry on the way back, and Chris would comfort her, tell her that he was going to make everything all right. Then, at home, he'd bathe her like a child, soaping her hair as she cried, sometimes crying too. Matthew wondered what had made Chris feel this tenderness toward her. Maybe it was because they had met when they were young. Before she had become like this. Maybe it was the memory of tenderness, of promise, of youth. He wouldn't know.

Outside the pawn shop, keeping watch, Matthew didn't see the cop car until it was too late. He knew he could run, and that maybe he could make it but he didn't want to leave Chris who had gone in with one of the kids. This time they'd had to back into the place over and over, as there were iron bars on the windows and the car had stalled at one point. But Chris wouldn't give up. It's part of why Matthew liked him. Why he loved him. He was full of life, while Matthew was filled with darkness, death. He didn't know why they were different in this way; it wasn't as if Chris had grown up any better than he had. His life had been one foster home after another, after his mother had finally and totally abandoned him. Once they'd finally gotten enough of the bars to bend and then break, Chris and the kid had scrambled in, a couple of giant black trash bags in hand.

"Don't move," the cops yelled, cars screeching to a halt in front of them, red and blue lights everywhere.

"Shit, shit, run Ishkehs!" Chris screamed running for the SUV, his short, muscular legs working hard.

Shots rang out. Matthew could swear that he felt a sting in his arm, and he could hear Damien cry out. He turned around and Damien had hit the pavement, his hand over his chest. Matthew froze as he heard another shot, the cops running toward them.

"Naw, naw son!" Chris cried, and Matthew felt another shot hit him.

THREE

"WE GOT MAD RESPECT NOW, YO!" CHRIS SAID. "AND WE ABOUT TO *blow up.*"

Though this made Matthew feel uneasy, he walked around posing in goofy exaggerated rap-postures, bending deeply to the floor like he was Eminem and posing for the camera, his lips kissing the air hard, his arms wrapped around his thin body. Chris laughed, smoke shooting out of his mouth as he did.

Prison had been all about hiding razors in his mouth, in his ass, about yellow cards outside his cell identifying him as a Native and in a gang, about fishlines moving toward him in the dark his first night in, about talking with Stanford, an OG in the 505s that had been in there for a few years and was about to be let out, about weeks in isolation living with your mind tearing itself apart, about learning. About throwing signs when he knew that no one but the person they were meant for was looking. About reading when he had a few minutes to himself in the prison library.

Most importantly, it had been about making new connections.

In prison, Matthew had finally been ranked in. It happened in the laundry room, the washers and dryers making a loud clanking noise that covered everything.

He was told he would be a *fucking woman* if he cried out just one time.

The man who hit him first was a homie who had been in for a good long time, and a survivor of a number of shootouts, José. He and

21

Matthew had talked in the weight room together, lifting, Matthew spotting for him. José was short but huge, and covered in tattoos, his arms spilling ink from one shoulder to the other: the roadrunner, New Mexico–style women with long black-eyelined eyes and huge breasts, the state of New Mexico with those distinctive lines on top indicating Aztec blood and language, the thunderbird with 505 in Roman numerals across his chest. And scars from bullets in his side, his leg, and half a pinky missing from when he was ranked in a few years back.

"Take it, bitch," one of the men waiting to join yelled. He was new. They were making all kinds of new friends, friends who could do things for them, friends who were part of the Mexican gang that was going to bring in new drugs, line up more junkies.

José's fist was coming down, hard, his face a sharp, expressionless line of grim determination, and Matthew waited for it like it was a sunset. He held himself up for as long as he could, taking the blows to his face, his shoulder, his sides, until José's friend began to kick him in the legs, and he buckled. That's when Chris came in. He looked over at him, keeping himself quiet, expressionless. He knew that this was a test for Chris too; they knew they were tight. But their ultimate loyalty had to be the 505s. Chris kicked him hard, taking turns with José and the other guy until he was all the way down, his arms covering his face like a child, and he began to bleed in earnest now, his mind blurring toward the gray until finally a great wave of something washed him ashore and mercifully, out to sea.

He'd spent a few days in the prison hospital, but though he was still in incredibly rough shape, his arm in a wide white sling, the prison budget was such that if a man could walk, he left the hospital.

In the cafeteria, over the brown plastic trays filled with government food not unlike the kind he'd grown up on, the guys smiled at him, and rubbed his bald head, and punched him on his good arm gently. Chris had convinced him to shave his head, which felt weird for him, as he'd always kept his hair long, which was black and shiny, like his dad's.

22

"Bro, it's your birthday tomorrow. Guess what we gonna give you?" Chris asked, sitting down and looking down at his soppy-looking hamburger and then back up at Matthew.

"That cuuuuute purse I been eyeballing in the mall?" Matthew asked, his long black eyes soft.

"Yeah the pink one, you pussy," Chris said, cuffing him on the head. "Nah son, we gonna get you a tat, sure, but we've arranged for a sweat. Yeah, that's right. Motherfuckas gotta give us our religious freedom. That they gotta do and so out back, some of the 505 are preparing that shit right now."

A couple of the 505s nodded communally.

Matthew sighed. Felt something rise up. "My mom said NAC was a bunch of shit, that that Road Men just took her money for ceremonies. That it didn't do her any good," Matthew said, squirming a little on the bench.

"Yo homes," Chris said, rolling his eyes, *"Fuck* yo momma."

The men at the table laughed, and Matthew felt a strange mixture of elation and hatred.

Chris had told him that he'd sit right by him and sing, Stanford leading the way with the peyote songs, and watch out for him like he was his own baby brother. And he did. And Matthew was strong, he sang with them and prayed, and when he came out, he felt new.

Matthew was allowed to recoup for a bit. It took a long time for his arm to completely heal, and he worried it wouldn't heal right, and that he'd be a liability to the 505s, to Chris, that they would have to get rid of him once he was on the outside. But it healed well, and the cast came off, and a month later, he was out. And three months later, Chris was out. And they were back in their old house, with some new guys. Matthew began to feel like a man. Chris had two new tears tattooed under his left eye.

"I wasn't gonna let that bitch fuck with us," he said, sitting on the couch and smoking a joint. He was talking about one of the men he'd had to kill in prison, the snitch. How he'd told him that he had some shit to tell him about getting some H in through the prison, in the kitchen, where both of them worked. He told him to follow him to the freezer. It had been a guard that the 505s bribed who'd told someone, an OG called Béésh who was in there for life, that the guy had leaked information. The guy had looked into Chris's eyes, Chris said, and at that moment, they both knew that he was going to die.

"You gotta earn *that shit son*," Chris said, pointing to one of the teardrops. Matthew felt cold.

The door opened, and Maria came in, looking good, like she had been off H for a while. She plopped down next to Chris and lit up a cigarette—the smoke floating up and around her head, her hand moving through her long, thick black hair. Mathew shuddered and lit up a cigarette of his own.

Chris and Maria had run into each other at a party, right after Chris got out, as usual. After a few minutes, they were walking off together toward a bedroom. Matthew didn't understand them. He didn't really understand love, though. When he had been out on the streets as a kid, sometimes he would have sex with junkies, even though those women could be rough. There had been one his age, a sweet girl from a family like his. A Mexican girl named Nita with black gloves and lots and lots of black rubber bracelets on her long, scared, skinny arms who he'd taken up with for a time. But one day, he'd come back to the edge of the park, and he could see that there was an ambulance, and he stopped. He watched from afar as they put Nita's blanketed, lifeless body onto the gurney, shoved her brutally into the ambulance, and slammed the doors shut. He began to drink even harder. Not long after, he found his way into Albuquerque, waking up in the bed of a truck moving south on highway 550. That's when Chris found him.

His feelings for Nita had been quiet. But the way Maria was with Chris, it was more like how his mother had been with her men, though Matthew felt uncomfortable whenever that thought would come. Chris told Matthew once that his mother had been a junkie too, that that's how she had died. That the foster homes he'd been in were where he'd learned about the 505s, that his foster mother worked for

24

them, that she had the kids she adopted doing errands for the 505s, and that it was the best home he'd ever been in. He still went over to see his foster mother, to recruit from there, see who he thought was good enough to leave the home and come live with them, so they could start on their way to OG, if they were lucky. If they lived.

Maria looked at Matthew and smiled, and he smiled back. She was wearing a pair of tight jeans and a lacy red tank top, her long, black hair sweeping down her back like an oceanic tide. She was looking over at Chris, her eyes narrowed. He was now going on about their new connections, the ones he'd made in prison with the Mexican gang. How they were going to go big. The whole thing made Matthew uneasy. He knew how it worked. Indian gangs had to stay small. That's how they survived.

Maria learned into Chris and kissed the side of his face.

"Nah," he said. He didn't like it when she gave him too much in the way of public affection. Or if she talked too much. But if she left his side at a party, he would become furious and start screaming for her. She leaned back, a petulant expression on her face. He really didn't understand why Chris had to do that. Maria was so beautiful.

Matthew had gotten a new tattoo when he came out. He looked at it, still healing and rubbed his hand down his arm.

"I like it," Maria said, and Matthew looked up, sharply. He hadn't realized she'd been watching him.

"Thanks," Matthew said shyly, and she smiled.

Thinking about his waterbird tattoo made him think about his grandmother, the Navajo one, the one he had loved to visit on his mother's reservation. She had held him in her lap in a big old stuffed chair, told him about Native American Church, about his clans. She had spoken to him in Diné, and she told dirty jokes. She was gentle and had soft, lined hands, and she would make him and his mother and sister blue-corn pork tamales in her tiny house, looking unhappily at her daughter, who would respond back to her angrily in English and Navajo and roll her eyes, asking her, "So will you watch the kids or what?"

"I got one too, you know," Maria said, lifting the sleeve of her small lacy red tank top just enough so that he could see it. The tank had mini-sleeves, just enough to obscure the design. The tattoo was red, yellow, and blue, and he wondered why he hadn't noticed it before.

"I like it," he said.

"I thought you would," she responded, cocking her head a little.

He laughed, and looked over at Chris. He was still going on about the dude he'd killed in prison, and Matthew was thankful for that. He turned back to Maria.

"You NAC?"

"Yeah," she said. "That and Catholic."

"Really?"

"Lot of Pueblos are both Native American Church and Catholic."

"You got a tattoo for that too?" he teased.

"I do."

Matthew couldn't help it, he wanted to see it. And more of her.

When his grandmother would fall asleep, he would turn the old black-and-white down, and he would read. One of his teachers had taken him aside in junior high, noting the books that he always had tucked under his arm with the stickers from the school's library on them, and handed him a worn copy of *Dante's Inferno*, telling him to keep it. When he had decided becoming homeless in Farmington was easier than putting up with his mother's men, he would go to the library to find the book, and he would sit down with it in one of the old, wooden chairs that they had in the lobby with the badly cushioned seats until the urge to drink or the malevolent looks of library patrons forced him outside. And one day he had snuck the hard-backed copy of the *Inferno* out, though he felt guilty about it.

He thought of that and of his Shimásáni and felt sad.

"Where is it?" he asked softly.

"Right here," she whispered back, and Matthew could feel his stomach tremble as she patted the thigh of her tight jeans.

"Harder to see that," he said.

"Only if you real real lucky," she said, laughing.

"C'mon," Chris said, standing up and taking her hand.

Matthew started. He didn't know how much Chris had heard of their exchange, and he felt guilty. Chris had been good to him.

Maria sighed and let Chris lead her toward the bedroom. He was the only one in the house who had his own bedroom, besides Matthew. Chris had made sure that Matthew got his own room, and that had made Matthew know he was special.

Right before they disappeared in the hallway, she looked back and smiled again at Matthew. He smiled back, almost involuntarily, and felt strange.

FOUR

"LOOK AT THESE FUCKERS RUN," CHRIS SAID, LAUGHING. THEY WERE watching a couple of guys from rival gangs run through their yards, their khakis cutting a path through the dirt, leaving red dust in their wake. They were on another drive-by because someone had done one in their neighborhood, and they had to have retribution.

Matthew nodded and hoped that no one innocent was hurt, was hit. He knew children died from these things. Of course, who was innocent. Who was a child. All of them were, none of them.

Chris and Matthew and a couple of kids from the house had left around sunset, the reds and the oranges crashing around them while they cruised over to the West Side of Burque in their old blue coupe. Chris had bought it for nothing at the dealer's because he liked the classics and because he knew how to work on cars. The mountains had faded in the rearview mirror as they went, the sun setting in front of them. It was spring. They could smell the sweet white-and-yellow honeysuckle growing in spurts on the edges of Central.

Chris enjoyed the drive-bys the most. He said it was like shooting fish in a barrel. He also said it was more exciting than smash and grabs, because that rarely involved people. But they were getting past the point of having to prove themselves through smash and grabs, drive-bys, random acts of violence. They were moving toward OG status, because they had survived. Soon it would be about the management of H. Not that they would escape the rest of it. In fact, Matthew knew the OGs had to be tougher on their own boys than on random people. Random people, people they held for money, people they fucked with, they were scared of them. The homies coming up, they had been born, most of the time, into this, and they thought they were invincible, even though they'd all seen people around them die. The key was to rough them up, then show them love.

And though it had worried Matthew, the connections they'd made in prison were paying off. They *were* getting big.

They had slowed down, and Matthew and Chris had pulled their guns out of their laps and took aim outside the window, the kid driving slowing just enough, the wheels whispering on the pavement. They had heard that a bunch of dudes from the gang who had taken out one of their own a week ago and shot up two of them really good—good enough to put the both of them in the hospital—were going to be out hanging in front of a convenience store, slanging and talking and generally doing business.

They were there. All of them slouching pridefully in front of bright signs of the store, each sign proclaiming in large, cursive numbers the price of fruit, Doritos, cigarettes. This gang had fewer Indians, more Mexicans, New Mexicans, though of course those things were gray. Matthew sighed, hard. There were women and kids there too, and Matthew aimed low, hoping to hit a few of them in the legs, teach them a lesson. Do what he needed to do. Chris, however, his gun was aimed high. Matthew sighed again, thought that if he squeezed a few off before Chris did, the driver would be forced to squeal out of there before the cops were called, before any identifications could be made. Matthew watched a couple of girls, with their long, highlighted hair and sharp nails, their shy smiles. One of them even kind of looked like his sister. These girls were tough, but they were shy in a way too. They would smash a bitch's head up against concrete if they thought she was looking at their man the wrong way, and Matthew knew women had gone to prison for killing women they found out had fucked around with their men. They went to prison over their man in one way or another, for holding drugs, guns, whatever their men needed. But even with their long, black-lined eyes and mouths set in tough lines he could tell they were just like him, all they wanted was softness, some kind of human moment to hold onto when they were alone at night, maybe in a cell, maybe in their own bedrooms they shared with sisters in the back of their mother's houses.

Matthew shot quickly again. Again. Screams ensued, and he could hear Chris firing off as many shots as he could and laughing maniacally and then telling the driver, "Go, fucking go you pendejo, before the cops are called!" The car screeched off into the night, and Matthew prayed that none of the girls, none of the kids were hurt. Or at least not too bad. But they had to learn. Many kids, women had been either killed or injured, some of them permanently, in their neighborhood. And the 505s were getting strong, getting a reputation for having money, for being ruthless. Matthew was a lot of the reason for this. He tried not to hit women and children. But the men, those he hit.

"Shit yeah!" Chris said. "Shit! I hope we hit those fuckers hard! So hard they think twice about coming back around. Stupid bitches!" Chris said, pulling a joint out of his pocket and taking a hit.

"Any sign of cops, Ishkeh?" Chris asked Damien, who was driving. He had been released from juvie and had come running back to them as soon as he could.

"No man," he said, and Chris nodded and took a hit and passed it to Matthew.

"Let's get fucked up. I wanna celebrate."

Matthew nodded, and Chris put the joint out and pulled his phone up, shot a couple of texts off. Soon they were inside Palms throwing signs on Academy and San Mateo, Chris giggling like a little boy as the women on the stage, coated in glitter and cheap vanilla-smelling lotion leaned down toward him, shook, danced, and made love to the metallic pole sticking out of the floor. Matthew often thought of Palms as a big, pulsing poisonous womb, one that Chris couldn't help but fall into, the building the color of a shirt someone had bought for a dollar at the local Walmart, pot-bellied men smoking outside, the music pulsing into the streets at almost all hours of the day. Palms was a place that they went for entertainment,

31

and it doubled as a place that helped them traffic. The owner was a friend, and the owner helped them sell a lot of H.

"Damn, I gotta get me a lap dance," Chris said. "Want one?"

"Sure," Matthew said. He didn't, but he knew he had to act like he did, or he'd never hear the end of it.

"That's my Ishkeh," Chris said. "Get that pussy."

Sometimes the strippers would go home with Chris. They knew about the 505s, and though the majority of guys in gangs were poor, lived with their parents still or lived in a house, once you moved up, once you survived, if you were smart, you could make some bank. And Chris loved to look like he had money. He loved to flash it. And he was making friends with the real OGs, especially a guy named Myron who knew that Matthew and Chris were a strong team, that together, they had made the 505s look good, had helped to really put their name on the map.

"Baby you smell so good," Chris was murmuring in a stripper's ear. He liked the dark ones, the ones with the big, ripe bodies like fruit, the ones with the least on. She was smiling back at him with her eyes lowered, her body rippling and smashing into his lap, her friend approaching Matthew.

He smiled at her. She began to do the same as her friend. Matthew knew that she was a lot like him: she wasn't really there. She had to act a certain way, but whoever she was, was deep inside. She did this to protect herself, but she also did it because the men around her didn't want to see who she was, didn't want her eyes to be too piercing, needed the disconnection to feel safe, to feel like men.

Matthew had gotten drunker than he usually did, he was in a mood. He hated the strip joint; it smelled, and it was sad, and he knew that Chris was going to take a girl home with him, his phone overflowing with texts from Maria all night long.

Matthew sighed and had another drink, and another, and realized eventually that Chris was yelling at him that it was time to go, that he was horny, that he had found some bitch to take home, some pussy that needed a good time. Matthew nodded and stood up, feeling like he barely knew where he was. He thought of his mother, about how sometimes when she would get drunk, she would dance and laugh and whatever man she was with would egg her on, and then punish her for it, would tell her that she looked like a slut, and she would slap him, and he would grab her hands and then they would fight; the next day the man gone, his mother holding a cold rag up to her bruised and swollen eye. The nights this would happen, Matthew and his sister would go into their tiny, sagging room and huddle together on the flattened pallet they shared, and Matthew would pet his sister's raggedy black hair while she cried. Honestly, Matthew preferred to stay in their room when the men were around, but his mother sometimes wanted him there, told him to learn to have fun, put a beer in his hands, tip his hand to make him drink it, the beer sloshing over the rim and onto his face, and into his lap, his mother yelling at him to not waste the beer, and then her hand coming out, connecting with his face. Sometimes though she wanted him gone, in fact, the older he got, the more she wanted him gone when the men were around. Eventually he was.

Matthew stumbled toward the entrance, listening to the sound of Chris's stripper giggling, and thinking of his mother, her dancing in front of her men and how she would fall sometimes and get up and get slapped on the ass and keep going, and he burned with humiliation. He turned around and looked at her, her painted face, her sparkly body, and he swayed.

"What you looking at bro?" Chris asked. "Yo, get your own."

Matthew frowned. "You stupid slut," he said.

"Fuck you!" she responded, and Chris roared with laughter.

"Don't mind him, brother's drunk. We just gotta get him home and into bed."

"No," Matthew slurred, sounding like a petulant child. Chris disentangled himself from the stripper and went over to Matthew. He put one arm around him and said, "It's cool bro. I got you. But damn kid, I was gonna have us all go out to Central and party. But we gotta get your drunk ass home now."

"No," Matthew said again, but weakly this time, letting Chris take him out. They had told Damien, who'd driven them, to park, to wait for their texts. It was Friday, and they had had Damien drive so that they could get drunk. Matthew worried about him driving at night in Albuquerque, where the streets downtown were shut down on the weekend; too many drunks, too many drunk drivers.

They waited for Damien to pull up to the door, Chris cussing him out already, the stripper and a couple of the guys standing behind them, and Matthew went silent. He felt bad about what he'd said. He just felt inadequate, like every man he knew.

"Not a fucking slut," the stripper said as they piled into the car.

"Take the front seat," Chris said, "and consider that a big deal. I gotta take care of my Ishkeh first."

"Whatever," she said. Matthew looked over at her, her fake fur coat, her long highlighted red hair and thought again of his mother. He turned to Chris, whose face was beginning to look like it was underwater. He opened his mouth and was violently ill on Chris's lap.

"Aw, fuck," Chris said, "pull over."

"Oh my fucking *God*," the stripper said, and rolled her window down.

Damien pulled over as soon as he could find a place to safely do so, taking a right onto a side street. Chris leaned over and opened the door and gently scooted Matthew toward it, supporting him as they got out. He held him steady while he vomited, and Matthew could hear the stripper complaining from the car. He started hating her again. He knew that he didn't really hate her, that he hated his mother, and that he didn't know who he really hated, but there was so much hate, so much that someone had to take it.

"You finished bro?" Chris asked, patting Matthew on the back, and peeling his oversized T-shirt off, using it as a rag, and throwing in into the darkness. "Yo, you're so skinny, I don't know how that much shit came outta you bro. Plus you always handle your booze like a champ. This shit's crazy."

He looked up at Chris, his face like a big, ugly balloon. "What about . . . Maria?" he said, and Chris's expression changed from one of some sympathy to one of pure rage.

"*What* you say, homes?" His hand moving from his back to his throat and tightening.

"Nothing, nothing, sorry Chris," he said, and Chris's hand loosened back up and left his neck.

They both knew that when Chris had first found him, he'd been barely more than a drunk, a bum, but Chris prided himself on cleaning Matthew up, and Matthew knew that this couldn't happen again. And that what he had just said should not have been said. Not if Matthew wanted to live.

"Sorry," Matthew said. "I was just . . . in a mood."

"Happens to the best of us," Chris said. That was the great thing about Chris. He could be a vengeful fucker, but he'd just as easily let things go if he felt like it.

Chris started leading Matthew to the car.

"I'm cool man," Matthew said, smiling weakly as they settled back into the car.

"Thank *God*," the stripper said.

"Shut the fuck up, you stupid bitch!" Chris said, "Or I'll dump your sparkly cheap-smelling ass out right here, or worse. My bro is right, you are a slut! You do like I pay you to do, and that is not to talk. There's only one thing I want you to do with that mouth." The stripper had stiffened and then sat back sharply.

"God! These bitches get out of line," Chris said, grumbling and reaching for a joint. Chris lit up as Damien pulled back onto the road and took a long hit, the green smell filling the car, and then passed it to Matthew. "It'll help with the nausea," he said, and Matthew nodded.

As the car made its way East, Matthew thought of his mother, and his sister. He thought about Nita, and the stripper and about Maria. The nausea began to subside, and he took another hit.

"Shit, I'm hungry," Chris said.

"You hungry?"

"Yes," the stripper said venomously from the front.

"Bitch! You think I was talking to you? Shit, the only time I'm talking to you is when I want you to get the *fuck* over to me and sit on my lap. Goddamnit."

Matthew began to worry for the stripper. The only woman Chris loved was Maria, and he treated her like shit half the time. One time, coming home like this, a stripper had talked back to him. She'd been Chicana and from L.A. And tough, and Chris and she had begun arguing, and Chris had pulled his gun on her. She had just laughed and said, "Go ahead homie. Then you gotta clean my guts outta your ride." Chris had blinked and then laughed, hard. Then he'd shot her in the leg. She had screamed and began cussing in Spanish that her homies on the West Side were going to kill him, and though Chris was ready to dump her out by the side of the road, Matthew persuaded him to take her to the hospital. They had pulled up, dumped her out, still screaming. That, later, cost them a couple of guys. Chris had known she was a favorite of an OG on the West Side, which is why he had flattered her, had offered her money, furs, dinner. He wanted to show a rival gang just how fucking G he was. And the stripper had loved the attention, but Chris just couldn't not be Chris. And a few days later, there had been a drive-by on their turf, and a couple of the homies, and little homies, had gotten shot. The homie had gone to the hospital. The little homie was pronounced dead on site. He had been eleven. Chris had shook his head and said, "Those fuckers. We'll get them back. That kid was a great look-out man."

Matthew looked over at Chris, who was busy taking another long hit. "Yeah. I think maybe some food would be good." Chris seemed to calm down then, telling Damien to drop them off at the Frontier and to join them, too. He told Damien to hand him the big, white T-shirt he was wearing, and the kid took it off, and Chris yanked it over himself, complaining that it stunk of pussy. He turned to the stripper.

"What you want, baby?" he asked her, and she immediately began to smile, to purr, to stroke his arm. "Nah. Not in here," he said, and she took her hand away and smiled and they sat down. Damien came in the door in just his wife-b and khakis, got in line and ordered for them, looked around and threw a couple of signs at some other homies sitting in a plastic red booth near the window in a way that only they would see, Chris handing him his card on the way up to the line. The glow of the lights made Matthew feel sober but strange in this restaurant shaped like a barn, its insides decorated like a bad Western from the fifties.

Matthew had ordered huevos rancheros, his favorite, and Chris was tearing his way through carne asada, the stripper picking her way delicately through a pile of green-chili cheese fries. He thought back to a conversation that he'd had with Chris in the early days. Matthew and Chris had been sitting on the couch, passing a joint around, waiting on a call so that they could go on a deal.

"You gotta keep these bitches in *line* yo. You know what I mean?"

"Sure," Matthew said. He remembered at the time how badly he had wanted a drink, how much he had to focus on Chris's words in order to stop himself from running out the door and finding one in whatever way he could. His hands had been shaking. He'd had the DTs pretty bad.

"It's like, you know how like, they say that cows would be eating us if we didn't eat them? It's like that, yo, I'm telling you."

"Cows?" Matthew said. He was confused.

Chris sighed impatiently and rubbed his head. He took a drink of the Pepsi he had sitting on the old seventies-looking wooden end table and set it down.

"Like OK, for example, I never, and I mean *never* let bitches get on top when we're fucking."

Matthew looked at him with an even more confused expression on his face. He didn't understand the switch from cows to women, and he wondered if he just wasn't really high, and so badly needed a drink that his mind was playing tricks on him. Also, he liked it when women were on top, partially because he could see their tits, but mainly because in the past, he was always so drunk that when they were on top, they could do all the work, and if he blacked out, they often didn't even notice.

"Like I don't ever compliment a bitch."

"Why not? Don't they like that?" Matthew asked. He really wanted a beer now. This conversation was making him feel weird. Sometimes he did hate women because of his mom. But it didn't feel good when he thought of them as something to hate. It made him feel ugly inside, dark, it brought on the black hole.

"Fuck yeah they like it. That's why I never do it," Chris said, sitting back on the couch. "Look well, OK, I do it at first. You know, to bring them in. Flowers and shit. Like I'm real good at first, because that way, when you start to assert your manhood, they get all desperate. They want that nice guy back." Chris began to laugh. "But then they don't get that guy, they get the *man*. But that's the thing, women don't want to be treated good, they want to know they place. If you keep treating them like that, they'll start seeing you as the bitch, and they'll cheat, and start taking you for granted, and then they on to another man."

Matthew raised his eyebrows and then shrugged.

"And you don't *ever* go down on a bitch. Shit, that shit makes a woman crazy. I mean, maybe once when you're first with them, but they gotta learn to go down on *you*. Gotta push their necks down and shit too, so they choke on it a little." Chris laughed again and sat back up and looked out the window over Matthew's head. "Though soon, fuck, I don't ever have to go down on any bitch ever again, woo any bitch at all. They all gonna be clawing each other's eyes out to get a piece of me," he said dreamily, scratching thoughtfully at his chest through his dingy wife-b.

He looked back down at Matthew. "You feel me?"

"I think so," Matthew said, squirming on the old beige couch.

"I mean, look, this shit's a war."

"A war?"

"Yeah it's a fucking war, Jesus, Matthew, bitches will run all over you if you let them."

Matthew pictured a herd of women, like sheep, running toward him, a lady-stampede. It sounded kind of good. He resisted the urge to laugh but he must have smiled because Chris looked encouraged.

"Yeah, I mean, I keep Maria in line. Otherwise that bitch would run her fucking mouth all day long, trying to boss me. And I ain't gonna be bossed, at least not by some fucking woman. I am the boss, and she knows that. And she loves it. That's why she keeps coming back. Like I said, women want to know you the man. They will try to push you, but it's bullshit, they're just making sure you know how to slap them down. It makes them feel secure and shit. Plus, it's natural. Like because of testosterone and shit."

Matthew thought of all the women he knew back home, like his mother, or his grandmother for that matter. His mother took so much shit from men, and she seemed to not be able to live without them, but she fought them hard, too. And his Shimásáni was quiet, but nobody crossed her, they had too much respect. And Maria . . . well, Maria cheated on Chris. And Chris was always digging her out of some shithole and cleaning her up. All of it was confusing. Often, at night, he had heard Chris crying. At first, he thought it was Maria, but Maria never cried, and after a while, when he would be getting up to go to the bathroom, or to get a drink of water, or to get more weed, he could hear it, and he knew it wasn't her. Chris would be crying and talking about how much his mother hurt him. Maria would comfort him, tell him that his mother had been a bitch, that Maria was here now, and she would hold him and rock him and that he could be her baby, and then he could hear Chris crying low and soft in a way that made him think his mouth was more than likely being muffled by a large, soft breast.

FIVE

A SHIPMENT WAS COMING IN. A BIG ONE, AND THE OGS NEEDED guys to guard, to escort, to be there in case any shit went down. One of the OGs, Myron, was handling this one. He asked Chris if they could trust their boys, if their boys knew how to sling, and Chris nodded and said, "Fuck yeah, those Ishkeh down."

The day of the shipment, about an hour from sunset, they gathered their guns and tucked them behind loose-fitting khakis, their belts holding their pieces tightly to their bodies. It was spring, and beautiful. Chris was excited, like he was a kid whose parents had finally saved up enough to take the family to Disneyland.

"Fuck we gonna show these motherfuckers how down we are, awwwww shit," he said as they piled into the SUV. After the last one had been impounded and ultimately lost to the system while they had been in jail; when he got out, he had gotten them a new one. Still a Ford, not an Escalade, but shiny and silver and large enough to hold four homies and two wannabe OGs.

They had been told to go somewhere east of Albuquerque at the foot of the mountains, at an agreed upon spot where the deal would take place. They drove, the air-conditioner on and Tupac blasting, Chris yelling the lyrics out in a near-hysterical state of bliss, smoking cigarettes and looking toward the mountains as he bounced his head and waved his arms emphatically.

"You know, Ishkeh, I knew these days was coming. I knew that ever since I was a little kid, and mom shit on me like she did, and I made a promise to myself to be an OG, the most powerful mother-fucking OG that this town has ever seen, that it would happen. It's destiny, man. Some shit is in the cards, some shit is just shit that's going to happen to you."

Matthew listened as they sped past the red and green of the desert, the occasional flash of yucca or some other flower in his periphery. His mom used to talk like this, about fate, about how she knew it was going to get better for her, because she was a good woman, because she deserved a good man. But that had never hap-pened. She had continued to pull her whole life apart for one deadbeat after another, to drink and to miss work and to treat her children like unfortunate accidents. Matthew didn't believe in destiny. But he believed in Chris, in Chris leading him, because Chris always seemed to know what to do, he always seemed to have a plan. He was good at making the OGs feel important, good at making them think he knew what he was doing, that he could do things for them, though he talked too much for some of them, and occasionally one of them, usually Stanford, would tell him to shut the fuck up and do what he was supposed to. Matthew knew that he was just excited for this life, for the things that drugs could bring him, excited to able to say he was a 505. Matthew didn't feel that excitement. But for the first time in a long time, he wanted to live, and sometimes he was genuinely happy, and that was enough.

Matthew slowed and took a turn down a dirt road, one that you could miss if you weren't looking, and the SUV began bumping along, rocks flying and dust swirling around the car. After about fifteen minutes of driving, Matthew could see a few figures in the shimmery distance. They pulled to a stop. There were three of their guys, including Myron. They were all older, at least in their mid-thirties.

"What's up, Ishkeh?" Chris opened his door first and walked over to Myron and stopped. Chris was a little guy, especially next to Myron, who was tall for a Nav dude, a little over six feet, Matthew guessed. Chris was around five foot six but muscular. He went to the gym and did weights every day, as soon as he woke up, before he did anything else, his short, thick arms covered in tattoos. The OG just looked over at him impassively and watched as Matthew and the other guys piled out of the car. There were nine of them total, and they all were packing. That Matthew knew. He also knew that although there was no reason that anything would go wrong, that the guys selling the H from over the border would be packing too.

They sat around in silence, smoking cigarettes until there was some motion in the distance. They watched as another SUV appeared and after a few minutes, pulled up and stopped. *Their* SUV was an Escalade. A huge, silver Escalade with souped-up rims and tinted windows. Matthew could hear Chris exhale in awe. The doors opened, and three men got out, one of them carrying a black suitcase. The guy with the suitcase walked behind another man, a man who was clearly in charge, and they made their way over to Myron. Myron nodded, opened the suitcase. He took a bit out of a package, smelled it, held it up into the light and then motioned one of his guys to come over. The kid pulled a lighter and some tin foil out of a pocket, melted a bit onto the tin foil and nodded over at Myron.

"Looks good," Myron said. "So, we're good with what we agreed upon?"

The man in charge looked at Myron for a moment. He was wearing a suit, despite the heat. "No. We need more. Three grand more. Shit went down. We had to take a lot of risk to get this to you."

Myron nodded. He had told Chris and Matthew on the way up that this might happen, and that as long as it wasn't upward of five grand over the initial price, they would deal. The agreement was, though, that they would make them wait, and request that one of their men go with Matthew back to the house and hang outside while Matthew got the rest.

They talked this over. A few minutes later, one of their men was sitting in the passenger seat of the SUV, Matthew driving. They were silent, the man looking down at his phone, texting. He was also wearing a suit, and he had turned the dial up for the air-conditioning as soon as they'd gotten into the car without looking up, without asking. Matthew wondered who he was texting.

It didn't take long to get to the house. Matthew pulled in, looked around and got out. The guy didn't move from his seat, his eyes moving briefly to check his surroundings out and then back down to the phone. Matthew got the extra cash, which was generally stashed under a loose plank under the dingy gray carpet in one of the back bedrooms, and got back into the car. He wondered if the guy spoke English. And if that mattered.

"Got it," Matthew said.

The guy nodded and continued to stare down at his phone as Matthew made his way back east. It was getting later in the day, the sun not yet exactly going down but getting there. There were big, black clouds in the distance, and though they looked ominous, unless it was monsoon season, often it only looked like it was going to rain but a few hours later, it was back to blue skies.

As they got closer to the turnoff, the guy began looking at his phone more urgently.

"Nothing from my men," he said.

"That bad?" Matthew asked.

"Don't know."

Matthew took the turn for the second time that day. Around ten minutes into the drive, he could see that something was wrong. Something was terribly, terribly wrong. There were too many cars. He came to an abrupt stop. There were cop cars in the distance, lots of them.

"Turn around now!" The man yelled, pulling his piece out of his side-holster. Matthew hadn't even noticed that he had one. He placed it on his lap and pulled the safety back. "Get the fuck out of here!"

Matthew was already turning the car around, dust spraying out in either direction, praying that the cops hadn't already seen him, that they would think he was some regular guy out for a joy ride. He felt like his heart was going to hammer out of his chest, and he tried to keep to the edge of the speed limit. The black of the pavement, as soon as he got back onto the highway, began to swim in his periphery, and he struggled to maintain calm. As much as he could without wavering, he looked in his rearview mirror, and the man stared at the side-view until they were a good twenty minutes down the road. The guy got on his phone, and began speaking rapidly but calmly in Spanish. He got off the phone.

"You will drop me off at the Frontier."

Matthew nodded. They had talked about if something like this happened, what Matthew was to do next. Who he was to call. They drove the rest of the way in silence, Matthew feeling sick, hoping Chris was at least OK, was alive.

He dropped the man off at the Frontier, the man whose name he'd never asked, whose face he assumed he'd never see again. Neither one of them said a word as he opened the door, got out, slammed the door after him and walked away and into the red-and-white doorway of the most iconic restaurant in Albuquerque.

Matthew drove back to the house. He made calls. There had been a leak of some kind, Stanford said. They assumed that it was one of the homies that had gone on the ride. Chris and Myron and the guys from the other gang were in jail. There had been some shots fired on both sides, and a couple of cops had been injured, and Myron had been shot in the leg. Matthew knew that when a cop got shot, somebody had to pay. He would have to wait to hear. He hoped that because Chris was only nineteen, that because his record was shorter than the other guys who'd been taken in, that if he hadn't been one of the shooters, he wouldn't be in for years. But Matthew knew Chris. Chris loved to play the hero, the defender, the one in front of God. He knew that Chris wanted to impress the OGs, and he knew that Chris would do anything to do it, including shoot a cop. He also knew that even if Chris hadn't been the one to hit a cop, that he'd take the blame for one of the OGs to show how down for the 505 he was.

Matthew looked at his phone in his hand, dead after an hour of listening to Stanford tell him what was up, and felt a great emptiness.

It was that black hole that he'd felt at the edge of his being for as long as he could remember reappearing in his heart like magic. He felt like vomiting. He felt like putting a knife into himself, and pushing hard. He got up, walked to the door, opened it as if in a dream, and began walking to the Walgreens, which was five minutes from the house. The doors of the Walgreens whooshed open, and cool air surrounded him as he walked in, took a left, and went straight toward the hard-liquor section. He picked up the largest, cheapest bottle of vodka he could find, stood in line behind a woman carrying a poodle and buying a gigantic bottle of red wine, two kids who barely looked twenty-one buying case of Bud and a bottle of whiskey and talking rapid-fire at one another, and one hardened-looking street Indian who pointed with his lips to the cheapest smokes and the cheapest little bottle of hard liquor behind the cashier.

The three homies who lived there, including Damien, who were leftover from the bust were nowhere to be found. Matthew was alone. He sighed with relief, slammed the door behind him and plopped down on the couch after getting a glass from the cupboard. He pulled the bottle out of the paper bag, the sound of its release almost sexual, and unscrewed the top and set it down on the old, wooden coffee table he and Chris had bought at a yard sale down the road. A little girl had been manning the table for her mom, and when they had handed the five bucks over she had smiled, her long black ponytails reminding Matthew of his sister's hair. Sometimes his mom would get in a good mood, a motherly mood, and would put his sister's hair up like that. Matthew had smiled back and the little girl had laughed and slapped her hands over her eyes. Chris had rolled his. He didn't like kids.

He turned the cheap Walmart glass that one of the homies had gotten at Chris's request over in his hand, his long fingers beautiful in the light reflecting off of the glass provided by the little window in the kitchen. He slumped into the couch for a moment and stared at the bottle, like he was staring at another human being, one that he'd known for years, one that he knew better than anyone else and that he didn't have to be anyone but himself for. Matthew sighed deeply and pulled up. He felt so much relief. Relief that it was over, relief that he didn't have to pretend to himself that this wasn't what he was born for.

He put the glass down and picked the bottle up to pour himself a drink. The lovely, clear liquid began to hit the bottom of the glass, and he heard the door open. He hung his head in irritation and stopped and put the bottle down, hard, onto the table. That's all he needed now. For one of the homies to come in, ask him for direction, ask him to be like Chris. Chris, the leader, the father figure. Matthew was nobody's father.

He blinked with surprise when he saw it was Maria, and she smiled and closed the door gently behind her. She walked over to Matthew and stood next to him, put her soft brown hand on his shoulder.

"Chris called me. The OGs have taken care of the legal shit. So he called from one of those illegal cells they got that probably lives up someone's ass to tell me to come over and stop you from doing this," she said, picking up the cap and screwing it back onto the bottle, her long red nails twisting artfully around the rim.

Matthew sighed and said nothing. He had learned to pretend to give people what they wanted. That way, he could keep doing what he wanted to do when they were gone. And they would go fast, when they figured they'd helped you.

"OK," he said, and she laughed.

"What?" Matthew asked, almost angry. His best friend was in jail, her boyfriend. What was wrong with her?

"Damn," she said. "It's like you really think I believe you."

Matthew was silent.

"Look, he told me not to leave your side. Not for a week. So I ain't going nowhere. And let me tell you something: I'm a junkie, so there ain't no way you can hide shit from me, so don't even try," she said, sitting down on the seat next to him. She leaned back, kicked her heels off and crossed her legs. She was wearing a pair of off-white short-shorts, and Matthew looked quickly away.

"Plus, now you really got shit to do. Chris will be lucky if he gets out in a year. You gonna have to take over." She picked the remote off of the coffee table and began switching though the channels.

Matthew felt the anger begin to surge in his chest, a fire building higher and higher, and his hands began to shake. But just as quickly as it had begun, the anger stopped, washed up, and broke. Chris loved him enough to send his woman to stop him from destroying himself. He turned to Maria and smiled shyly. She smiled back.

"It's going to be OK, Matthew."

"Yeah."

"This shit happens all the time. It's part of this life. I mean ... shit I'ma Ride or Die. Let's smoke some weed and then get out of here. Let's go get something to eat. I'm starving. Shit, stressful shit always makes me hungry. That, and being pregnant." She looked over at Matthew, and Matthew blinked.

"Ayyyyeee, just kidding! I really had you going there. Oh damn, that woulda been some serious drama, right?"

"Yeah, it really would have," he said, sighing with relief.

"You think I'm crazy now right?"

"No ..." he said, still aching for a drink.

She laughed and elbowed him hard in the ribs, just the way his sister used to. "I'm just trying to distract you, that's all. Make you think about something else."

Matthew laughed uneasily. He liked Maria—too much. But she wanted to help him. And she loved Chris, just like he did, even though she cheated. But Chris cheated too. Maybe it was just part of how they worked, like the way Maria would get all fucked up, and then Chris would clean her up. He wondered why this time was different for her. Why she wasn't on her way to getting fucked up, and instead had listened to Chris and decided to come over and help Matthew, to get him to not drink. Matthew wasn't sure.

He looked over at her again, her long legs, and realized he would be alone with her for a long, long time.

SIX

STANFORD WAS SITTING ON THEIR COUCH. IT HAD BEEN A COUPLE of months since the incident, and though Chris was going to serve time, he was only going to get a year. He hadn't taken the fall for Myron or anyone else, and he also hadn't said shit about shit, which was smart. It was what his lawyer had told him to do. Admit nothing. Sometimes it was hard, because if the lawyer wanted a kid to take a fall, a kid took a fall. But Chris had become too valuable; he was good at what he did. They had let another kid take the fall, one of the homies who had gone along with them. Sure enough, the other homie had been the leak, and he was somewhere else now, a different state, in one of those group homes for wayward boys. Matthew was sure that kid would end up back in trouble. That's the way it worked. Those homes were great for trafficking. They were understaffed and underbudget, so there was always someone to bribe. But the kid who'd taken the fall was fourteen, and his record was short. He said he'd done all the shooting, and since it'd gone down as the sun was setting and with everyone at a distance, and wearing uniforms, the cops theirs, the OGs theirs, the cops didn't have any definite proof either way. Though they knew what was happening. But they had someone to blame. Myron and the OGs from the other gang would be in for a few years—there was no way they could get out of that. They had clearly been the ones buying the drugs. But even though their rap sheets were long, they had been able to negotiate down, because the cops had really been after the dealers from Mexico. They were part of a vicious cartel, a rival of the MS13s that the cops had been trying to take down forever. And they would be in court too, for a long time, the debate about which country they should be tried in going on and on. And there were more where they came from. There were always more. That was something Matthew learned early on: he was not unique, there were more of him, more and more—a line leading out into the desert, a line of brown men who looked just like him, who had backgrounds just like his, full of anguish and abandonment and pain.

Stanford smiled. Matthew could tell he liked him. Nav guys were usually quiet and so was Matthew. They joked about how Matthew was Apache, those old tribal jokes, and how he would think that meant that he could take over, start raids like in the old days. And Matthew would laugh, because in a way, the OG was testing him. Wanting to make sure that he was loyal, that he was down. That he wasn't necessarily trying to permanently replace anyone. Matthew just wanted to do his work, the work that would allow his way of life to continue until Chris got out. Whenever they were allowed to, he and Maria would visit Chris, and they'd talk about the future in careful, coded terms. Chris looked OK. He was part of the inside network now, dealing from the inside, networking, getting closer and closer to Béésh. And he was doing sweats, praying.

"Your Ishkehs are doing well," Stanford said, lighting up. He was a chain smoker. He talked a lot about his kids, his woman, who was also Nav, and who had been with him almost since he was a Pee-Wee. They had grown up down the street from each other, both of their mothers single mothers, both of them part of the gang network.

"Yes," Matthew said. They had gone through their networks, gone to the moms in the neighborhood who were down, who would hold for them, start and maintain connections for them, their kids Pee-Wees that turned quickly into homies, watch for them during deals. They figured out who was ready to move out and into the house. They would talk to people, see who had a shitty home life, who was full of rage, ready to move out, make money, be down for whatever the 505s wanted. They had new, loyal boys. Matthew was proud of them.

And Damien was getting better every day. But he missed Chris. He couldn't help but feel like he would have been a better father figure to them. The way Chris would talk to them, instill them with pride, pump them up, Matthew couldn't do that. But they respected him.

"Sales are up, and there's a new shipment coming in," Stanford said, putting his cigarette out in one of the ashtrays they had sitting on the coffee table. It was overflowing with old cigarettes, the stained white ceramic barely visible.

"That's good," Matthew said.

"You're doing well. We're happy with you. Come with us this time and this time, won't be no cops to fuck it up."

"OK," Matthew said. He knew that he had three homies who would ride along, who could be trusted, one of them being Damien of course. Another, a young Pueblo kid, reminded him of Chris. He was ambitious like Chris was. He was a little more chill though, and that was good. Matthew didn't want any more trouble. There had been enough. He had let this kid run a number of holdups and smash and grabs and they'd all gone off without a hitch. The kid was smart, calculated, like a mathematician. That's what they called him actually, because he did everything like clockwork, including take care of the 505's dogs. And he wore glasses, big old glasses that he seemed to have plucked out of the mid-seventies. The kid had also done things in front of God, walking into a couple of rival neighborhoods, walking straight up to a couple of rival members and stabbing them in broad daylight and then not running, just waiting silently for the cops to come while they beat him almost to death, take him to juvie, try him, let him out and into a halfway house and then when he could, he'd go right back into the house with the rest of his homies. He also had a side business that he ran for the 505s, pulling credit card applications out of people's trashes and starting them, and it had bought them guns, gear of all sorts, and miles of khakis and white wife-bs. He also liked to use them to get people gifts. He'd given Matthew a pipe, Maria loads of jewelry, and the OGs all kinds of things. And then the mathematician would make the cards disappear, untraceable.

Maria sat on the couch with Matthew, just far enough away to show she wasn't being disloyal to Chris, but she was allowed to stay, which was a big deal for a woman, especially a junkie. But she hadn't gone back to the H for a while now, and she had quietly helped Matthew take Chris's place, so she had come to be trusted. The OG looked over at her. She was filing her nails into sharp little points, looking down at them without saying a world. "You miss your man," he said, his eyes squinting thoughtfully. He was a short, lanky guy, with smooth, dark skin and a little pot-belly that poked out of his wife-b like he was pregnant.

"Damn right I do," she said, and Stanford laughed. "Bout to stab a bitch if he doesn't get out soon."

The OG laughed again. "Chris always did like his women crazy," he said, and shook his head.

"Yeah. I am crazy," Maria said, going back to filing her nails. "Crazy *fun*," she said and Stanford laughed.

Stanford stood up. "I'll call you," he said, and Matthew nodded. He left, and Matthew sat back down. Maria stopped filing her nails and looked up. She smiled at him.

"What?"

"You're good with them, you know that? They trust you. That's important."

"You think they trust me?"

"Shit yeah. See, I love Chris, but he's so fucking arrogant and always fucking wanting to impress the world with how bad-ass he is, that sometimes they're like, man, what are you all about? I mean, shit, it's all about the money. Who gives a shit about anything else. Chris always watching too many of those old gangster movies and shit, and that's Hollywood, that ain't real." She went back to filing and then stopped and looked out the window. "I do miss his ass though. He always finds me when I'm all fucked up, and cleans me up. I never had anyone in my life like that. Men are happy to fuck me, use me, dirt me, and sell to me. Chris isn't like that. He wanted ...

wants me to be clean, to be a good girl. No one's ever thought I was a good girl."

"I think you're a good girl," Matthew said, smiling shyly.

Maria smiled. "Yeah?"

"Of course."

Maria bounded up off her end of the couch and walked over and hugged him while he laughed awkwardly, the smell of her musky cologne covering him like a fog. She let go of him and looked deeply into his eyes. "We gotta get you a woman."

"Yeah. I heard they're on sale at Walmart," he said, and Maria punched him softly in the arm.

"No really. You a good-looking guy, you got needs like any other man. I have a girlfriend. She's hot. Mexican. Really good chick too, her man just died, and she's in need of some comfort you know?"

Matthew squirmed. Sometimes, he would go with one of the women hanging around, usually a girl at a party who kept eyeing him and who eventually would come up to him, her whiskey breath a living thing. He would take them to a back bedroom by the hand and they would do what they needed to do, and it was clean and short and efficient and without fear. He liked it that way.

"No. You don't want that. If I finally found a woman, I'd probably lose her. Like as in, I'd be walking around and around like I do, and suddenly, I wouldn't be able to find her. Women, they don't like that. They like you to know where they are," he said, lighting a cigarette, a Marlboro Red. He liked the taste of them.

Maria's eyes got large, and she twisted her lips in an exaggerated fashion. "What? That's bullshit. You're exactly what a woman wants. You're a *man*, like a real man. You're successful, you nice and you good-looking. You got that silent masculine thing going on too, and when you're not quiet, you're funny. Women like that. We gotta get your confidence up is all. Don't be crazy."

"I'm telling you. I'd be calling you from Las Cruces crying because one minute my woman was there, and the next, gone. I have some kind of magic, like some kind of backwards woman magic. It's horrible," Matthew said, but Maria was already shaking her head.

"All I'm *saying* is that you should meet her. She's really pretty and shy like you. You'd like her. Let's just go to this party tonight that my friend Macina is having, and she'll be there. No pressure. Have a couple drinks, hang out, no big thing, no pressure."

He blinked coquettishly. "You think I'm pretty?" he whispered in a sweet little girl voice, and Maria punched him in the arm as a response.

Maria had said no pressure twice, but it was clear that there was pressure. Matthew hated pressure. He liked it when other people made decisions. Whenever he tried to make them for himself, he got lost in his own head. But women, they were all about pressure. They always seemed to want something from him that he couldn't understand, and certainly couldn't give them. But he also knew that Maria wouldn't give up unless he said yes, so he nodded, feeling resigned, and she jumped up and clapped her hands like a little girl.

"OK! I'm gonna go over to my mom's and get ready and like, you get ready. Take a shower, do your hair, and like, wear something nice. Not like a tie or some shit," she said, laughing, "but like you know, your best shirt. Like something buttondown."

"I'll get out the clown suit," Matthew said, defeated, and she immediately turned to her phone and started walking out the door, nearly bumping into it on her way out. She looked up, turned around and rushed over to him—Matthew looking on with a confused expression on his face—and leaned down and hugged him again, her long arms wrapping around his head, mostly. She stepped back then. "I'll text you the address!"

"Backwards magic," he said, but Maria just giggled, and as she shut the door, made a little girlish squealing noise, and he knew she'd would be texting her friend, telling her that she had a guy for her. Matthew picked up a joint and lit it, letting his cigarette smoke itself out. He thought perhaps the right thing to do was just not to show up, tell Maria the next day that he'd had work to do, that he was busy, that something had come up. But he knew that if he did that, he'd never hear the end of it, and she would just try to fix him up with her friend again and again. He always thought of himself as a sorry sack of shit. He figured he'd show, and that the girl wouldn't be interested, and that it would be over, and he and Maria could continue like they always did.

He made a couple of necessary calls. He waited for a scheduled call from Chris in prison, and another to Stanford to continue the arrangements for the next shipment, and then he smoked a joint down to the nub and took a nap, reading a little bit before he did, curling into his sheets like a child, his long hands tucked behind his neck. He woke up a few hours later, showered and looked at himself in the mirror, feeling strange. He had a shot of whisky from a flask he kept under the sink, just one, and shuddered as he wiped his mouth, watching himself in the mirror. He did look like his dad, the cheater, the one who abandoned, the silent one. The lanky Apache with the slick black hair. He missed his long hair still, thought it was stupid that he had to shave it off. He was nearly covered in tattoos now himself, many of them mirror images of Chris's tattoos. He had a Columbus and skulls tattoo, that was completely his though, and a Zia, and 505, a thunderbird. He did have a few Apache hieroglyphics, and that made him happy. All his life, he was surrounded by Navajos. They were everywhere, there were so many of them. He figured if NASA ever made it to Mars, there would be a colony of Navajos already there, quietly herding sheep and inviting them to have some frybread and mutton. He shook his head. Smiled awkwardly in the mirror. He wouldn't be any good for a woman, and he knew that. What he didn't understand is why Maria didn't. He should have just told her no. Women loved to fix their friends up. Matthew began pulling his clothes on. He knew he was too distant, too cold to love, to really love someone you needed to have a thing inside of you that really wanted it, that really needed it. He loved Chris, that was true, but that was different. He was a guy, he didn't expect the same things. Women wanted to crawl inside of you, root around, make themselves a part of your heart. And he felt best when he functioned as if he didn't really have a heart, not in that way. The last woman who had really gotten into his heart had been his mother. She had taken his love and torn him up with it, and he had had no choice because he had been born with his heart in her twisted, alcoholic hands. He would never let himself feel that way again.

He walked out of the bathroom, gathered his keys, his wallet, his piece and walked into the cool New Mexican evening. He loved the smell of the desert, the dust, the huisache dulce, and the way it combined with the smell of the city. He got into the old coupe, trying to put Maria and her friend out of his mind. He stopped at a corner store to get a case of beer and a bottle of whisky. Maria had texted him the address not five minutes after she'd left the house, and Matthew knew where it was, right in the heart of 505 territory. He only had to drive for about fifteen minutes, Necrophagist blasting from the speakers, when he pulled into a house alive with people yelling, laughing, drinking, their long nails clinking around their glasses, their shaved heads glowing in the light. Matthew parked behind the line of other cars parked in the street, many of them SUVs, and walked up. He nodded to a folks as he entered the circle, threw up some signs, and exchanged a few complicated handshakes and *what's up homes*, a couple of side-man-hugs, his eyes darting furtively around for Maria. There were people from various gangs there that they were basically friendly with, though that was always changing, and everyone always had their eye out, and kept as much to themselves as possible. He saw Damien and Math, who lifted their chins in greeting. Math had one of the pits with him. He always did, for some reason. The pit was sitting faithfully by Math's side, panting joyfully, looking up at Math. Math never pet the dogs though, at least not as far as Matthew ever saw.

Finally, he spotted Maria, his chest growing tight. She was standing by a short, cute Mexican girl who was staring anxiously into the crowd. "Hey! C'mere homie!" she said, and Matthew walked toward her, anxious to get the whole thing over with. "This my friend

Sharina. She's the one I told you about, ayyyee!" Maria said, elbowing him hard in the side.

"Hey," she said, looking him up and down. She was wearing a tight pink dress and heels, and she looked a little like Nita, his junkie girlfriend from his days in Farmington. He smiled. She gave him a tight, unhappy line back. Clearly she wasn't impressed.

Matthew still had his booze in his arms. He lifted the giant cube of cheap beer and said, "Gonna go put the baby in the bassinette." Maria rolled her eyes, and Sharina just wrinkled her forehead and looked off into the crowd. Matthew squirmed.

"Anyway!" Maria said, and as Matthew and turned to leave, he could hear Sharina loudly whispering, "What the fuck did that mean? I got a baby! Didn't you tell him that? And he's too *skinny*. And young. My man was in his thirties. A real OG."

Matthew hoped that this would be the end of it. That had been movie-bad. Like the kind of movie where people met and hated each other and then fell in love. He was pretty sure all of that was true, except for the fall in love part. No woman in her right mind would fall in love with him. He didn't understand why this kind of thing was so urgent for women anyway, it was like it was a hobby for them. They always said that they wanted you to be happy, as if getting a girlfriend ever made anyone happy. Or a boyfriend for that matter. Chris and Maria fought like hell, and most of the OGs he knew were gone half the time, doing their shit, their women left to live with their mothers, the other half dying and leaving them with children. Is that what Maria wanted for her friend? Matthew thought about having a child, and he shuddered. The thought of bringing another person, another innocent person into this life was beyond his comprehension. This life was evil, it was cruel, it picked you up like a tornado and tortured you like a killer. There were still times when he thought of dying, about how he couldn't wait to do it, so that even the pain that he kept tucked deep inside would stop.

Matthew went into the house, negotiating the throngs of people yelling and drinking and laughing, and set his booze down on a table, taking a beer from the case and cracking it open. He drank long and hard, his throat working like a machine. Drinking for him was always a gamble, he knew he probably shouldn't do it at all. But it was weird with him, there were different places that he was in, emotionally, and more or less though he fucked up sometimes, like that one time at Palms when he was in a good place in general, he didn't want to drink and drink. That was something that Chris had given him. He missed Chris. They had promised one another that when he got out, they were going to get more tattoos together, identical tattoos of the state. He walked through the party, talking to people, and feeling generally removed. Everyone was so young. Everyone was scarred, tattooed, missing parts of their bodies, but they were laughing and having a good time. That's what teenagers did.

He walked out and over to Damien and the Mathematician. The Mathematician was looking at his phone, and Matthew figured he was working some kind of scam, as usual. He'd told him that shit like that was going to eventually replace gangbanging, though Matthew didn't believe it. Damien was trying like crazy to get into a girl's pants, telling her that he wanted to take her out, treat her good. The girl just kept laughing. Damien's nickname was Romeo, because this was Damien's jam, getting with the ladies. Matthew figured eventually the girl would be won over. They almost always were. Damien was good, and he had a sad, sweet face, with long eyelashes that pointed down over his big, black eyes. He had a shy little boy in love with the world quality, and chicks loved it.

The Mathematician smiled at Matthew, asked him if he was having a good time. Matthew nodded, and he went back to messing with his big bright phone.

Matthew was walking in to get another drink when he spotted Maria's friend, Sharina, and sighed. He knew she didn't want to see him again. But he wanted another drink, and she had migrated into the house, where the booze was. He walked up to the table where she was standing alone, looking awkward, and smiled politely.

"You seen Maria?" she asked, and he shook his head no.

She looked around at the party, her eyes empty, flat. Matthew began to feel sick, wondering where Maria was, what she might be up to. Drugs of all kinds were everywhere, and definitely H. Maria seemed to be in a good place, but that was the thing about being a junkie, and an alcoholic, it could take you by surprise sometimes, when you were least expecting it, when you thought the thing inside you had died, and there was no turning back. Sometimes it was because you were sad, other times it was because you were happy and you wanted to celebrate, and that's how you always celebrated before. But sometimes it was just a shadow in a corner, waiting, a person asking you if you want a drink, some H. And you would say yes.

"Shit," Matthew said, and Maria sighed.

"I been her friend since we were little. It's always like this. It makes me so fucking mad at her. But I love her, you know?" she said, her mouth tightening and her eyes looking wet.

"I know," Matthew said, patting her on her small brown arm awkwardly, and without thinking. He didn't touch people very often. He worried that she would recoil, but she didn't, she looked up at him gratefully. "It's OK. She's OK. She's probably off somewhere. But let's go find her?"

Sharina nodded and they began walking through the large, sweating crowd, stopping at different people that they knew, asking if they'd seen Maria. They got a lot of nos before a yes. One guy said that he'd seen her heading out with a couple of other guys, that they were doing a beer run. Matthew and Sharina looked into one another's eyes, and Matthew sighed.

"I been texting her and nothing," Sharina said, looking down at her phone, which featured a picture of five-year-old boy, his large dark eyes already looking pained, vulnerable.

Matthew sighed again, deeply. He picked his phone up, dialed. She didn't answer. Both of them began texting, and without a word, started walking toward the front of the house in the hope that she would return by car soon, that she really had just been out for a beer run. Matthew and Sharina stood outside drinking, talking to people as they came around, watching everyone get progressively more fucked up. He looked over at the Mathematician, who was making the pit sit patiently as he fed him scraps of meat. Damien was gone, and Matthew figured he'd left with the girl he'd been hitting on. Matthew had picked a bottle of Patrón on his way out, and though hard alcohol was generally his enemy, he'd only had one beer, and he thought to just sip a bit to steady his nerves. Not only did he need Maria to continue to run things without Chris, Chris loved her. Matthew knew that he'd go crazy if he knew she was fucked up again, that he'd do something stupid and end up in solitary, or with an extended sentence. Plus, Matthew liked Maria, though he tried really hard not to think about that.

"Sometimes I feel like she doesn't have feelings for other people," Sharina was saying. She sipped at her glass of Patrón. Matthew had asked her if she wanted some, and gotten her a glass. "I mean, I remember when this started, we were in junior high. And she would run off without me. At first I didn't know what was going on. Thought she was just ditching me for guys, you know?" she said, looking out into the street, squinting and then back down at her phone. "But then one time I caught her. I thought it was just coke. But it wasn't the right color. And she didn't act like she was fucked up on coke or speed, you know the way it makes you. She was sleepy, like all of a sudden, and I knew she didn't want me to know. But I knocked on her door one day and no one was home, so I let myself in, and then when I walked into her bedroom, the door was open. And she was snorting it. Soon, it went to needles. Her mom kicked her out. She lived with me, but when she got pregnant, my mom kicked her out."

Matthew was surprised to hear this. He didn't know Maria had a child.

Sharina could see Matthew's confusion, and shook her head sadly. "Her body was too fucked up. It died while it was inside her. Now she can't have kids at all." She looked down again at her phone, the image of her little boy. "I can't imagine life without my little Manuel."

Matthew ran his hands down his black jeans. He had a Megadeth T-shirt on, and he felt more like himself in it than he ever felt in the uniform Chris always wanted him to wear, the khakis and white tank and white T-shirt. He thought about going over to Math and telling him what was up, but he wasn't sure he trusted him completely. There was just something too quiet, too intense about the guy. He figured he'd wait until he felt like he had to tell him.

"You're different, ain't you?" Sharina asked. She had watched him rub his jeans nervously and had ended up staring at his outfit, at his face.

"Yes'm. Differen'," he said in an exaggerated Southern accent. "I'm differn' alright."

She stared at him blankly for a moment, and he thought he'd ruined it with her again, but after a second, she giggled, just a little bit. "I think I'm kinda different too," she said. "Though not *that* way. Sometimes I don't . . . feel like I belong, or like I'm here at all."

This surprised Matthew. She seemed like the rest of them, with their tight jeans and deep V-neck T-shirts and their kids and their lives that revolved around the money that boys could make selling H. He was about to ask her why when a car pulled up and stopped, and a bunch of people got out, including Maria. She was laughing and talking with a guy, a fucked-up looking G in a pair of khakis and tank. She always did like her men in uniform. Sharina went stomping up to her.

"The fuck didn't you answer your phone?" she yelled.

"Your wife's a *bitch*, homes," the guy said and people laughed. Sharina turned to him and gave him an evil look, and he shrugged and walked away, Maria's eyes following him as he went. Matthew walked up, wondering what had gone on between them. Something. None of his business. Still, it made his gut twist.

Maria lifted her phone out of her big, red purse and stared. "Damn! What the fuck you two? Like fifty million missed calls, you fucking psychos. I was just on a beer run, damn!"

"You shoulda told one of us," Sharina said. "We was worried!"

Maria cocked her head and smiled, first looking at Maria, then Matthew. "Jeeez. Sorry *Mom*. Dad. I swear I'll get home from prom before my boyfriend knocks me up."

Sharina cocked her head disapprovingly.

Maria sighed. "Look. That's sweet. Crazy, but sweet. C'mon, let's get a drink."

"You know why we were so worried," Matthew said.

She stopped, looked at him. "Yeah. But I'm telling you, I'm clean now, OK?"

Matthew stared at her, her toughness and vulnerability all coming to the surface at once. It was something he understood, that combination. But it was explosive because the toughness tried to cover the softness because it had learned that it had to, but when the softness needed out, it destroyed everything.

"Just *tell* one of us next time," Sharina said, shaking her head. "Shit."

"Fine," Maria said. "Damn, thought I was too old for babysitters. Guess not."

They sat in some beat-up old lawn chairs, the broken pieces of plastic sticking up and poking Matthew in the ass, and Matthew talked a little business with other homies—who was planning on what, what rival gangs were up to, who had died. Maria pulled a fat slightly-charred joint out, and they passed it around. Matthew poured her a glass of Patrón. Sharina and Matthew began to talk, and Maria watched silently. Matthew wondered why she didn't go talk to some of the other girls that she knew. He and the Mathematician talked about what he'd been up to on his phone.

"Check this shit out," Math said, handing the phone over to Matthew.

"I don't understand," Matthew said, handing it back.

"Well, what you were looking at, it's code. It's how I run all my credit card scams—I send a bunch of people emails all at once, and then if they click the link in the emails, it goes to ... hard to explain, but it breaks into their accounts."

"Damn," Matthew said, looking at Math with respect. Math could see that respect on Matthew's face, and he smiled slightly, the pit still at his side. It had followed him everywhere he went.

About an hour later, Math waved goodbye. He was mysterious. Always disappearing with one of the dogs.

On the way home, Maria asked Matthew about Sharina, and he shrugged awkwardly and said nothing.

"You get her number?" Maria asked, turning to her phone to text furiously.

"I guess," he said.

"We gonna double-date when Chris gets out," she said, then went silent. "I guess until then I'll have to be a third wheel."

"Oh," Matthew said, thinking of the guy from the car.

Maria went silent again. He dropped her off, and went home. She had caught a ride to the party with Sharina, but Sharina had had to go home earlier, because she needed to get up, take care of her kid. And her mother had told her that she needed to come home. Matthew thought about Sharina. He *had* gotten her number. He felt like he shouldn't have done that, but she was nice. And he didn't have to do anything. Maria had looked funny when she was talking about being a third wheel. He knew she was happy for him, it had been her idea after all, but he knew that she was lonely too. And it made Matthew nervous, the way she made him feel.

SEVEN

"DAMN, ISHKEH, GET LAID," CHRIS WAS SAYING, HIS VOICE BREATHY over the phone.

"It's not like that, she has a kid," he said, shifting the phone so that he could smoke.

"Well then, give that bitch another one," Chris said, cackling maniacally.

Matthew was silent.

"Dumb bitch'll get more from the system with another kid. And shit, you can hide all kinds of drugs in a baby's diaper."

Matthew was silent again. Then, "I do get laid. I fuck women all the time."

Chris sighed dramatically. "Look, whatever, Maria's going on and on about it. That bitch drives me crazy. Sometimes I think I just gotta get rid of that bitch, but she needs me, so I guess I'll keep her around."

"Yeah," Matthew said. Then, "Why don't you and Maria have kids?"

Chris was silent, and Matthew felt bad. He didn't understand why he had said that. He wished he hadn't.

"Bitch is sterile. Because she was pregnant . . . with me, when we were, like, kids. And she was so fucked up her body rejected it. But some of it got left behind and scarred her all up inside."

"I'm sorry," Matthew said, meaning it.

Chris was silent again, and Matthew was sure he was going to change the subject but he then he said. "It was a boy, yo."

"It was?"

"Yeah. And like my foster moms had bought all kinds of boy shit, you know basketball shit, little shirts. But I just couldn't get that bitch to clean up," he said, and Matthew could hear him breathing hard on the other end. "Yeah. I was fifteen. She was fourteen. Real shit show. It's cool though because now I can fuck her all I want without a condom and bitch can't get pregnant, right?"

"Right," Matthew said, feeling sick.

"Times up bro, but you remember what I said about that one restaurant being the bomb, right?" This was code. They were trying to move some H into the prison, and there was to be an exchange.

"Yeah, I got it."

"You're good man, you're really good," Chris said. "When I get out things are gonna get loud again, they're gonna get crazy. I'm practically OG at this point. Everyone respects me."

"Bye, Chris," Matthew said. He hung the phone up after Chris responded, and stared at his, at Sharina's number.

"Hi," he texted and looked at his phone. The minute that he sent the text, he wished that he hadn't. He picked up a baggie of weed, pulled some out and began to roll himself a joint. He sighed. He had to get his homies together for the shipment tonight. He couldn't afford to have his mind somewhere else. He knocked on doors, talked to his boys, made sure they were ready. They were. They had hustled that last batch of H out the door so fast, they'd run dry. It was crazy how much this town loved its H. He went to his room, lay down, listened to some Megadeth, tried to sleep. He pulled his phone out of his pocket and stared at it.

A few hours later, they were getting in the car, pieces tucked in the back of their pants, Damien in the front driving, when he got the text from Sharina. "Hey! Sorry, was at work." he sighed. He didn't know why this was so unnerving, but it just was. Anything to do with women was unnerving. He decided to text her after the shipment. It was something to look forward to. They drove off, Matthew calm, all of them silent, the homies joking about girls, partying, weed in the back, all of them giving Damien shit about the girl he had gone home with the other night, and then falling silent as they came to yet another pull-off. Obviously, this was in a different location, with different men. They'd all had to lay low after the last time, and it had taken a while for things to start up again. They pulled up, and there was Stanford and a couple guys, guys they could barely call homies they were so young, waiting, smoking.

It went fast, the men coming in from the other side, drugs being exchanged for money, nods on both sides, talk of next time. The homies were excited on the way back, they were ready to get selling and were already busily texting people on their large, shiny phones, asking them where they wanted to meet. When they got to the house, Matthew divvied it all up and they went on their way, almost as if they were girl scouts, and what they were selling was thin mints, not drugs. He smiled at Romeo, aka Damien, on his way out, and he smiled back, wiggling his eyebrows in a way that made Matthew know that he had a lady lined up for tonight. Matthew laughed, punched him in the arm.

Damien rubbed his arm. "What. It's not my fault the ladies love these pretty pretty eyes."

"Oh my god you pussy," another homie said.

"You mean, getter of pussy," Damien retorted.

"I'm going to bang you on the arm harder than you're going to bang that poor bitch tonight if you don't cut it out, get out the door, and get to slinging," Matthew said and Damien laughed. He knew Matthew was gentle, that he'd never hit anyone. Not a 505, anyway.

Matthew sat down and stared at his phone. He texted Maria instead.

"What's up?"

She texted right back. "What's?!? Fool, why u wait so long to get back to Sharina? She thinking ur not interested! I'm coming over."

He started to text that she shouldn't, but he knew she would anyway, that was just Maria's way. Plus, she handled the money, and some of the sales. Dangerous as it was to let her have a portion of H, she knew how to sell, she knew where the junkies were, and which ones had the money. The best ones were the ones who would do anything to get it, or the ones with some kind of family money. The worst were the ones that didn't know how to get the money, and were all fucked up, and wanted it anyway. Matthew often worried for Maria, because he knew that some of those junkies would kill for it, if she wasn't willing to give it. But years ago Chris had taught her how to use a piece, just like he had with Matthew. She had Chris's gun in her purse at all times. And she was like a gunslinger pulling it out, Matthew had seen her whip it and hold it on a guy so fast he hadn't even seen it coming. And she was even faster with her knife.

The old wooden door, the paint peeling off, opened and shut about five minutes later. Maria lived only three blocks away.

"What's the holdup? You like her, right?" she said, sitting down next to him and picking up the joint that was sitting in the ashtray, lighting up and taking a hit. She coughed, and Matthew took it from her.

"Just tell her to come over. Fuck it, no, I'll do it," she said, picking up her phone. Matthew let her. She was only trying to make him happy, he knew that. She pushed the bottom of her jean shorts farther down her long legs, as they'd clearly ridden up when she'd sat down, and pulled her phone out.

"Wait," he said, staying her arm. She looked at his hand on her arm, and Matthew felt himself shiver. Instead of pulling away, she smiled at him. He pulled away.

"What?" she said softly.

"I . . . I—what are you going to say?"

She laughed. "Damn, Ishkeh, trust me. I know all about women—I am one if you haven't noticed."

He had noticed.

She typed into her phone and then watched it. It lit up.

"I told her to come here, that we were just chilling. She said she would ask her mom if she could watch Manuel for a while. I'm sure she will. Her mom loves that fucking kid. It is pretty cute," Maria said. Matthew wondered if looking at other people's kids made her sad, but she didn't look sad. Sometimes, though, people were good at hiding things, how they really felt.

"Let's have some drinks, like, and do you have anything to eat?" she asked, and Matthew walked with her over to the kitchen. Maria opened cabinet after brown wooden cabinet, pulling bags of chips out. She opened the yellowing refrigerator door.

"Aw damn, you guys need to clean this thing," she said, shutting it hard, and with a disgusted look on her face. She looked like she was thinking and then said, "OK, you got plenty of tortilla chips, and you got some Patrón. So, I'ma go to the store, get some mix and a bunch of avocados and some shit to make guacamole. At least that'll make you look classy," she said, and Matthew dug into his pocket, pulled his little black faux-leather wallet out and handed her two twenties.

She stared at the oily twenties in her hand and then back up at him. "Damn."

"It's not enough?" he asked, digging for his wallet again.

"No, no, Papi, it's plenty. Stop. It's just that . . . well, with Chris, I always gotta beg for cash. I mean, you kinda can't blame him, I mean, with the way I used to spend it," she said, laughing. "But still. He likes to fuck with me, and I hate that."

"Yeah," Matthew said, not knowing what to say. They had a strange relationship.

"So thanks," she said. "I'll just walk to the store around the corner. By the time I get back, we'll still have plenty of time to get shit ready before Sharina comes."

"OK," he said, feeling nervous.

Maria was gone and back in a flash, and when she came back with bags, she set them down on the counter and got to work making guacamole, drinks, and then cleaning first the kitchen then the living room up. Matthew helped her, taking direction and laughing with her. Maria was funny. And she made him feel good. They had already started on a Margarita by the time Sharina got there, a tentative knocking marking her arrival.

Maria bounced off the couch and went to answer the door, hugging her as she came in.

"Hey," Sharina said shyly. She sat down on the couch opposite him as Maria went into the kitchen to make her a Margarita and bring the chips and guacamole out.

Maria and Sharina talked about work. Maria worked in a corner store, though she made her real money by helping the 505s, and Sharina had a kind of clerical job in a hospital, though her family had been involved with gangs for generations. He wondered how Maria had convinced her to even give him a chance. She seemed so ... good. Matthew was content to let them talk. They talked about people they'd known growing up, who they thought was a bitch, who was fat. They talked about the men that had screwed them over, how much they didn't like their jobs, how much they hated living with their families. Maria and Chris lived together off and on, but it was tough, they would fight, and it would get physical, and then she'd move back in with her sister. And Maria's sister needed her. She was diabetic, severely so, and on disability, but she still needed someone to help her get around, to cook for her. Matthew had never met her, and she didn't talk about her much. But when she did, it was clear that she didn't want her sister to have any part of this life, any part of drugs, gangs, violence.

Around 11:00, Maria looked at her phone and said that she had to go.

"I ... I should too," Sharina said.

"No, girl, stay!" Maria said, and Matthew squirmed.

"Oh, I gotta get home to the baby," she said and stood up, straightening her jeans and looking at her phone.

Maria looked at Matthew with that *do something* expression on her face that women were so good at making.

"You could stay, for a bit, I mean, if you wanted to. It's I mean ... I'd like that," he said, meaning it, and not meaning it. He lit a cigarette nervously. She sat back down, looking at Maria.

"OK," she said, "but just for a minute or two."

"OK!" Maria said, practically running out the door, "I'll see you two later!"

They were silent for a few minutes and then Sharina began to laugh nervously. "Because that wasn't obvious. Dang," she said.

"Right?" he said. "I'll go get us more drinks." He set his cigarette down into the ashtray.

"That would be great," Sharina said brightly, and he got up from the couch and walked into the kitchen. He poured the drinks the way that Maria had showed him, his hand shaking just a little, his pour heavy.

He handed Sharina her drink and sat down. She thanked him, and they were both quiet, nervous. Without Maria's constant chatter, they were lost.

"So, Maria said you like to read. I like to read," she said nervously.

"Yeah?"

"Yeah, I mean, I just finished the latest Harry Potter. It's pretty good."

"Oh." Matthew felt nervous. "I just read cereal boxes. That's my thing."

Sharina stared at him for a minute and then said, "You're weird homes."

"I know," he said, thinking that he'd messed things up totally.

"But you're nice," she said. "You really read just cereal boxes? Why?"

"Ha. No. I was just trying to you know, be funny. Lighten the mood or something? I uh . . . just read this book. It's called *A Farewell to Arms*."

"Dang. That sounds scary. That a zombie book?"

"Oh. No. It's like, about war," he said, taking a long drink of his Margarita.

"I don't usually read that kind of stuff. Too real," she said, laughing. "My life is real enough, you know?" she said, running her hands through her short, highlighted hair.

Matthew had never thought of it that way. But he nodded.

"I could let you borrow my Harry Potter book if you want," she said, looking shyly into his eyes. He smiled at her, a small, furtive thing.

"I'd like that," he said, lighting another cigarette and thinking about Maria.

They were silent for a moment, the air filling with the smoke from Matthew's cigarette.

"You think she and Chris will make it?" Sharina asked, breaking the silence.

Matthew drew breath. He'd never talked to anyone about this.

"I shouldn't . . . say," he said.

"Oh, I'm sorry. I know he's your friend," Sharina said, gulping her drink. She pulled at some fuzzballs on her jeans and looked at the door anxiously, her round black eyes narrowing unhappily.

"They fight a lot," he said.

"You don't know the half of it," she said, laughing nervously but with obvious relief.

"The hell I don't," he said, and she laughed some more. "You don't live with it."

"Well, I practically do," she said, and he picked his cigarette up and inhaled deeply, looking over at her, hoping that she would take the lead.

"Yeah, that's true. You've known her since you were kids."

"I have. And Chris too. Never liked him. Sorry, like I said, I know he's your friend."

"It's OK. I know everyone doesn't like Chris. But he—he saved my life. For example, he introduced me to my first cereal box," he said, and Sharina laughed, just a bit.

To his own surprise, Matthew began telling her about himself, more than he'd told anyone in a long, long time, including the things about his mother's boyfriends, the men who came to him at night. Matthew didn't like telling people about his past. It didn't matter, and it just gave someone something to have over you. But he could tell Sharina was sweet, she was kind, and he knew that she wouldn't judge him. After all, her last boyfriend had been in the 505s.

"I understand. My ... uncle ... he did things to me," she said, touching him on the arm. He was drunk. He began to tear up, she moved over and held him and they began kissing, softly at first and then with more urgency, and soon he was leading her to his room. She was very sweet, shy, tender. She let him pull her clothes off of her, and she kissed him lightly, with fear.

"Do you have condoms?" she asked. "I don't want any more babies." He nodded, feeling a sheet of pure, deep relief wash over him. He didn't want any babies at all. As he began to pull it over himself, he felt something from her, and he stopped. She had a worried expression on her face, like she looked like she needed to say something.

"What is it?" he asked, "We don't have to do this."

"It's just ... I can't ... please tell me we're not just hooking up."

"No. I like you. It's OK. You understand my cereal boxes," he said, and she laughed again, her laugh like a tiny silver bell.

She seemed relieved, and Matthew slid her on top, and it was quiet, gentle. They did not love one another, and they never would. But there was something almost better than love there—compassion, understanding. This Matthew decided, was enough. More than enough, it was good. But as he came, he thought of Maria. Maria in her red tank top, Maria in her short jean shorts, Maria's eyes on him when he touched her arm.

Sharina cried out, and then leaned into him, panting. He patted her back. She curled around him and asked him to set the alarm for a few hours later, so that she could crawl back in her bed, be there when her boy woke up. He told her he would, but he knew he would probably be awake, his eyes searching the ceiling for something, something to tell him what he was, where he was going, how he had gotten there. He didn't like thinking about the future, and normally that was really easy, not to think. He'd set things up in his head that way, and it was good. But things like this, people in your bed, they made you do this. He wondered what he would feel if he loved her.

He would probably feel worse. He would probably feel much more panic. Because he knew he could never love her, it was easy to keep a distance from her, even with her little arms wrapped around him. But it still made him think about a future with her. And then there was Maria. He picked his phone up in the dark, as he'd brought it with him in his pocket, stopping as they went to pick it up from the coffee table, and stared at the few texts that were waiting in his phone. They were about deals, about money, about H. But he was looking to see if there were any texts from Maria. There were not. He set his alarm. He did not sleep.

EIGHT

SHARINA BEGAN COMING OVER ALMOST EVERY DAY. IT WAS EASY to be with her. So much easier than he thought it would be, because of the way he didn't feel. At first he had been afraid of that, that hanging out with a woman would do that, it would force him to feel, and this would bring on the blackness, and this would make him start to drink hard again. But that wasn't the way it worked with her. She was nice, and she liked him. But she had a job, and a life, and she had already had her heart broken, so there was a way in which she not only didn't expect love, she didn't want it, and once Matthew realized that, it was so much better. Not cold exactly, but not hot. Like a lukewarm bath. And she was totally down to help them move H. And with Maria around too, it became like a party, like a family within a family. And Matthew liked Sharina's kid. He was three, and strangely well-behaved. He liked to sit on the floor, a fraying beige blanket underneath his solid little body, and play with his toys, occasionally needing to be picked up and fed, or held, his little brown arms wrapping easily around him. And Matthew didn't mind sitting him on his lap, bouncing him while he giggled. Most nights, Maria would come over, and Sharina would join them when she got off work; then some of the boys would hang, some OGs occasionally, usually Stanford but sometimes Rudolph. Rudolph was quiet, even for a Navajo guy, and Matthew wondered about him, because though he would never look directly into anyone's eyes, he was watching.

They would all smoke weed, cigarettes, sort money, talk shipments, field calls, homies floating in and out of the house. Damien liked to sit on the couch and talk about the newest girl he was in love with, until he got a text to go out and sell. Matthew would laugh at him, and Maria and Sharina would tell him he was too young to be such a ladies' man. He would just smile sweetly at them and bat his long, black eyelashes.

Sharina found them connections through the hospital, which added to their business. Maria would chat people up at the convenience store—she'd been doing that for a year—and that helped too. It made their network big, but not too big to worry the MS13s and the gangs that were loyal to them too much, and with Chris gone, though it was not as exciting, it was quieter, though Matthew was worried about how big it had already gotten, how big Chris wanted it to be. Chris was always talking on the phone about the tats he was getting, about how much mad respect he was getting from Béésh, about what he was going to do when he got out, which was go straight to Palms.

"Yeah," Matthew would say, and update Chris about how things were going, how the girls were helping him.

Sharina and Maria were like sisters, and they liked to laugh, and this made Matthew happy. They would go to the park, and throw Frisbees around when they all had time off, and Matthew would treat them to dinner on Fridays, or they would come over and make dinner. Sharina had introduced Matthew to her mother, and she liked him, didn't mind that he was in the 505s, that he was a homie, because she had been helping the 505s all of her life. Her boys were little homies, her husband had been in the 505s, though both she and Sharina had clerical jobs. It was a tradition. Both of their men had died in the 505s, and though there was sadness there, there was also pride. And besides, Matthew was quiet, polite to her and to her mother, and he made good money. And when he died, there would be another.

"HEY. WANNA GO UP TO SANTA FE THIS WEEKEND? THEY GOT THAT big Indian Market thing going on. I mean, shit, you're the one who should wanna go," Sharina said, laughing.

"That's true," Matthew said. It was hard for him to think about traditional things, like Native American Church, though Chris liked to do sweats in prison, or Powwows. Those were things his mother hadn't bothered to introduce him to. He couldn't dance traditional to save his life. But he could buy Sharina some turquoise jewelry, eat some greasy frybread. His mother had made frybread sometimes, when she was in a good mood, or when she was wanting to impress a man. He loved frybread; he also loved a lot of the traditional foods, like tortillas with green chili and mutton or the blue corn mush you could get at the flea market outside of Farmington. He liked to wander along the vendors, talk to them, see who he was related to. When he'd been out on the streets, sometimes he would get a ride up to the flea market, and sometimes a distant relative would give him something to eat for free, shaking their heads and telling him that he needed to get free of that life. He had always nodded earnestly and thanked them profusely, and though he'd never asked anyone for money, sometimes they would hand him a few dollars and say, cousin, don't spend it on booze. And though it had been hard, he hadn't.

"But . . . let's just go up, you and me," Sharina said.

"OK, but why?" he asked. Sharina always wanted Maria with them, and frankly, though it was a bad idea, so did Matthew. Things were nice with Sharina, and he was happy, was even able to push his feelings away most times. But that didn't mean they weren't there.

They were sitting in his living room, a couple of the homies hanging around, drinking, smoking weed, texting little homies about where they should be, waiting for calls. He picked up a cigarette and lit it. Maria had a late shift. The Mathematician was sitting on the couch not far from Matthew, and he had looked up when Sharina had asked if they could not include Maria. But he had quickly looked back down at his phone, as he knew better than to get involved in any kind of G drama, especially when it came to their women.

"You know I love her, but sometimes you know, it's just more romantic when it's just you and your man," Sharina said, and Matthew nodded. He inhaled, was silent. Then he smiled playfully, "I'm your

MAAAN," and he got up and stood in front of her, and began pulling his arms up into his armpits and hooting like a gorilla.

Sharina looked up at him and smiled, and hit at him with her little arms. "Shut up you monkey," she said, and he did a few more loops around and stopped.

"I mean, I donno, her man's in jail. And that's the thing, it's sad. And she introduced me to you, and I love hanging out with her. But she gotta understand about being a couple, you know?"

At this point the Mathematician got up and walked outside, one of the pits following, and Matthew assumed that he'd gotten a call for a deal, as he was bringing the phone up to his ear while he shut the door. Math still made him uneasy though.

"Could you get us some drinks?" Sharina asked sweetly, and he went over to the kitchen to pull a couple of cold, golden beers out of the refrigerator for both of them. He stood looking out the window for a while, thinking about how it had been when it was him, and Chris and Maria. Matthew always came first. He never told Matthew to get lost. In fact, a number of times it had been the other way around, and though it had pissed Maria off, she had gone, telling him that it was cool because she was busy, she had shit to do. Then, after a few hours had passed, even if they were at Palms with Chris stuffing bills down some stripper's bright-blue thong, he would text Maria, and it would start. She wouldn't text him back. Or she would, and she'd say things to piss him off, make him think that maybe she'd found someone else, or was doing H, or simply just didn't need him anymore. He would go crazy, calling her over and over then, screaming over the phone when he finally got her, telling her she was a whore, that he didn't need her. But after a few drinks, or the next day, after the stripper had left, he would call, and they would get together again. Sometimes she would almost catch him with a stripper, because she liked to come over in the mornings, and there were times when the stripper had just left, and Maria would scream that she could smell pussy, and that he was a cheater. But many times Chris was alone and sleeping, and Matthew could hear his noncommittal grunts, and her laughter, and then finally their labored, mutual breath.

He walked back over to the couch and sat next to Sharina, and put both beers down on the coffee table. Matthew realized that he had to do this. That it was better for him, better for all of them considering how he felt about Maria, no matter how hard he tried to push it down, no matter how much he liked Sharina.

"Let's do it," Matthew said, putting his hand on Sharina's knee and giving her an awkward smile. She smiled back and looked like a little girl, and Matthew felt his heart move, just a little. It was OK, though; he kept his hand on her knee, and Sharina scooted closer to him and then leaned into his side. About ten minutes later, the door opened, and Maria bounced in, slightly slamming the door behind her.

"Hey guys!" she said brightly. "Daaaamn work was a bitch. I just ordered pizza. Double-cheese and pepperoni. Hope that's OK." She seemed sort of flustered, and tired looking, but strangely excited, and her hair looked messy. She closed the door, and looked over at them, combing through her hair with her long, brown fingers. She looked at Matthew's hand on Sharina's knee.

"Hope I'm not interrupting something," Maria said with a touch of irritation in her voice, and sat down and lit a smoke. Even though Chris smoked, he hated it when Maria did.

"No, not at all girl," Sharina said. "We were talking though, you know about, how like, we wanted to go up to Indian Market Saturday. You know—"

"Damn! I was just gonna ask you guys about that! Let's go. I used to powwow you know, I was good. I used to fancyshawl, shit, no one could beat me. We should go up to my Rez on feast days too, I got lots of relatives that would feed us."

Sharina looked at Matthew, and Matthew looked down at his feet, then back up at the beer on the coffee table. He picked his up and drank deeply, set it back down and asked Maria if she wanted one.

"Sure," she said, and Matthew got up and went back into the kitchen. He could hear Sharina talking rapidly and nervously, and he felt nervous too. He pulled a beer out of the refrigerator for her, and walked back to the living room and handed it to her. The case of Dos Equis had been on sale at the convenience store and it was his favorite.

Maria took a long pull of her beer and said, "Cool. So let's head out Saturday morning. Do the homies need the SUV?"

"No," Matthew said.

"I'm so excited you guys! I would be so lonely and fucked up without you two."

Sharina sighed and went over to Maria and leaned down and hugged her and then pulled up and stared at her, smiling.

"What?"

"It's . . ."

"Oh my God, you pregnant?" she said, standing up. "That would be great! Oh my God, little Matthew or little Sharina! And Manuel would have a little brother or sister! I could be the godmother!"

"No! I mean, girl sit down, it's nothing like that," Sharina said, putting her little brown hand on her forehead, her sharp pink nails bending into her hair. "It's that, you know maybe after going up to Santa Fe, like, me and Matthew were thinking about staying up there that night—"

"Shit, that would be great! Let's do that, I mean we could get a hotel room, party all night in Santa Fe and then crash at the hotel. Man, we should because I've been looking to get away, I mean even if it's just to Santa Fe."

Matthew got up, went to the kitchen and came out with a bottle of tequila and set it down, with the three glasses that he'd brought out with it. He had realized that the beer wouldn't be enough.

"What's this?" Maria asked, and Matthew poured a glass for all of them.

"The thing is, Maria, like, why don't you come up to Santa Fe with us that day, and then maybe me and Sharina might stay the night you know ... on our own," he said, working hard to not feel the pull of the alcohol on his heart. He wanted more. A lot more.

Understanding came over Maria's face, and she closed her eyes. "Oh shit. Oh shit. I'm so sorry. You were trying to tell me and ... I'm sorry. I been hanging around you two too much, I know. It's just that, with Chris in prison..." and she started to cry. Sharina had backed up and sat down again on the couch, but she got up again and walked over to her and leaned down and hugged her.

"Girl, we love having you around. I would totally go crazy without you, you know that? We just thought for one night, you know?"

Maria continued to cry, and Matthew felt guilty. He poured himself another shot and drained it quickly. They sat and talked, and the pizza came, and Maria dried her tears and everything seemed to go back to normal, except that it didn't seem normal at all now. Matthew started to think that maybe he should've have let himself get so close to Sharina. He began to feel resentment toward Maria, a burning in his chest, and he quietly took shot after shot, the girls gossiping and talking around him. A few hours in, Maria looked down at her phone.

"Yo. I gotta—I mean, I'm supposed to go get something. Hook you guys up maybe, you know? So I should go," she said, standing up. She was wearing bright red shorts, and they made her long brown legs look like something out of a cartoon. They were long, so long. Matthew felt that burning feeling again. This time, it wasn't resentment. But he was drunk, confused.

"You guys, I'm sorry. I know it's important for couples to have some alone time," Maria said, and she stood up and hugged Matthew and then Sharina. "We'll have a great time at Indian Market, and then I'll get my butt down here and let you guys have some sex, am I right?" she said, and Matthew felt embarrassed as Maria elbowed Sharina hard.

"Whatever, girl," Sharina said and they watched her go. Sharina sighed heavily as the door closed and looked over at Matthew. "Baby, you drunk."

Matthew was surprised. Usually, and almost always these days, he felt like no one would really know unless he wanted them to.

"I'm going to join you," she said. "That sucked. I mean, I want her around but it's just that you know, sometimes it's good with just you and me, that's all."

Matthew nodded and poured her a large shot. She sat down and drained it in one gulp, and wiped her mouth. "Keep 'em coming," she said, and he poured her another until they were both so drunk that it was all they could do to stumble over to the bedroom, and collapse into each other's arms, the sounds of the homies coming in and out, the smell of their vinegary sweat everywhere, the image of Maria's face when they had told her that she shouldn't stay with them, the glow of her brown brown legs in the white-hot light.

Matthew woke up with a pounding headache. He wanted a drink. Instead, he got up, went to the bathroom and walked into the kitchen to make coffee and eat toast. Sharina was gone. She had gotten up early to go home and get up with Manuel.

"What's up Math?" he asked. The kid had already made coffee and was looking at his phone intently.

"Nothing much. Up and ready to work. Gonna go feed the dogs first though."

"Good," Matthew said, getting a cup of black coffee and sitting down on the couch. He didn't like dealing with the dogs. Chris had instructed the little homies to keep them mean, hungry. It made him sad. But Math didn't seem to mind. In fact, he had completely taken over because he was so good at it. He looked down at his own phone. He had some calls to make, some figuring out to do, especially if he was going to go up to Santa Fe tomorrow with Sharina and Maria. He thought about what had happened last night and felt bad. He sighed hard.

The Mathematician passed him in the hallway on his way out the front door, the smell of cologne Harvey in his wake. Matthew had noticed that lately, the Mathematician had been using some sort of expensive cologne. He didn't remember that when he'd first moved in. Matthew went into the kitchen for more coffee, made himself some toast and sat back down on the couch and began to eat. He felt a little better as his stomach was finally settling, and the pounding in his head was diminishing, at least to some degree. Matthew thought about how ambitious the kid was, how good he was at his scams, his codes, at taking care of the dogs, who for all of the shit he gave them, seemed to give him a quiet kind of respect. He hoped he'd make it, hoped he'd survive. He was cool too. Never talked about anything personal, never fucked around, though he did like to do things for show. But the OGs liked that, especially because unlike Chris, Math was all about doing, less about bragging.

He picked his phone up and saw that there were a series of texts from Maria, most of them asking for forgiveness for hanging with them all the time and not realizing that she was in the way, and telling him that she had a friend she was going up to Indian Market with the next day, and not to worry. She liked to end all of her texts with that winking face. He smiled and texted her back that she should come with them, that it was no big deal, that he and Sharina could just have dinner alone. But Maria texted back that she really felt like it was important that they had time alone, as a couple. He simply texted, "k." He felt sad, and the whole thing seemed ominous in some way, but he went about the business of his day, falling asleep that night hard. He'd told Sharina that he'd rather take the night off, that he was still hungover enough that he thought sleeping on his own would make him a much better boyfriend the next day when they went up to Indian Market, and she agreed. She told him that she was hungover too, and that her mom wanted the company anyway, had been nagging her for a mom and daughter night, and that they were going to have Chinese takeout and watch *Selena*. He said that sounded nice and told her that he'd pick her up around 9:00 a.m.

The next morning Matthew got up feeling amazing. That was the thing about drinking too much, the only good part about a hangover was that the next morning, when you weren't hungover anymore, it felt like a miracle. When he'd been in Farmington drinking every day, and almost all day, that had stopped being the case. He had felt like he just had to maintain drunkenness, that it was all about not vomiting, or passing out, about keeping in the cloud.

Outside of Sharina's door, in the SUV, Matthew sent her a text and a minute later, she came out with Manuel in her arms, her mother behind her. She gave him a tight squeeze and handed him over to her mother, and Manuel began to cry, his solid brown arms reaching for Sharina. She comforted him for a bit, kissing him on his head, but he began to cry louder, and it was clear that she just had to go ahead and go, or it would turn into a scene. She got into the car and turned to him, smiling, her little lips pink with lipstick. She shut the door and buckled in. "I'm so happy," Sharina said, looking at him and giving him a quick kiss on the cheek. "I got a text from Maria saying she'd found a friend to hang with, and I told her that she should come with us, that we could all hang together and then split for dinner, but she told me no, that she was sorry she hadn't seen that we needed alone time together before."

Matthew nodded and patted Sharina's knee and then turned on the sound on the iPhone, which was connected to the stereo. It was tuned to the station that Sharina liked. She didn't like his death metal, said it was too rough, too depressing, and Matthew understood. They always played her music, which was mainly Chicano hip-hop and ballads in Spanish, and Matthew didn't really mind it. The hip-hop reminded him of the stuff that Chris liked.

The drive up was beautiful, and they passed all of the pueblos, one of them Maria's, and he thought of her, hoped she really was as OK as she sounded. Maria did have a lot of friends, but some of them were bad, a lot of them were junkies, from her junkie days, and that worried Matthew. As they began pulling into the plaza and wandering around, trying to find a place to park, Matthew wondered at the beauty of this town, the money of it, the short, beautiful adobe houses everywhere. There were loads of tourists wandering around, plates from states far, far away, and he knew that in many ways, a lot of these people were here just to look at Indians. He laughed.

84

"What?" Sharina asked.

"Nothing," he said. He had laughed because he was thinking about the fact that so many of the people in this town were Indians, or in Albuquerque, and yet, unless they were in their full regalia, or perhaps were wearing jewelry and sporting long hair, they wouldn't look at them that way, which was fine by him.

"There's a spot!" Sharina said, and Matthew parallel parked into the spot that had just become available. Chris had taught him to do it.

They got out. Matthew had found a place on a side street. He paid the meter, and the two of them started walking toward the crowd. There were so many vendors in the park, and Sharina squealed excitedly. The park was in the middle of downtown, which was old—each building a tiny, little masterpiece, a circle of buildings surrounding the park, the church with the "miracle staircase" that always spooked him smack in the middle.

"We should also check in," Matthew said. He had splurged and gotten them a room at the La Fonda, which was on the plaza. As with everything Santa Fe, it was an old, beautiful adobe building. It suddenly occurred to him that he could have parked in their underground parking facility. He shrugged. He told Sharina that, and she asked him if he wanted to get back in and do that first.

"Nah, let's wander around for a bit, have some lunch," he said, putting his hand in hers. She looked up at him and smiled and again; he felt his heart move.

The day was beautiful, hot and dry, but lovely, and Sharina exclaimed over every earring, preferring the long and dangly or the large hooped. She also liked colorful things, bright reds and blues, dyed shells, which she would hold up to Matthew's ear as he laughed and looked stoic, his arms across his chest.

"You'd look good with one of these," she said, holding a peach-colored shell to his ear.

"Like Geronimo good? Like stoic as fuck good?" he asked, and Sharina giggled.

"Yeah, super-manly," she said, and kissed him delicately on the cheek.

They had stopped for lunch, frybread and mutton, and sat under a tent with large, cool Pepsis. A couple of 505s had checked them out, and Matthew had flashed them his tats, some signs, quietly, in their secretive way. They'd nodded at one another and moved on. This was not a workday, at least not for him. And they could see that he was an older homie, approaching OG status, so there was respect. He'd also seen some guys from rival gangs, and they had eyed each other attentively, micro-aggressively. But this was Santa Fe, and no one wanted to start any trouble. He and Sharina had decided to walk around a bit more, then check in for a nap.

"I see a lot of Native guys with one of these in their ears, and it looks cool," Sharina said, holding the earring back up to his ear, his shaved head tilted toward her tiny hand. "It looks . . ." she said almost shyly, "hot."

"I'd have to get my ear pierced," he said thoughtfully. Then, "Oh my gaahhh, we could do it at like, Claire's? Like in the mall? And then like, you could get that totally totally cuuuuute swimsuit you were talking about and like we could check out guyyyyys!" he said, and Sharina giggled.

"For real though, you should pierce it. You could take it out when shit goes down, so it wouldn't get ripped out or nothing," she said pragmatically.

Matthew sighed. "I don't know if Chris would like it."

Sharina rolled her eyes. "Chris," she muttered, but let it go, as she knew how much Matthew loved him. "I guess that's true. And what if you did forget to take it out? I don't want anyone pulling my man's ear out. I need that ear. I like that ear," she said. She looked pretty. Like so many women Matthew had known, she had insisted on wearing the jewelry that he had bought her, taking off the big faux-gold earrings and bracelet that she'd worn out the door that day. She'd wanted a long pair of turquoise earrings and an intricately beaded bracelet.

He looked at her and smiled.

"What?"

"You look so pretty. You know, you have to be Native too."

Sharina laughed. "Don't tell my grandma that. She's so racist. She goes on and on about how Spanish we are, and mom always rolls her eyes. I know we Aztec, at least. And plus, my family's been in New Mexico for I don't know how many generations, maybe we're Apache."

Matthew frowned. "I hope not," he said, brushing dust off of his black jeans. He'd wanted to wear something that he liked, not the khakis and white tank, but now he had to admit, he was hot. He was ready for a nap.

"We could be related," he said.

Sharina laughed. "I doubt it."

"You Apache?" she asked, and Matthew paused, thought about how close they were and how incredibly far apart. They had never talked about this, or about how Matthew was becoming a father to her child, about whether they would ever move in together, about what would happen if he didn't live. Because he probably wouldn't.

"Yeah. I'm Navajo too," he said, letting go of her hand and leading her toward La Fonda. "And white."

"You Navajo?" she asked, looking incredulous.

"Yeah."

"Wow," she said, shaking her head. "You don't look Navajo."

"I know. I look. more like my dad," he said, frowning. He realized that they'd never talked about that either, and that he didn't want to.

"It's just that I donno, like Navajo, they're like, real Indians and shit," she said, and Matthew didn't know what to say. "Or they're like, you know, street Indians."

Matthew felt sick. He wanted to lie down. "You ready to check in?" he asked.

"Yeah, I am," she answered brightly, taking his hand. He let her, and they walked back toward the car.

After a long nap, Matthew felt better. He had to field calls from some of his homies, and from Stanford. They were talking about how Chris was going to get out in a month, and how they were going to get both him, and Matthew into a new place, maybe let the Mathematician take over where they were at now. Get Chris and Matthew more into the business side of things. Chris had been doing right behind bars, kowtowing to the Chicano and Mexican gangs they were affiliated with, using the fact that he was half Mexican and the fact that the Chicano gangs identified strongly with their Native roots. Trying to make them feel like the 505s were there to serve them, and never to take over. Because if they thought that for even a second, Stanford had told them, and they knew, they would be stomped out fast and violently. There would be nothing left. Matthew had been holding it down outside. It was time that they started taking over some of the coordination of shipments from Mexico, time that they started working on bigger projects when it came to the money side of things.

"Get some work done baby?" Sharina asked, rolling over on the crisp, lavender-scented hotel sheets and pressing herself into his side. He had laid back down after he'd been done with his calls.

"Yeah," he said. "Hungry?"

"Very," she said.

"Let's eat in the restaurant here, it's really cool," he said.

"Sure," she said, and they both got up and began getting ready. That wasn't a long process for Matthew, but for Sharina, who loved to dress up, it involved curling long dark hair, applying make-up, pulling on pantyhose; a dress going over her bare brown shoulders, and a zip that needed zipping with Matthew's help, her tattoos disappearing as the dress slid on. He watched her get ready, thinking about how lovely she was, how nice she smelled, how easygoing she was about him, his life. Maybe that was why he could be with her. But it was also why he couldn't love her. There was so little in there. She was a survivor, but she wasn't a fighter. She was too much like him. In all honesty, he liked his women a little rough ... like Maria. But he knew better than to get involved with them. They were like his mother, they would only take that soulful roughness and turn it on you.

The restaurant was packed, and they talked about going else-where, and quickly decided that that would be best. Outside they wandered, hand in hand, Indian Market closed up for the evening, tourists out in their newly purchased turquoise, some of them so obviously wealthy it hurt Matthew's eyes to look at them, their newly purchased velvet shirts, their silver conch belts.

Sharina was talking about Manuel, about how excited she was that he was going to be in preschool. Matthew thought about himself at that age. Someone had come to the door, someone from the state. His mother had never bothered to enroll him and his sister, and when the woman had come, his mother had been drunk. He didn't understand why he and his sister hadn't been taken from her then. But he was glad. Cruel as his mother could be, the system was even crueler. He and his sister would have been separated, and foster homes were filled to the brink with children, the foster mothers almost always fostering for the check from the government. And children were hurt in there, by adults, by other children who were brimming with rage and pain. And though there were the men who had come at night, his mother's men, going into the system almost guaranteed that someone would touch you at night. And there would be no sister then to comfort you after. Just other silent, fearful children, glad it wasn't them.

They were rounding a corner, Sharina was still talking happily about Manuel, about the school supplies she was going to get him at Walmart when they saw them. The Mathematician was wearing the usual khaki but he had a nice button-down shirt covering most of his tattoos. Maria was in a short, red dress. They stopped. The Mathematician tried to play it cool, but they knew what was up. It was obvious.

"Hey, Ishkeh," the Mathematician said, and Matthew went silent.

"This is your friend?" Sharina asked, and the Mathematician looked down at his phone and then away.

"Yeah! I mean, he had nothing to do and I was trying to give you guys some space—"

Matthew punched the Mathematician in the face so hard, he went straight down into the cobble stone streets, his legs bending out comically out from underneath him as he did.

"What are you doing?" Maria yelled, pulling on Matthew's arm. He threw her off. "You whore," he said. She began to cry.

"Matthew stop," Sharina said, and he turned to her with rage in his eyes. "This is work. You stay out of this."

"And you," he said, turning back to Maria, "you're coming with us. We're all going home. And you, *Ishkeh*," Matthew said bitterly, "stay down. And wait for me to call your bitch ass to tell you that it's OK to come back. If I do. And I might tell Chris. I'll decide later."

Sharina and Maria followed Matthew back to the hotel silently. Once they got to their room, Sharina packed their things, tears running down her cheeks, while Maria sat in the big, antique chair, looking out the window, her expression that of a petulant child's.

In the car on the way down, Maria tried to talk a few times, to lie about what they'd seen, but Matthew knew. He'd known for a while now, or felt like he should have. The cologne, the way they were almost never in the room together at the same time and when they were, the funny looks, the way they avoided talking to one another. Matthew's rage built. He wanted a drink.

"Shut up!" he'd yell every time she opened her mouth. He hated her. Hated her for making him feel for her, for being just like his mother. A slut who used men, who had no feeling for anyone but themselves.

He dropped Sharina off at her house first, telling her that he'd call her tomorrow. On the way back to his house, where he planned on taking Maria so that she couldn't go off somewhere and shoot up, he tried to bank the rage inside of himself but he couldn't, it just kept building. He parked and barked at Maria to get her ass in the house. It was silent, the homies either in bed or out on a deal.

"Sit down," he said to her, pointing to the couch.

She sat, that angry, petulant expression still on her face.

He went into the kitchen for the tequila and a couple of glasses. He brought it all out, set it down on the coffee table, poured them both a drink. He drank his first in one gulp, then poured himself another.

Maria did the same, holding her glass out silently and letting him pour.

He sighed, hard, his anger beginning to boil down, simmer. "Why'd you have to go to Santa Fe? At least answer me that."

She opened her mouth. Closed it. "I was jealous."

He shook his head, "God, you dumb bitch."

"Stop calling me that shit!" she yelled. "You sound like him!"

"Shut up," he said, standing up, "Or I'll tell Chris, even though it will start shit, even though it'll kill him. Fuck, he's getting out next month? And you start up with one of his homies?"

"So what! He cheats on me all the time! And with fucking whore strippers!"

Matthew stood over her and sighed. "And you cheat on him."

"*So fucking what*? That's what we do. We're both cheaters and I'm a junkie, what the fuck do you care?" she asked, pouring herself another shot and downing it. "Why do you even care what he thinks?"

"He saved my life," Matthew said. "And the least you could do is not make it so fucking obvious Maria, Jesus, I mean, why did it have to be him? And why did you take him to Santa Fe? You could have had the run of half of Albuquerque, if you'd been careful."

She began to cry. "Because I wanted you to see!"

He narrowed his eyes in confusion. "Why? So that I'd tell Chris? Jesus, what the fuck is wrong with you?"

"*Don't you get it, Ishkeh?* I'm tired of being clean," she said, tears running down her face. "I just want him to leave me the *fuck alone* so that I can finally die. I want to die. I just hate living clean, I hate living at all."

Matthew stood in silence, and then sat down next to her and poured himself a drink. He was feeling incredibly drunk now, and he was sure she was too. They were both sweating, and Matthew shook his head.

"I used to feel that way. I feel that way sometimes still," he said, nearly whispering, even though they were alone. "Why are we like this?" The anger had turned now. It was gone.

Now she was silent. Then, "I don't know. I feel sometimes like I was born this way. I mean I grew up bad too ... I mean, sorry, Chris tells me things."

Matthew tensed up. It horrified him to know that she knew about the men.

"Men touched me too you know. My mother's boyfriends. She liked white guys. And they would beat her, and ... take her. Sometimes they would prefer me, and she would let them," she said.

He hung his head. She patted him on the shoulder. He put his arm around her and drew her in. He felt something wild light up inside of him, and he knew she could feel it too. She turned her face to his and they kissed and immediately he knew that he was in love with her, that this was what love was, and he could feel the thing inside him move, fly free. He pulled her by the hand off the couch and into his bedroom, knowing that he would hate her the next day, avoid her, hate himself and that this was the worst thing that he could possibly do. But that there was no way he was not going to do it.

NINE

"WE CAN'T TELL *ANYONE*," MATTHEW WAS SAYING. "AND IT CAN never, ever happen again."

Maria was looking at him, her eyes slit like a snake's. She had left the next morning because she had to work and had texted him around noon that she loved him, that she wanted to see him. That they needed to tell everyone. He had not answered. She had come over after work, and he had had to lead her to his bedroom, as the homies were around, Damien sitting on the couch and watching TV, and he still didn't know what to do about the Mathematician. Matthew was just as guilty now.

"Fuck you we can't tell! Why not? I love you!"

"Well I don't love you," Matthew spit, and Maria began to tear up. She was sitting on his bed.

"That's a lie," she said, her lip quivering.

"No, it's not. I couldn't love you anyway, after the way this happened."

"That's stupid," she said, "and another lie."

"Think what you want," he said, looking over her shoulder and out the window. He went over to it and closed the aged blinds. It was bad enough that the homies had seen her come in and act like she was his girlfriend, greeting him by coming up to him and hugging him tight, the way she had. Especially Damien. He loved Chris. He had to do damage control now. Get her to see reason. Get her to *go away*.

"Why are you doing this?" she asked. She was looking up at him, her long black eyes filled with despair. "You know we belong together. Fuck Chris."

Matthew laughed, and Maria's eyes narrowed even further. "Stop that. It's mean."

"Mean? What about Chris? He loves you! He's come after you a million times, cleaned you up a million times. Me too."

"You don't get it do you?" she asked, her expression one of wonder. "You still don't get him." She shook her head, her lips a small, tight line.

He looked down at her, irritation in his voice. "What do you mean? Of course I get him! We get each other, we're homies and we'll be OGs together!"

It was her turn to laugh. "No. You and me? We're nothing but things to him. Things he owns. He did all that shit for you so you would have mad loyalty. I've seen him do it before," she said, scooting back on the bed so that she could lean against the wall, the blue and yellow sheets still dirty from their night together, and she pulled her long brown legs up and crossed them, folding her hands on top of them and leaning forward.

"Before?"

"Yes. With plenty of boys like you. He finds them, he cleans them up. Boys with no daddies like you. Like him. And then he puts them in the line of fire so that he isn't, and usually they go down. But you survived."

Matthew thought about this, his mind racing through all of the times that he and Chris had been on shoot-outs together, shit they did in front of God, smash and grabs ... he thought about how it'd gone down. He couldn't say she was right. But he couldn't say she was wrong either.

"I don't know..." he said, shaking his head. "You're just trying to make me paranoid. You're jealous of us. Chris always says that women are jealous of what men have, that they want to break up our friendship."

It was her turn to laugh. "Jesus, you his man now? Is that what you want?" He walked up to her rapidly, and made to slap her in the face but stopped. Her face was turned toward and up at him, her expression defiant, strong. *God* he loved her so much.

"Go ahead, I know you want to. You want to hit me because you scared I'm right. And you want to hit me because you never got to punish mommy for all the shit she did to you. And you want to hit me because you love me, and it hurts."

He sighed and lowered his hand slowly until it was at his side. It wasn't him. He had never hit a woman, and he didn't want to start. He hated her then, hated her mouth, her words, the fact that she was taking all of the things he had worked so hard to bury and pull them up with her long brown hands, her pointed red fingernails. He lived, maybe badly, but he lived by standing on top of those things, by pushing them down, keeping them down.

"If you think so bad of Chris and the 505s, why don't you leave?"

She turned to him and sat up. "You fucking think it's that easy? Shit, I might as well be one of the 505s, you idiot. They'll find me. They'll shoot me full of holes. That's another reason why I want to die. Only way out when you know as much as I do. But shit, at least I was willing to try with you. Willing to see if we could do it. I felt like . . . you were brave. I guess I was wrong."

Matthew sighed and his anger began falling away from him, like some kind of black powwow shawl someone had draped around his shoulders without his knowing. He sat down next to her.

"I'm not brave," he said.

"You are," she said. "You just . . . don't know any better. You don't know anything different." She leaned into him.

"I'm a fuck-up Maria," he said.

She laughed softly, without cruelty this time. "No baby. You're like . . . like one of them clowns we got at home," she said, running her hands over his head. Her palms felt like velvet. Like brown velvet.

"I'm a clown?" he asked.

"No baby. Like, you not silly like the clowns back home are. But you're something crazy so that all of us can see how crazy we are without being crazy. Even Chris. He thinks he a clown, but he's just a fucking idiot. You a real clown."

He was silent. He didn't understand. She pulled him to her, put his head in her lap. Stroked his hair. "I know. It ain't fair, this shit. And men. Damn, you guys are so stubborn. You get shit in your heads and you just run with it like you're bulls." He felt it again, that deep, unbearable beauty inside him that he felt when her hands were on him. It felt like he was burning up from the inside, like he was a supernova but he didn't know which way he was going to go, explosion or black hole.

Matthew laughed and then he went silent, he let her touch his hair, his face. He closed his eyes and fell into the beauty. It felt like . . . like love. His phone began to go off. He was sure it was Sharina. This was a mess. A horrible, horrible mess.

"Maybe we could get out together," she said. "Tell the cops."

"No," he said. "That's no way out. And besides, I don't want out. I like being a 505, even if what you're saying about Chris is true. I like having a family. I never had that before."

She stopped stroking his hair. "Then you as stupid as he is."

"I guess so," he said, and she began to kiss him.

"This is wrong," he whispered, pulling her jean shorts off and pushing her up to him.

"Everything is wrong," she said.

He sighed and moved into her, his body singing, his phone beeping insistently.

After, they lay on the bed. He had tried to urge her to be quiet, and had tried to be quiet himself, but it was difficult. He hoped the homies were too busy with their own shit to care, but he was sure they were storing the information up in case it could be used later. She picked his book up from his bedside table and looked at it, pulled it open like she had him.

"You smart," she said.

"Nah. I just like stories. You wanna borrow that? I'm done. It's a Hemingway."

She looked at the book thoughtfully. Read the back. "I read this one. I used to like to read in school. Teachers thought I was smart. That I was gonna get out." she laughed. "I guess they were right." She put the book back onto the table.

"What are we going to do?" he asked.

"Nothing. This. Since you don't want to tell the cops. Since you don't want to tell Chris and everyone in front of God."

"I don't want to tell the cops. I ain't no tattletale. I know that's wrong. And Chris would kill us both, and you know it. And it would hurt him, you're wrong about that. He does love you, and I'm a fucker for fucking his woman."

She sat up. "*His* woman? Again, you act like you and I both are his things. He's got you fucking brainwashed," she said. "And as for telling the cops, why is that so wrong? You think drugs are so great? Why don't you shoot up then. I'll help. We can be junkies together. That would be nice."

He sighed. He was too tired to be angry. He didn't even like being angry, it didn't come natural to him. He looked down at his long brown hands, at the deep purple-and-white scars, at the ache that was already coming from hitting so many people, so many things that he had never even wanted to touch. "I don't like junk. I like booze," he said, laughing bitterly. He was silent then. He thought about Chris. About Maria. About what she was telling him about calling the cops. His stomach began to burn with hope. With betrayal.

"Two peas in a fucking pod," she said, rolling away from him. He closed his eyes, tried pushing her away inside himself, but he couldn't, not now. He pulled her toward him, and she curled into his side. She felt like alcohol, like too much alcohol, like that warm place that he knew, that he used to be in when he was drinking in Farmington. That golden spot where he was so drunk, and he'd find a place, maybe a big green desert bush with a spot that some other drunk had smoothed out before him underneath, and he'd pass out and sleep and sleep and dream and feel like he was in his mother's arms, the few times she would hold him.

"This feels so good," he whispered.

"Yes," she said, and they made love again. He couldn't help it.

After, he got up and picked his phone up and texted Sharina that they should hang tonight, texted the Mathematician that he should come back and get the fuck to work, and he called Stanford, who was, supposed to come over that night to talk about a shipment, and to talk more about what was going to happen when Chris got out, when the transition was going to take place.

"You need to leave, before the Ishkehs really start to suspect what's up. Plus, your little boyfriend is coming back, Mr. Mathematician. I'm letting him come back because I need him. Because he's good at what he does," Matthew said, standing over her. She was still in bed, naked, lying there with one leg bent at the knee.

Maria laughed. "He was never my boyfriend. He was there because I was jealous of you and Sharina."

Matthew was silent for a moment, his eyes narrowing in confusion. "Why did you introduce me and Sharina then? That's really fucked up. She's your friend. And so . . . so am I."

"Because I was trying to make myself not like you. I was trying to throw her in your path. Plus, she deserves a good man, and you a good man," she said, leaning over the side of the bed and getting a cigarette from the end table. She lit up, blew smoke. "But then it just made me want you more."

Matthew shook his head. "I don't think you really love me. I think you think like a junkie, and junkies just want everything, they don't care who they fuck over. I know, because that's the way I am about booze. Or how I was, before Chris."

"Come here," she said, and he shook his head. He had to learn to control his feelings for her, to let her know that he was in control, the way Chris was always telling him. She looked up at him, and he couldn't help it, he came over to her and sat down.

She sighed, pulled herself up to him, rested her small brown chin on his shoulder. She was so close in height to him, and he liked that. He'd always ended up with short girls, but it's not what he preferred. "Look. I'll go," she said, the heat of her body pure hozho, hozho, his Shimásáni's word. "But I want you to just think about what I'm saying. About the cops. About getting out of this shit. 'Cause I do love you. 'Cause you and me, we the same."

He was silent as she pulled her clothes on, that ache in his stomach, so unfamiliar, relighting. Hope. He had already put his clothes on. He walked out with her, though she stopped at the bedside table and after looking thoughtfully down at his book for a moment, plucked it from the table and tucked it into her bag. He was ready to make it look like it was nothing at all, start talking as if he'd had to pull her into the bedroom to talk business if the homies were out in the living room, but it was empty.

"I'll call you later," she said. "And dammit just *think* about what I'm saying," and Matthew realized that he was nodding. He watched her open the door and leave. He stood for a while and looked at the big, wooden door, framed by the two blue-curtained windows on each side. The windows were open and the wind was blowing the curtains inward, the motion of it punctuating the feelings of loss and emptiness he felt at her absence. He had to find a way to not feel those feelings, he had to find a way to gain control.

The Mathematician came back around noon. The door opened, and Matthew was sitting on the couch, his piece by his side. He had texted the other homies to stay lost for a little while, and they had silently obliged. The Mathematician shut the door and looked at him. Matthew picked his gun up, didn't look at him, let him squirm, though the guy was pretty cool. He just stood there, quietly, waiting either to die or to go on.

"This is what we're going to do today," Matthew said, cleaning his gun with a rag. "There's this guy. He and his friend owe the 505s a lot of money. He hasn't paid it, but he kept asking for H. We gave him more, telling him that he had to pay. This has gone on too long."

The Mathematician was silent. Matthew thought about how funny he looked with the bridge of his glasses all taped up, his nose swollen and blue.

"So we're gonna go over there, and we're either gonna hurt him a lot, or kill him. I'll figure out how I feel when we get there. But you gonna do the hurting, you get me?" Matthew said, pausing in cleaning his gun. He looked up.

The Mathematician was cool, he nodded.

"You got your piece?" Matthew asked, standing up and walking over to the kitchen, opening a an old wooden drawer and throwing the rag in it.

"Shit yeah," the Mathematician said.

"Let's go then," Matthew said, tucking his gun in the back of his khaki pants.

"Wait," the Mathmatician said, and he walked down the hallway and into the room he shared with the other homies. He came out a few minutes later with a big, black gym bag.

"You think we're going to play some ball?" Matthew asked, confused.

"Hell nah, Ishkeh," the Mathematician said. "This my hurt bag. But it look like a gym bag, huh? That's what's so great about it," he said, looking almost cartoonish with his taped-up glasses. He'd been lucky that Matthew's punch had only broken the bridge. He opened it up, after setting it down on the couch, the unzipping loud and unsettling. There was a length of pipe, brass knuckles, and a few other things that looked basically like long, surgical needles.

"Shit," Matthew said.

"Yeah. Sometimes people need to be shown who the fuck is in charge is all. And when you show them pain, they not only know who the fuck they are, but who the fuck you are, too."

Matthew realized then that the Mathematician wasn't just a 505, a little gangbanger, he was a straight-out psychopath. The rest of them grew up in violence, bad homes, drugs—they got used to this shit. But the Mathematician, he enjoyed it. But they needed people like him, that was the thing.

"Let's roll," Matthew said.

On the way there, they smoked a blunt, one hit after another, Matthew silently taking a flask of vodka out from underneath the driver's seat and taking a swig, and passing it to Math, who shook his head no. Matthew took another swig and put it back.

The house was a piece of shit, there was no other way of putting it. It was in the North part of Albuquerque, a small sleazy part that was not far from one of the best parts, and when they got out, Matthew looked around to make sure there were no witnesses. There were kids out playing, as it was around five o'clock, and maybe a few cars on the street, but no one was paying attention.

Matthew didn't knock, he just walked in, the Mathematician silently following, his hurt bag clutched firmly in his short, strong brown hand. There were three junkies, one passed out on an ancient blue Lay-Z-Boy, and two, a man and a woman semi-curled together on a couch, watching TV. It was MTV2, and there was an old Smashing Pumpkins video playing, the light of it flooding eerily throughout the house, which was otherwise dark, as the curtains were pulled and the lights were off. They jumped when Matthew opened and then shut the door.

"What—?" the guy said, as Matthew locked the door.

"Shut the fuck up *now*," Matthew said. The guy swung his long legs out from under his woman and set them on the floor. He was wearing black jeans and an ancient Megadeath T-shirt that looked like they hadn't been washed since the T-shirt was first issued. The woman, sensing that something was about to go very, very bad, crawled back into the corner of the couch and crossed her legs. She was skinny, and white, and wearing an old pair of shorts and a faded pink tank top.

"This place fucking *stinks*," the Mathematician said, letting his bag go. It landed on the floor with a large whumping noise.

"I . . . I . . ." the guy said. The other dude in the Lay-Z-Boy was still asleep.

"Where is the money," Matthew said, walking up to the dude on the couch, and staring down at his rat's nest of greasy hair. The guy began to pick nervously at his acne. "Yo, I mean, look, I'll get you the money. I mean, that's not the issue—" Matthew stopped him by round-housing him once on the chin, the guy falling back into the couch, his mouth splitting and bleeding.

The Mathematician starting laughing. "You ever notice that white junkies bleed the most? Damn, that shit genetic?"

Matthew stared at the junkie, and his woman began to whimper.

"The money," Matthew said. "Now."

The junkie scooted back far into the couch. "I know I owe you. I know. It's just that I don't have it right now," he said, and Matthew looked back over at Math and nodded. The Mathematician unzipped his bag.

"No, no man! I hearda you! You torture people and shit!" The junkie said, his voice rising. He got up, Matthew's hand shot out, and he held him by his crusty shirt. The man began to squirm.

"The money," Matthew repeated.

"I don't got it! But don't do this, man, I mean, I can call my uncle. He's rich. And like, he likes me, and I know I can get some money from him, I just haven't been trying hard enough—"

The Mathematician had come forward with his length of pipe, and with one hard whack, he hit the guy so hard in the arm that Matthew heard a crack. He drew back as the man screamed, and Matthew let him slump to the floor.

"What the—" the guy in the Lay-Z-Boy said, finally waking up, his face covered in his own spit.

"You sit tight and shut the fuck up," Matthew said, and the guy nodded, his dirty blond hair swinging.

"The fucking money. Now," Matthew said and the junkie began to cry, hard.

"OK, OK, you come back tomorrow and I swear to God, I'll have the money. I'll have five-fucking grand, I swear to God."

"What if your uncle won't give it to you?" Matthew asked flatly.

"Yeah, what about that?" the Mathematician said, his arm holding the length of pipe raised high.

The junkie looked at Math's hand nervously.

"You know your brain calculates shit?" the Mathematician said.

"Wh-what?" the junkie asked.

"Yeah. It's like a fucking computer. Like, it knows exactly how hard, and like what kind of arc I need to have, like in fractions and shit, that it needs to have in order to hit you in the same spot in the other arm and shit. And the last time, I'm pretty sure I broke your arm."

"No, no, please don't hurt him," the girl whimpered and the Mathematician swung around toward her. She put her arms over her face and started crying hard, loud.

"Maybe I should break your woman's face. Maybe that'll motivate you to give us the fucking money, you stinky, fucking junkie," Math said.

"No! Dude, no I promise. Tomorrow I'll have it. We'll have it."

"Why should I believe you? I think you're going to run. I think if I let you go, tomorrow, I'll knock on your door, and you won't be here. You'll be somewhere else. How the fuck do I know that that won't happen?"

"Yeah. Tell him how," Math said.

The junkie looked panicked, his eyes darting back and forth.

"Now, man!" the Mathematician said, raising the pipe again.

"Wait! Wait! You could . . . I'll chain Linda to the radiator, and—"

"What?" the woman said, sitting up and looking at her man. The Mathematician started laughing wildly. "Man, these fucking junkies. They don't give a flying shit about the people around them, do they? Go on, tell me how that would fix this," the Mathematician said. "And you!" he said, pointing the pipe over at the women. "You shut the fuck up, now! You can't even imagine how much I want to break your face. That's like coming to me, you get it? So you shut up!" Her wide pink mouth slapped shut in one quick, hard motion, making a clapping sound.

"Yeah, see, I'll chain her here, and then you know I'll come back."

"You stupid fucking junkie, that's the stupidest thing I've ever fucking heard. You willing to chain this bitch up, so we supposed to think you care enough about her ass to come back for her. That's it, I'ma fuck you up."

"Wait," the guy in the Lay-Z-Boy said. "Wait. I can get the money. Now."

The Mathematician grunted and began swinging his arm up toward the junkie's unbroken arm, but Matthew stayed his hand. That's what he was good at. Control.

"How?" Matthew said.

"Look. We're junkies. We know it. We've drained our families and sometimes we get jobs, but we don't keep them. So we figured we could start holding people up. That's what we were gonna do. And the thing is, I own this piece-of-shit house. It was my aunt's, and I was her favorite, and when she died, she gave it to me. You're over there harassing my friend Craig, but the fact is, we all owe you. Craig's just the guy who's bought it for us. He buys it, I give him and Linda a place to stay, and he gives me some of his H. I don't like it as much as he does, is the thing. He's crazy for it, and eventually he'll OD, and I'll have to come home to a dead man. But you don't give a shit about that, you give a shit about the money. And that's your job. I'll get you the money. Today. Now. If you can stay here an hour, watch him, I'll be back."

Matthew thought about this. Ultimately, this fucker could be lying. But he figured if he was, that the junkie who owed the 505s money would rat him out, because that's what junkies did. He wouldn't let him go.

"This true?" Matthew asked and the junkie on the couch, Craig, nodded. "Yeah."

104

"You've got an hour," Matthew said, turning back to the Lay-Z-Boy junkie. "If you aren't back in an hour, you'll come home to two dead bodies now, instead of one dead body in a year. And maybe I'll kill them and call the cops on my way out, and tell them I saw you do it. And make it look like you did. I'm good at that. And if you try to run, I'll tell them what you looked like. Oh, and you're going to leave your license with me."

The junkie nodded and got up off the Lay-Z-Boy. "I gotta use the little boy's room, OK?" he said, and Matthew nodded at the Mathematician. He walked into the hallway, the Mathematician following. Craig had begun to cry. Matthew was sure he was in junk-pain as well as pain from the broken arm. The Lay-Z-Boy junkie came back, and handed Matthew his license from a an old black wallet that was sitting on an end table that was also covered in needles, lint, candy wrappers, old bent-looking spoons and lighters.

"What a fucking life," Math said, and the junkie from the Lay-Z-Boy looked like he wanted to retort, but changed his mind. Matthew knew that was a smart move. No matter the cost, if he had, Math would've fucked him up for it.

The Lay-Z-Boy junkie left, and Matthew stood against the wall, watching the TV. Now it was a Metallica video. More Matthew's speed. The Mathematician sat on the Lay-Z-Boy, first checking it for needles.

They were silent. Matthew wanted to look at Craig's arm, see if it was broken, see if there was anything he could do, but he knew better. He knew he had to be tough on them, or this would keep happening. If they really were going to start holding convenience stores up, eventually, they would get caught, go to jail. But they would cease to be Matthew's problem then. The TV blared and then Craig moved close to his girlfriend, who began whispering in his ear and telling him that everything was going to be OK. That Mike would be back in time, and that he'd get the money, and that then they'd take him to the hospital. She was stroking his hair, and Matthew couldn't help but think of Maria, and he shuddered. He pulled his phone out of his pocket and saw several texts from the homies, but nothing from Maria. Or Sharina for that matter. He looked at the TV. A Pink video came on, and he watched her sing and dance and cry about a relationship that had died a violent, ugly death. It felt ominous, this whole house felt like the inside of a horror show—its dirt, its sadness, its sickness. There was a part of Matthew that wanted to gun them all down, spare them from their own lives, let the poison that was inside of him out, but he wasn't that person. He didn't even like doing what he was doing now. He looked at his phone again. The Lay-Z-Boy junkie had been gone for a half an hour now. He knew he'd let him have more than an hour, but not much. Because if he did run, they would get the reputation for being soft, and that was the last thing that the 505s needed.

"Your friend better get back soon," the Mathematician said, breaking the silence. "I really like to fuck people up. And you don't want to know what else is in my bag." Craig and Linda looked over at him as he said this, and quickly away. Matthew could feel their fear like it was a palpable thing. About twenty minutes later, the Lay-Z-Boy junkie, Mike, came back, looking surprisingly calm.

"I got enough to pay you back, and enough for some more," he said, after he'd shut the door. Matthew figured he'd left some of the cash in his car, because he knew that whatever they had on them, they were going to take, which was true. He also knew that if he were with Chris, he would tell him to take him to the car and to dig through it until he was satisfied that he wasn't hiding any cash in there. But that wasn't Matthew.

He handed them the packet of H, and they left.

As they were getting in the car, Math turned to him. "Why didn't you run his ass over to his car, make him search through it?" He looked suspicious, calculating.

"Too tired. Plus, if there was money in there, we'll get it."

"I guess," the Mathematician said, shoving his hurt bag into the back of the car. Matthew looked at him sharply. The Mathematician looked back, nearly defiant. Matthew was ready to pull his piece out and pistol whip him. Math looked away.

Matthew thought about how much he hated this, hated Math. Chris. How guilty he felt for feeling that last one.

Back at home, he sat down on the couch and cracked a beer open, texted Sharina that she should come over. The Mathematician and the other homies were out dealing, and he had the place to himself. He had made it clear to Math that he should get lost. Sharina texted him back that she would be over in an hour, right after work, that she had talked to Maria and that they were planning on bringing something to make for dinner. Matthew's heart began to race. What had she told her? If she'd told her anything, Matthew would deny it. Would kick her the fuck out. But then what was he going to do about Chris? He went over what Maria had told him, wondering what was true. He felt sick. He had another beer. He thought about what she wanted them to do. He waited. Turned on the TV. Turned it off. Looked at his phone. Composed a long text to Maria. Deleted it. About an hour later, the door opened, and it was Sharina.

"Hey sweetie!" she said, walking into the kitchen first and putting down several grocery bags. He followed her in, and when she set them down, she turned to him and wrapped her arms around him. "I brought stuff for enchiladas. And Maria's bringing stuff for Margaritas."

"Oh yeah?" he said.

"Yeah," she said. "I'll go ahead and get started."

"OK," Matthew said, and she began talking about work, about the people at work who she hated. About people at the reception desk who gave her trouble. About her supervisors, who she mainly liked, except for one. Matthew began to relax, though he didn't know how he felt about Maria coming over. It was risky for a variety of reasons. Sharina might see through them, or Maria might get drunk and reveal everything, she was unpredictable like that. The door opened, and he tensed.

"Hey guys!" she yelled, coming into the kitchen. "Damn, it smells good!" She came over to Sharina and hugged her, and then started making Margaritas, and she and Sharina fell into their routine. They talked and laughed, and Matthew mainly listened.

This is what they began to do. Pretend. They hung out at night just as they always had, all three of them, though Maria mysteriously didn't come over on Fridays or Saturdays anymore, and Matthew figured this was something that the two of them, Sharina and Maria, had discussed.

Sharina and he started talking about moving in together. Maria continued to work on Matthew about going to the cops. And he began to listen.

Chris was getting out, and they were about to get their own place. They would live together, but it would be just them and it would be somewhere nice, in Rio Rancho, in the suburbs, with money leftover to get Maria's sister a nurse to help with her diabetes. Sharina was ready to take it a step further as she put it. And . . . she made him happy. Or more precisely, she made him not unhappy, not too happy.

Maria came over in the afternoons, in-between shifts, and they would fuck in his bed until he was delirious, and Maria told him that there was a cop she knew, a nice one. He'd been undercover years ago, and right before he got out, he'd told her that she could get out, that he wouldn't tattle if she didn't but that she could go with him if she wanted to. But that she hadn't because back then, she'd believed Chris loved her. But that she still had his card.

They would talk about their childhoods, about the book she had borrowed to reread to, as she put it, remind her of who she had been, who she wanted to be. She told him it made her sad but in a good way. They talked about what they thought about things, and they laughed; they laughed a lot. They did not talk about what was going to happen when Chris got out, and they did not talk about what Maria did on Friday or Saturday evenings. But all of this was about to come to an end, one way or another, Matthew knew that. Chris was getting out, and when he did, everything was going to have to change, absolutely everything.

MATTHEW TOOK THE SUV TO PICK CHRIS UP AND WAITED, THE volume on the radio turned up. He had the iPhone set up to play all of Chris's favorites. And he knew what he was going to want to do as soon as he got back. He was going to want to go to the Frontier, eat carne asada, and then head straight to Palms. He had told Matthew that this is what he wanted many, many times. He sighed. Thought about Maria's long, brown legs trembling around him, her cries, the way she talked about her childhood on the pueblo. About the cop whose card she still had.

He heard a bus pulling up, stopping. He watched as people got off. And there was Chris, stepping off the bus, walking toward him with a smile, his eyes looking dangerous, restless, full of what he wanted out of life.

He opened the passenger door. Slammed it shut. "Drive this fucking thing," he said, "Drive it to so fucking hard, Ishkeh."

Matthew hit the pedal, and Chris laughed wildly as Matthew handed him a splif. Chris lit it, took a long, poetic toke and handed it back to Matthew who inhaled hard, like someone had handed him a tall, cold glass of water on a hot day. They sped north.

"This shit is going to get real," Chris said.

TEN

THE MOVE TO RIO RANCHO WENT QUICK, QUICKER THAN MATTHEW thought it would, the girls squealing over the new, large Mexican-tiled bathrooms, the big plushly carpeted bedrooms. Rio Rancho was a suburban dream, and the girls were more than happy to move into it, leaving behind a life of shitty apartments and houses crowded with relatives and their children, with cockroaches and faded, frayed, musty-smelling old towels, other people's boyfriends, cracked walls, ancient, stained kitchens.

The morning after he had picked Chris up, after an evening of strippers, booze, coke, and more body glitter than Matthew thought existed on this planet, they collapsed into their respective beds, thank God, around 5:00 a.m. Chris had not brought any strippers home with him, and at first Matthew had been very grateful for this. But his heart had sunk when he heard Maria coming in thirty minutes later to what became a tearful reunion, one that culminated in loud sex. He felt sick, angry. And he wasn't sure who he should be angry at, though he knew in that moment that he hated them both.

That night, the two sets of couples had their first double date at Little Anita's in Old Town. Chris and Sharina both looked ecstatic. Matthew kept giving Maria furtive looks over the rim of his Margarita, of which he had four in an hour and a half. She looked cooler than he did, joking and talking and wrapping her right arm around Chris occasionally, though he could see she was uneasy. Uncharacteristically,

Chris allowed her small affections, though Matthew knew if she went too far, he'd push her off with one of his, "Nah, babys."

As Sharina and Maria talked about moving in together, about how they would be a family, about how Maria wanted to be like an auntie for Manuel, Matthew wondered if Maria and he would still be together, and if so, how. He wondered if it had all been a bunch of shit on her part, if she loved him at all, or if she had just needed attention during Chris's absence. She turned to Chris, called him, "baby," and waved the waitress down frequently, telling her that "her man" needed more salsa, or another Margarita.

"Aren't you excited?" Sharina asked Matthew, leaning over in the big, plastic red seats and elbowing him.

He blinked. For a minute there, he'd almost forgotten she existed.

"Oh, oh, yes. Of course," he said, leaning over and patting her knee. She smiled, content, and Matthew felt sorry for her. He looked over at Manuel, who was busy pushing the little bits of soggy enchilada that Sharina had cut up for him around on his plate. He smiled, laughed, and then joyfully hit both hands against the high chair and began to wail. Sharina got up and comforted him, then took off to the bathroom. Matthew felt sick. It wasn't right to bring a child into this kind of life.

"Damn, man, we OGs, now," Chris said. "What I tell you, Ishkeh?"

"You're right," Matthew answered, feeling drunk. "We're OGs now." Maria looked at him, and he looked directly into her eyes, the sorrow and anger that he felt a palpable thing. She looked away.

"Can we get some good furniture? You know, like the good shit? Like the shit they got in furniture stores on Nob Hill?" Maria asked Chris excitedly.

"Course, baby," he answered, and she clapped her hands like a little girl.

Maria liked expensive things. Matthew remembered walking on Nob Hill once with her and Sharina, Sharina talking about the new things that Manuel was doing, and Maria nodding distractedly, walking toward the furniture stores that featured big, expensive, often antique pieces in their windows. She had begged to go in each one, and she could spend hours in them, asking the salespeople about the different pieces, their histories. She particularly liked anything French. She scoffed at New Mexican–style furniture, said it was for old people and tourists. Matthew didn't know anything about furniture, and he had no opinion about it. But he loved Maria, and so he would listen as she would go on and on about how someday, she would have all the things that she wanted, a dishwasher, a maid, pretty clothes, a house to match. Sometimes she'd fall silent in the middle of talking about this life, and Matthew could tell she was dreaming awake. Matthew couldn't understand. He did like a clean house, that was true, but the house they had been living in was clean. And was only a short distance to downtown, Nob Hill or the South Valley when they had business there.

His mother had never really cleaned anything, except here and there, when a new man was on the scene, and Matthew had hated that, the cockroaches it brought, the dirt built up in the corners, the mold, the fact that his sister had once ended up with lice, and he had had to get it out for her as she wailed, her tiny body pushing him away as he held her and pulled the little comb through her long black hair while she sat in the old, blue bathtub, the bodies of the lice pooling around her.

They finished dinner, and Math was waiting for them outside in a car, Parisian hip-hop blasting from the speakers—the Mathematician liked the foreign stuff. Matthew narrowed his eyes, thinking about this commonality between Maria and Math. Math, who was now their special homie: the homie who was going to come around every week and tell them what the boys in the house had been dealing, how much money they were making, he was going to be their liaison to the house they used to live in. He and Matthew had come to a silent arrangement about Maria. Which was, don't talk about it. But it made Matthew uneasy. All of this was becoming uneasy. It had been perfect, paradise. Now it was all plummeting toward hell. And Matthew hated the way Math treated the pits. He would starve them, hit them hard when they did the littlest thing wrong, and sometimes he would make them fight when he had decided they weren't good enough guard dogs. And he wouldn't even bother to bury the bodies. He just let them pile up in a corner in the yard.

The ride to Rio Rancho was simple, usual, with Maria and Sharina talking about all the things they were going to do for the house, Chris talking at Matthew about how they were going to set things up from here on out. Chris had made a few new connections in prison, most importantly with a couple of rivals of the MS13s, who had connections to some big cartels in Mexico, different than the ones they'd dealt with before in location. And because this group had people from areas where the population was much more Native in culture, in language, they gravitated to the 505s more easily than the MS13s, who were more Spanish—Spanish speaking, Spanish identified. With this new group, the transition of H from the towns the H was grown was even smoother, it was part of the local economy. In this group, they didn't pray to Malverde, the patron saint of drug dealers in much of Mexico, they prayed to vaguely Catholicized versions of Native Gods, and there had been no effort on the part of the local, mountainous population to form autodefensias. Much like with the 505s, these villages, these people, grew up with gangs, with cartels who paid for their schools, their medicine, and recruited directly from those schools. They too saw the sacrifice of their boys as part of a resistance to Spanish Mexico, and they were more than happy to find routes via buses, planes, and cars filled with drug mules who were filled with H, the H eventually making its way into the waiting arms of the 505s. The people that Chris had made friends with were going to be their new best friends, Chris said. And with their new best friends came girls, young drug mules Maria and Sharina were going to help them with, which is why they had quit their jobs, why they were all going to live together. They knew they would be making better money living in the house, and helping the mules who came in because those women needed places to stay, people to pick them up and women to tend to them and the H that they would be carrying. Both Sharina and Maria spoke Spanish.

When the girls started to come though, often they only spoke a little Spanish, and spoke more of their indigenous languages. Maria would teach them bits and pieces of Pueblo, and they would teach her bits and pieces of their language, using Spanish and the little English the women knew to help them along. The strangest thing was when some of their words would sound like Navajo or Pueblo.

They set up the extra bedrooms downstairs to accommodate the women and the secondary kitchen downstairs up to process the H. But upstairs was pristine, it was pretty. Not that it was bad downstairs, but there was a practical element to its construction, one that sort of looked like it had been set up for children by those in the military. There were bunk beds, and baskets of samples for the girls, and it was clean. But it was bare. The kitchen was purely for processing and in fact, food was not allowed in it at all. Upstairs, the girls began to buy things for the main kitchen from the little boutique shops in town—mixers, food processors, thick blue hand-crafted hand towels, a solid, brass steel rack that hung from the ceiling for pots and pans. The bedrooms began to fill too, the beds four-poster, imported, and at the ends of them were little tables or couches, which Matthew didn't understand the need for. He began to feel like the house was something he'd broken into and that soon someone would find him and take him out of it.

"I'm so happy," Sharina was saying. She had just gone in to check on Manuel, who seemed to be getting larger every day. He was a huge baby, his head was huge, his arms wide and fat, and Matthew felt, if not love, something close to it for him. He began to wonder about his father. Sharina rarely talked about him, it was strange. Matthew wondered if he had done anything to her, but he wasn't about to ask. Although they had been together now for more than a year, Matthew still felt like asking her would be wrong, as if it was just none of his business.

"Yes," Matthew answered noncommittally. They were sitting around the kitchen table, Chris out meeting with OGs, and Matthew, Sharina and Maria waiting for some girls from Mexico to come in. The Mathematician picked them up from the airport and brought them to Rio Rancho. He was also the first to know if something had gone wrong at the airport, if the drugs the girls carried in the different parts of their bodies had been discovered, although that hadn't happened yet. Math and Maria would nod at each other politely when they crossed paths, and go their separate ways, though there was always something awkward in their gaze, and Matthew could see it, though Chris, with his gigantic ego, could not. All he did was praise the Mathematician, talk about how if he survived, he would be big, he'd be OG. How great he was at training the dogs.

Maria had gotten quieter. She had never completely quit reading, but lately, she had really begun to read in earnest, and she'd sit in the big, plush couch that they had bought at one of the boutiques downtown and read. She had liked his Hemingway, but her thing was detective novels, though she often complained that she could always predict the ending. Sharina had told her that she should start writing them. Maria would always scoff at this, and say something like, "Shit. I ain't no writer. Those fuckers got degrees." Matthew didn't know about that, but her increasing silence made him wonder. Chris had been back for a few months now, and she was often shut up in her own room if Chris was gone. They had hardly talked at all since Chris's return, and there had been absolutely no discussion about what had gone on between them. He wondered if she was still disappointed in him for not wanting to tell the cops, and he wondered if she thought about that. He should tell Chris. She was a liability. But it just wasn't in Matthew's nature to do something like that, not to mention that he was still tremendously, painfully in love with her.

"Ain't you happy?" Sharina asked Maria. Maria was sitting on the couch, a cup of coffee in her slender brown hand. She had just eaten some toast and fruit with them. She always insisted on fruit

116

now, fresh fruit. Matthew liked it. He had rarely had it, or fresh vegetables, growing up as they had mainly on commods.

Maria finished sipping from her cup, put it down and looked up. She had one of her detective books in her hand, her finger wedged into it to save her place. "Yeah," she said. "I am."

Matthew tried not to look at her but he could feel her staring at him. He looked up briefly, gave her a look of pure, unadulterated grief, and then got up. "I'm going to get things ready downstairs, for when the girls get here."

He could hear Maria sighing deeply as he left, and Sharina asking her what was wrong. Women were always asking each other what was wrong, what they were feeling. It unnerved Matthew when they did that. He went downstairs and began opening the cabinets that held the large metal bowls and setting them down around the table. They were for cleaning the condoms full of H, after they had come out of the girls. He pulled drawers, got razor blades for cutting them open out, and the plastic gloves that they all wore. He sat down at the table and waited, made some calls, listened to the girls chatting happily above. He thought about Maria's naked body, about her long brown form arching at his touch, her mouth open and begging, and he wanted a drink, badly. He went over to the cabinets, and opened some of them, where they kept a lot of hard liquor, the closest thing to food that was allowed on that level, as it was the level where they kept the drinks for their parties, when they weren't using the area for processing H. He pulled a bottle of Grey Goose out, which had been Maria's choice, and a glass and sat down at the table. He poured. It felt good. He poured a little more. Looked at his phone. Looked away. Poured again. He began to feel it, that thing, that large gray thing that made him feel so good, *so right* start to hover around him like a cloud of light. *This is who I am*, he thought. *I'm tired of fighting this. This is who I am.* He felt guilty briefly, the feeling spiking through his chest like a bullet almost, but then he pushed it down with another pour. He picked up his tattered copy of the *Inferno*. He liked to read down there, as it was quiet when they weren't processing H. He tried to concentrate but he couldn't, so he put it down and turned the TV on, telling himself that he wouldn't go through the whole bottle, which, he told himself then, if he did, it's not like it was a very big bottle anyway. There were images on the TV, but when he was drinking earnestly, it was hard for him to focus on them, though sometimes whatever would come on TV would be something he found over-whelmingly sad or hilarious. He began to laugh bitterly, and sud-denly he felt tired. He walked up the stairs, reeling, the bottle still in his hand, thinking about Maria, the grief now overwhelming. He thought perhaps when he got up the stairs he would tell her that, right in front of Sharina. Right in front of God. His heart began pounding. By the time he got all the way up the stairs, he wasn't sure anymore. He didn't feel the conviction he'd felt just moments before, when he'd started his climb. That was the thing, he thought, that was also who he was, the silent one, the one who had to be lead, the one who couldn't do anything for himself. He drank again from the bottle and came out on the landing. It was empty. He didn't know where the girls were. He sighed deeply and walked over to the bedroom he had with Sharina, hoping she was gone so that he wouldn't have to share in his humiliation. He just wanted to be alone. To read one of Maria's detective books. There was one she really loved that was really more of a thriller called *Nothing Short of Dying*, which she had asked him to read right before Chris had come back. Luckily, Sharina wasn't in their bedroom. He assumed she was out shopping with Maria, the baby in the stroller, their mouths clacking away like typewriters. He lay on the bed, on the soft, clean sheets and feminine blue bedding and felt his head swim. That's what he was, he thought, as his head began to swim, he was an ocean, not even a person. He picked the book up, but had to put it down, as a few minutes later he needed to get up to puke, and he did, and this was repeated several times throughout the day until he was empty, and then he finally slept, and hard.

He woke a few hours later to the sound of women's voices. He felt dried out, and he had a headache, but he was surprised that he didn't feel worse. He pulled a joint from the end table, lit it, took two heavy pulls and then saw that there was a little bit of vodka left in the bottle and drank that. He swung his legs over the side of the bed and sighed and put his head in his hands. He got up a few minutes later and went into the bathroom to drink water, lots of water, and then shower to try to rinse the stink of booze and vomit off of himself. He felt better coming out of the shower, and he lit the joint and took another long toke. He was going to be OK. He walked into the main living room and then into the kitchen and started a pot of coffee. The women were already downstairs, he could hear the laughter and chatter. He watched the coffee percolate and, when it was done, poured himself a large cup, drank half and then filled the cup again. He went downstairs.

Women were sitting at the table, some of them carefully and delicately slitting condoms full of heroin over bowls with their slender dark hands, some of them washing them in other bowls, some of them were still waiting for the bathroom. Maria and Sharina were talking to them in Spanish, and Matthew was struck again by how beautiful they were, their hair so thick and black it practically hurt to look at it. Their hands were beautiful too, as they did the work that they had come here to do, though their main job was in getting the heroin to the United States.

A few hours later, Math arrived to get the H, and take it back to the house, where it would then go to other houses to distribute. Once Math did this, he was going to bring a few of the homies back to the house in Rio Rancho. They were going to have a huge party at their house that evening, and parties like this were some of the reason they had relocated to Rio Rancho. It was quieter here, true, so they had to try to fit in, but a little bit of noise was assumed to be another suburban get together, rather than a bunch of gangsters who were probably up to no good. The girls continued to work, chatting, and Matthew did his part, pulling the H into little plastic baggies, putting it all down on paper. That was the thing, they ran it like a business, the OGs insisted on that, and when there was any deviation, even a little one, someone paid. But they didn't have to worry about that with Chris—he lived to impress the OGs, and Matthew lived to impress Chris. Matthew wondered though sometimes about the Mathematician, who was quiet and calculating and sneaky. Chris still had no idea that he had been fucking Maria, though when Matthew thought about that, he thought about the fact that he had been fucking her too, though he had thought about it as so much more. And he had no idea how Math thought about it. As far as Matthew could tell, and it was hard with him, he guessed that Math got off on it, saw it as some sort of secret way he was bigger, better, more of a man than Chris. Matthew often wondered what else the Mathematician might be up to, what other way he wanted to quietly emasculate Chris, while at the same time, nodding and acting as deferential as possible to his face. Every once in a while, Math would catch Matthew staring at him, and he would stare back, directly, and blankly and then he'd finally look away.

Matthew looked at the table again, the girls were laughing now, and Maria and Sharina were coming out of the bathroom, the last of the girls done in there, the cleanup over. They were like some sort of perverse, global Native family, a tribe of drug dealers that dealt mainly to young white kids, but also to Latinos, other Natives. Once, Matthew had said something about that to Chris, when Chris was going on about Native pride, how the 505s were all about being proud to be Native. Matthew said that there were Natives who had died because of the drugs they'd sold them. *Nah, bro,* Chris had said, *Don't think like that. We gotta weed out the weak for the future, man. We don't want no weak-ass Indians around. We set to take over the world. Or at least, the continent. You ever hear those old Indian stories about how we'd get this country back? Fuck, we are. I don't wanna hear shit from those elders who complain about Mexicans. Fuck, Mexicans, Guatemalans, Salvadorians, shit. They're Indians. And they're all moving here. Soon this place is gonna be an Indian fucking Nation again, Ishkeh. And we gonna rule again. And we gonna do it with shit like this. And if it bad? Fine. That's what we gotta do to get where we need to be. That's not our fault. We ain't got nothing. White people have had everything for five hundred years man. We taking it back, any way we can.*

Matthew thought about this as he watched the girls deal with the last of the heroin, as he helped to sort it into little baggies of brown dust, brown, rocky dust that was going to move into the arms of the people of Albuquerque, though some were still at the stage where they thought if they sniffed it, they weren't addicted. The Mathematician's favorite spot to deal was the Launchpad. He had told him that everyone who worked there, and loads of the people who came there, were junkies. He said it wasn't even like selling there, it was like sitting down in a dark corner and waiting.

Matthew understood junkies, though there was something about H, the feeling of it, as he had tried it once on the streets in Farmington, that he just didn't like. It was too much, too dark, too serious. Alcohol made him feel light, sweet, funny, happy. He felt like dancing. Most times. When the sadness came it was big, that was true. But junk was like falling in love, and Matthew didn't want to do that. He looked over at Maria, feeling hungover and sad. Even though he didn't like junk, and booze was his thing, that thing, that big, fat, wet overwhelming need to let yourself be swallowed by something else was what had made him fall in love with Maria, because she understood it too. It was funny, really. All of them, all of the alkies, the junkies, all of them with that need, they were the ones so afraid of human love that they would do anything to be in the state that seemed furthest from it, but was really the state that was the most immediate, pure form of love. Maybe it was about control, about knowing that you could get that feeling when you needed it, when you wanted it, not when someone else decided to give it to you. To take it away. The way Maria had. She looked up at him, feeling his long, slanted eyes on hers, and she smiled faintly. He smiled back and then looked again at the table of women. One of the girls there looked sort of like the girl he'd known in Farmington, the girl who had died. The girl who hadn't forced love out of him. She looked over her shoulder at him and smiled. He smiled back. Maria saw this and got up to put her arms around Chris.

"Nah, baby, I'm working. We talked about this," he said, shrugging her hands off of him.

"Why you gotta always be like this?" she asked, putting her hands on her hips and glaring down at him. He continued to work, to sort and to count, and she finally threw her hands up and walked over to the couch and plopped down next to Sharina. Sharina petted Maria's arm awkwardly, and Chris ignored her. He liked to answer her needling with silence, Matthew noticed. He assumed it made him feel powerful.

"I'm talking to you, you fucker," Maria said, leaning forward. Chris did nothing. The girls around him could tell something was wrong, even if they didn't speak English, and they began to fall silent. Matthew was sure that this was something that they'd all seen before.

"You just gonna ignore me? Is that how this is gonna work?" she asked, her mouth a thin, angry line.

"Just stop," Sharina said, putting one of her tiny hands on Maria's shoulder.

"No," she said. "He shouldn't be like this, and he knows it. The whore."

"But maybe we can just talk about this later?" Sharina said, her voice pleading. She got up and went to the liquor cabinet and pulled a bottle of red wine out of it and two glasses from above.

"Come upstairs with me. Let's have some wine and some snacks," Sharina said, and Maria settled farther into the couch.

"Not until this fucker pays attention to me," Maria said. "Not until this puta does something beyond act like he's king of the fucking world, when all he is, is a fucking pussy."

That did it. Chris got up quickly, the chair he'd been sitting in falling back. He swaggered quickly over to Maria and pulled his fist back, and that's when Matthew intervened. He caught Chris's wrist with his hand, Chris looking back in surprise, Maria's angry, petulant expression changing to one of shock, worry.

"Homes? Are you fucking kidding me homes? You ain't gonna let me take care of my fucking woman? What the fuck is wrong with you, Ishkeh?" Chris said, struggling to free his wrist.

The girls around the table stopped working. They went silent, their hands paused in whatever they were doing, razors in air, bowls still.

"We don't got time for this, that's all I'm thinking," Matthew said, and Maria looked over at him with her eyes narrowed, as Chris worked his way around toward Matthew.

"I decide what we got time for," Chris said, his wide brown nose curling up like an angry little dog's.

"All I'm saying is like you said, we got work to do. Don't waste your energy on her. She ain't worth it anyway."

Chris shook his head. "Let go of my hand. And don't say shit about my woman, serious."

Matthew let go of his hand and began walking away, and he could hear Chris's arm come around and connect with Maria's face. Her sob after, and then her rage. The sound of Sharina comforting her, telling her to let it go, come with her. Matthew resisted the urge to turn around and slam his own fist into Chris's face. He knew Maria didn't want that anyway, and he knew this was part of their routine. He kept walking up the stairs to his room, and a few minutes later, he could hear the girls in the living room, Maria sobbing and furious, Sharina gentle and comforting. Matthew hated Chris truly in that moment. It was a moment he'd remember because all of the love he'd had for Chris had turned backward, went inside out, and come out the other side. He saw him as small, stupid. A man who'd gotten more than he deserved by pure malice, childish manipulation. He saw him as the kind of man that his mother used to fall for, over and over again, the kind of man who used to bully him as a child.

Things settled down, were put away, sorted; H was delivered to various places, and the house went ominously quiet. A few hours later, workers from the local grocery came with food, booze. They set trays down and pushed beer and wine into refrigerators and coolers, hard alcohol into cabinets and left. About an hour after that, people began to show. 505s. The two OGs that weren't in prison: first Stanford and finally Rudolph. Wannabes. Friends of the 505s. Women, lots and lots of women, their black and dark highlighted hair pouring over their shoulders, cigarettes and joints perched on their long colorfully manicured fingernails, though Chris told everyone coming through not to smoke cigarettes indoors or he'd kick them the fuck out. Chris put music on, rap of course, some old and some new. It was a mix he'd put together himself and people began to dance, to drink and laugh. Matthew sat in his bedroom smoking a joint and empting another bottle of vodka, trying to read. He had come out a few times to talk to people he knew, do business really, and to see if Maria was back on Chris's arm. But she wasn't. He actually couldn't find her or Sharina. He looked at his phone. He'd texted Sharina a few times, but he suspected that she was at her mother's with the baby. Possibly with Maria. He didn't know why she wouldn't answer him, though he feared that it was because Maria had decided to tell her about their affair. He felt a tremendous bitterness in his heart, a hatred toward both Chris and Maria. Chris for being a piece of shit who'd fooled him into taking on this horrible life, and Maria for making him love her. He suspected she didn't love anyone. He heard a knock at his door. He went over, opened it, expecting Chris. Though the last time he'd gone out, he'd seen Chris with several of the drug mules. He had been sitting on the couch, two of them in tiny dresses on either side, giggling at whatever he was saying in bad Spanish, his hands on the legs of each girl on either side. Damien was hovering in the periphery and batting his long silky eyelashes at the girl that Chris seemed less interested in. When one of them went in to whisper something in Chris's ear, he nodded and smiled, and Matthew had decided that he was done with the party.

"Hey," Maria said, walking in and locking the door behind her.

He sighed and put his book down.

She was silent for a while. Then, "Math is out back doing a dog fight. That fucker gives me the chills."

"Don't talk about him," Matthew said, and she drew breath sharply, and then was silent again. She walked over to him, sat next to him on the bed and lifted his near-empty bottle of vodka up and looked at it. "Didn't save none for me, huh?" she asked, laughing bitterly.

He stared at her. "Not here to tear that out of my hands this time?"

She looked up at him. "You know, Chris wanted me to do that, that one time. But I was sad too, you know. I don't want to see you stuff your life in one of these and throw it into the sea. 'Cause ain't nobody gonna pick that message up."

Matthew rolled his eyes. "What do you care? You want to do the same with H."

Maria hung her head. Put her hands in it. "Look," she said, her voice muffled, "I didn't come here to argue. I came here to tell you something important."

He looked up at her sharply. "Where's Sharina?" he asked.

"She's at her mom's with Manuel. She don't want her kid around this shit."

"Well, he is all the time anyway."

Maria shook her head. "Ain't you one to judge."

Matthew was silent for a moment, then, "I am. I thought she was different. Had a real job. I was raised in shit. This is how I turned out. She want her kid to be like me? Like her last man?"

It was Maria's turn to laugh. "You stupid. Really. She was raised in it too. Sure, she had some sort of outside job, it helped to pay the bills. But she was hoping her last man would advance, move up. You *know* that. She just got that job to help her out while he did. But instead, he died. Shit, it was Chris's suggestion I hook you two up. I didn't want to at first. I thought maybe once her man died, she might get out, that maybe if she wasn't useful to the 505s, they'd let her go. That maybe they'd figure she didn't know too much. But I knew that wasn't true. That was just some sort of stupid fantasy," she said, looking up at him defiantly.

"I thought you said you fixed us up because you didn't . . . didn't want to let yourself be with me . . ."

"Yeah. That too. But see, Chris likes to keep everyone in, everyone tight. You raised 505, or you get in the 505, and you stay. And I help him."

Matthew opened the door and walked out into the party wanting to find Chris, to punch him in the face over and over. He felt blind rage. He wanted to punch him as many times as he could until someone shot him, put him out of his misery, put him down like a dog, put him out of this.

He could feel Maria behind him. She put her hands on one of his arms. "No. Come on. Just let's wait. I'm telling you, I got something important to say."

He shuddered and stopped.

"I'm going to get us another bottle, and we're going to go back to your room and talk."

"I don't want to talk."

Maria was silent. Then, "Wait here for me."

She threaded through the bodies, the people talking and laughing and drinking and a few minutes later she reappeared with a bottle of vodka. She took his hand, and he worried for a few minutes about who would see them, but then he didn't care. He was so tired. He suddenly felt so tired. She led him back to his room, closed and locked the door. She pulled him to the bed, unscrewed the cap and drank, and then handed it to him. He drank hard until she stopped him with her hand, and then she drank again. She began to cry. He held her, pet her hair, pulled her clothes off and began to make love to her underwater, their bodies swimming against the inevitable tide. When they were done, he turned to her and smiled weakly.

"What was so important?"

She smiled back. "I called that cop."

ELEVEN

THIS WAS THE TIME OF HIDING THE FACT THAT HE AND MARIA WERE in love, were fucking every chance they could get, in bathrooms, in bedrooms—hers, his, the downstairs bedrooms when Chris was entertaining OGs above—with Matthew's hand over her soft mouth to quiet her like a child. When Chris was at a drop-off. When Matthew was at a drop-off, and he could take Maria with him because Chris was busy sorting H or money, or making a call. They often spread a blanket on the cracked concrete floor at the old Railyards after the drop-off had been made, the orange of the pipes above swimming in Matthew's line of sight, the shattered clear and green glass making it look strange and lovely as he entered her while the sun came down, and he knew who he was, he lost who he was completely.

It was also the time of planning. Of Maria telling him about what the cops wanted them to do. Of feeling at every turn that Chris was going to find out what they were up to and kill them both. They would do a drop-off, then wait for the cops, who would come in at night at the Railyards after the junkies they dealt to would get their shit and go, and after the cops would go, Matthew would read to Maria from the *Inferno*, and she would listen like a child listening to a bedtime story. Sharina noticed his distance, but because he was there nearly every night, unless he was out doing business, and because he took the time to be with her and Manuel, she began to do what women do every day—tell herself that she was paranoid, that she was making it up. It wasn't hard, as their relationship had begun this way, kindly, sweetly, but dispassionately. And even though it made things riskier in some ways, it also made it easier too that they all lived together, as many of their meals were together, their outings to the park, their parties. He never had to text Maria to see when she was leaving and vice versa, they could watch one another, and the others. They had a system. And the house was so often full.

As scared as Matthew was about being caught, being with Maria was good. She made him laugh. It was hard to make Matthew laugh, only his sister had. When she was a baby she used to clap her tiny, chubby brown hands on his face, and he'd pretend to eat them, and she would laugh and laugh and so would he. As they got older, they would sit in their room and make fun of whoever the new guy was in Mom's life, stumbling around and shaking their fingers in each other's faces. She would pretend she was their mother, and she would stumble around too, and dance pathetically with an exaggeratedly drunken look of seduction on her face, finally falling, while Matthew would cheer her on like the men did, and they would laugh and laugh until their mother would yell from the other room to *shut the fuck up would you two, I have a hangover!* This would make them laugh harder, and they would cover each other's mouths and giggle until the fit had passed.

Maria had started it. They were in the Railyards one day after a drop-off, and they had some time before the next. Matthew was reading her a few passages from the *Inferno*, sipping from a few wine coolers. Sharina was at her mother's with the baby, and Chris was off getting a new shipment far, far west of there.

"He's so pompous you know," Maria said.

"What?" Matthew asked, putting the book down.

"Chris. It's all I'm such a fucking OG muthafucka I'm so fucking important and shit, it gets on my nerves."

"On my nerves, giiiirl. Like I'ma *cut heem*," Matthew said, standing up and waggling his head. Maria died laughing at his impression of one of their favorite comedians. He laughed with her, and when he stopped, he looked west at the setting sun, the light coming in through the glass of the building. "Look," he said. "The light. It's magical."

"What?" Maria asked, running her hands absentmindedly through her long, thick black hair, her hair looking reddish in the light. Sometimes she would nod off on the blanket, and he would hold her until he followed her into sleep. She would curl up on top of him, and when she would, he felt like they were floating in space, like he could feel everything at once. She told him that she was never at peace except when she was in his arms like that. When they would wake up, they would hold each other for a while, breathe each other in, maybe have sex. Maria would massage his lanky body, and he would sigh, and whisper as quietly as he could that he loved her.

"The light," he said insistently, pointing.

She looked west. She walked over to the tall glass walls, the light coming through her hair, making her look so angelic that Matthew began to tear up. It seemed to make her glow, that light, and he knew looking at her that she would die someday, and so would he but that it was OK because of all of this beauty, this hozho. He stood up, walked over, held her from behind.

"I wish I . . ."

"What?" Maria said, leaning into him. It felt so good. So warm.

"You looked like an angel."

She laughed. "You're silly."

She leaned into him, and he kissed her neck.

"But what were you going to say. What you wished."

"I was . . . I just . . . wish I could give you a baby."

She was silent for a long time, and Matthew worried that she was going to cry or be angry. But then she sighed heavily. "Me too. Never wished that with Chris. 'Cause if I could have babies, you and me would have some cute Indian babies."

"If," he said.

"Yeah, if," she said. Then, "Probably best, I guess."

"Yes," he said, and then they both went silent.

"I'm a fucking OG, I mean, shit, like OG and *shittttt*," Maria said, turning to Matthew and making a face that Matthew knew to be a Chris-face. It was arrogant and childish all at the same time, and it was perfect.

"Shit, all the bitches love me. They been loving me so long I got body glitter permanently ground into my skin," Matthew said, and Maria threw her head back and laughed hard. "Shit, I'm so OG that the *OGs* think I'm OG as fuuuuuck," Matthew said, lamely.

"That last one was not that funny," Maria said, laughing.

"You're just not OG enough to appreciate how OG that joke was, *Ishkehhhh*," he said, and she shook her head.

"We should be getting back. I got another drop-off, and then weren't you and Sharina going to make dinner?"

"Yeah, I told her that we would cook something nice," Maria said and they both looked west again. The sun was gone, and the land looked cold, forlorn. They gathered their things, finishing the last wine cooler before they left.

On the way home, Matthew got a text. Maria was sleeping next to him, the light of each passing storefront, streetlight, sweeping over her closed eyes in a way that made his heart swell more and more dangerously.

"Maria," he said, sad to wake her.

"Mmm?" she said, opening her eyes and smiling.

"Guess what? Next drop is off. And it was the last one for the day."

"Ohhh," she said, sitting up and flipping the visor down to look at herself in the mirror.

"Do you ... want to go to Santa Fe?"

She looked over at him thoughtfully. "Why not?"

"Yeah, I was thinking that Chris will be gone until probably midnight. He's off getting a shipment, and then he was going to go and have dinner and then, well, you know, entertain the guys. He thought, they'd ..."

"Want to go to Palms?" she said, frowning.

"Yeah," he said softly.

Maria laughed. "Don't worry, Ishkeh, I know all about Palms. Shit, Chris is always talking about it." She looked in the mirror again, and smoothed red lipstick over her lips, which were full, especially for Native lips. God, he loved them. He had Maria text Sharina from his phone, telling her that there were more drop-offs and that he wouldn't be home until late, maybe even not until the next morning. After a few minutes, Sharina texted, "K," and he sighed heavily.

She looked out the window, at the storefronts as they moved onto Central, the light flashing in the glass as they passed each one, Matthew already deciding that they were heading to Santa Fe for dinner, no matter what. They deserved some beauty. And things were getting close with the setup. Maria had talked about how it was going to go down. How they would wire their bodies under their clothes, the things they needed to get Chris, and especially the big gangsters—the ones from Mexico, the rival gang of the MS13s that they were now affiliated with, to say. And though Maria said that they promised them a life somewhere else, promised them safety, she had told him that they had warned her that if they wanted to be together, it would make their lives after this one riskier. Because these big Mexican gangs, they were everywhere, and they would be very angry.

"At first it would work," Maria said, lighting a cigarette and rolling the window down. Matthew did the same. "Him making me jealous. He's not some kind of damn genius like he thinks he is. He's just a bulldog. He knows how to pout, how to dig his paws in. But after a while, you realize he just an animal. A selfish one. And we fight still, I know. But that's just habit. Not love. I remember for years, I would live to hear the phone go off—just one text from him would send me flying. But then he would go missing, and I realized, 'cause I'm smarter than him—a lot smarter—that he did it on purpose. He thought it would keep me," she said, inhaling. "But eventually it just made me realize that I'd never loved him."

Matthew was silent. Then, "That's the way I feel about my mom."

She turned to him, and tears began streaming down her face. And his. She touched his face as he drove, and he pushed his chin into her palm, his heart exploding.

"I love you so much," he said. "It hurts. I mean it really hurts me."

"I know baby. I love you too. I'm sorry it hurts. I'll make it not hurt anymore," she said, running her hand over his head, that head that had once contained so much beautiful black hair.

On the way up, they listened to a band Maria loved. She was into alternative music. Nirvana. The National. Anything sad, anything with heavy guitar. The music beat into him slowly, his hand on Maria's leg, the back of her hand gently stroking his neck, the side of his face, so soft, his body humming.

At the Ore House, after they had ordered their drinks, Maria talked about when she was little, how they used to go here sometimes, after they were finished selling jewelry on the square. How exciting it was if they'd done really well, and how fun it was to celebrate by going out, which they didn't often.

"We'd sit there on the blankets, answering questions, you know, listening to the tourists talk about how much they loved Indians, or were part Cherokee, that kind of shit. Talking to relatives, seeing cousins, Natives we were related to. It was OK. We were OK. My mom was real good, she did these baskets, and my dad, he did earrings, necklaces. They were pretty. I still have some. But then he got cancer. And when he was gone, my mom kinda fell apart. Started drinking. Couldn't take care of me and my sister, and that's how we ended up in the system. 'Cause even though we shoulda gone with an auntie, 'cause that's the law, all of my aunties were messed up. And my grandmas were dead by then. There was no one but a distant relation living in Albuquerque, who was already a foster mom. And fucked up. Real fucked up. Lots of kids, lots of guys around, all the time. And no one really checking up on anything. Most times, my sister and me had to fend for ourselves. And she had the beets so bad that she didn't go out much. I did. 'Course, that's what got me in trouble."

"I'm sorry," Matthew said, holding her hand. "I didn't know that."

132

"I don't talk about it much," she said, signaling the waitress and ordering another Margarita for the both of them.

"Sometimes I'd hitch a ride up to the Rez to see my mom," she said, looking down at her hands. "But when I'd find her, she was all drunk. Finally one day I went up, and she was dead, they told me. Not long after that I met Chris," she said, frowning, and Matthew took her hand.

"My family is dead too," he said. She nodded, and dipped a chip into the bowl of salsa and chewed thoughtfully, a sad expression on her face. She finished and looked up at him, a light in her eyes.

"Let's be each other's family from here on out. Forever."

"Yes," Matthew said.

"Promise?"

"Yes. Promise."

"Because I want this. I mean, I know I can't have babies, and I don't know what life would be like without Chris and the 505s, but I want this. I want a chance."

Matthew nodded. When she talked about a life, some kind of life somewhere far from here, the kind of thing she said the cops talked about setting up for them, a job, an apartment, new names, the only thing that Matthew could picture was a vast grayness. He would see people like this in Albuquerque all the time, normal people, Indians like him, who did their jobs, and came home to people. But it was like they lived on another plane of existence. Matthew had to remind himself that this was all terribly average, normal. That it was his life that wasn't.

Back at the hotel Matthew pulled Maria's clothes off her, and she ran her hands over her his head and cried, and he cried, and she comforted him as he held her, and she moaned and trembled like a child, and he began to feel the grayness parting—a little light coming in like it was one of those days where it's been gray for far too long and the beauty is too much to bear and you stop believing in the sun and then suddenly, yes, there it is, coming up over the clouds so perfect and new, parting the gray forever.

TWELVE

"YO, I'M TELLING YOU, ISHKEH. LET'S DO THIS SHIT."

"I don't know, Chris. We're doing really great right now. I don't think it's a good idea. I mean, if we start shit now with the Zias, they're closer with the MS13s, and there could be some real serious shit. You know how they are in Mexico. And what they do to people . . . you know how close we are to being stomped. The only reason we haven't been is because we're useful to their rivals, and those guys are constantly on the edge of being stomped out."

Matthew couldn't believe it. Just when things were going well, were going perfectly. They had a shipment coming in, and Matthew was going to be wired, get everything. But then this.

"This *ain't* Mexico. This is the fucking United States. That shit doesn't fly up here. Yo, they try to bring the noise like they do down there, and there will be like, fifty-fucking swat teams—"

"Are you listening to yourself? You're saying that we should count on the law, which we break every day, to protect us. Secondly, that's exactly fifty fucking swat teams, what we don't want. Chris, sometimes I think you just like showing off."

Chris had been pacing the living room, and he stopped and stared at Matthew, who was sitting on the couch. The girls had left when the discussion started. They knew that this had been going on for weeks, what Chris wanted to do. Maria had told Matthew to stop it any way he could, that this would only be trouble for them, would ruin what she had set up with the cops. She told him that they

135

shouldn't even tell the cops, that Matthew should just try and stop him. Sharina would just tear up whenever they talked about it and leave the room. She did that a lot lately.

"Bro, that's part of what we do. In front of God, yo! Come on! You used to be down for this shit! What's got into you? This soft life? Man, don't let this shit define you, this shit we bought, because you know what? We bought it with violence. We bought it with blood, with guns, with smash and grabs, with fucking people up, but this is our shit! Ours!"

Matthew knew that Chris would never let it go. And Stanford was into it, ever since Chris had brought it up one time when they were all at their house, talking about how it would make them the real deal, epic, how it'd gain them respect. Chris kept talking about how Indian gangs didn't have the kind of respect the Mexican gangs did here, that they barely existed, that they were just throwaways as far as the Mexican gangs were concerned. That they needed to do some real, visible damage if they wanted to be in the eyes of everyone. Stanford had nodded hard as Chris talked, finally yelling drunkenly, "I'm sick of these Mexicans getting all the attention!" Chris had responded with, "Damn straight!" Rudolph had sighed and leaned into the couch, and Matthew suspected that though he'd go along with whatever Stanford decided, he wasn't really for it. Even at the time, Matthew knew it was trouble, knew that this was something Chris wasn't going to let go, that this wasn't one of his fleeting ideas, especially as Rudolph, the oldest OG who wasn't in prison, was responding so well to it. Matthew had been silent. He'd hoped that he could talk Chris out of it later. Or that he'd move onto something else, some other crazy shit. But every time he brought it up, it only seemed to make Chris more excited about it. And of course, his little protégé, the Mathematician, was pumping him up about it every chance he got, telling him that he had some serious bank coming in from his scams that could help fuel the battle gear. Matthew wondered about that. About whether he was hoping Chris would go down, and he could take his place. Math was over a lot now, and Matthew would fall silent around him and stare, and Math would act like it wasn't even happening, like it was all cool. Matthew wanted to punt the fucker in the face, right out of their fancy, plate-glass windows. Because what Chris wanted to do was something that rival cartels did to each other all the time in Mexico, which was raid another cartel's stash. And if he did that, one of them could go down, could die. If Matthew didn't, and Chris did, the deal that Marina had gotten them with the cops would be off. She had told him that they wanted the guys above Chris, but they wanted Chris too, and they wanted him alive. Chris was the key.

Matthew and Maria began to talk about it when they got away. She would lay in his arms, her long, sweet body like a bird in his palm, and try to plan.

"You know what, since he won't let it go, and since nothing you say will stop him from wanting to do it, maybe you could ... maybe just delay him? Make him think that you're down, but not until the shipment comes in?"

"Man, I don't know how we could get him to do that," Matthew said. "I mean, the next shipment isn't for a month, and Chris is hot to do this. Like, I can barely get him to not do it *tomorrow*."

They were done with a drop at the Railyards and were laying on their blankets. If Chris weren't so involved with the 505s, with what he wanted to do, he would have noticed how much they were gone, how withdrawn they were, how secretive. Sharina knew what was up. At first, she'd tried to deny it to herself, that was obvious. But finally, she'd pulled them both aside while Chris was gone and told them that she knew they were together. Matthew had almost felt relieved—because that was all she seemed to know. When he denied it, she cried, her tiny brown hands covering her face. Then she began sleeping in another room. And not talking to either of them. Matthew knew that if she hadn't quit her job, and if she wasn't afraid of what the 505s would do, she would be gone. How could he tell her that Maria was the only woman who had ever really gotten inside him, and made him feel OK about that, feel safe? That when he lay with her, her head crooked in the corner of his elbow, listening to him read from the *Inferno*, he could rarely think of anything but the way her hair smelled, the scent of her skin, her breath on his neck, her sweetness? He felt like he was bathed in light.

Maria was silent for a while, and Matthew wondered if she hadn't nodded off. But then she spoke. "You could tell him that you want to get some more gear. That you got a new connection and that they got machine guns. You know how he loves that movie gangster shit."

Matthew thought about this. Sat up, took a drink. "That could work. But Math, he looks at us funny, Maria. He's smart. And he's with Chris wherever he goes now, he's like . . . the new me. But with dogs." Matthew knew he should feel bitter about this, and he did, but not enough. He didn't know what was real now, if Chris had ever loved him, or if it was like Maria said, that he'd been only trying to use him from the beginning.

"Yeah. That fucking guy," Maria said, sounding angry and strangely sleepy all at the same time. "I forgot about him. I don't know how I did. But I can take care of him, don't you worry about it."

At this, Matthew's stomach tightened. He tried not to think about the fact that Maria used to sleep with Math. He told himself that she had only done it out of desperation, to get his attention, to piss Chris off. But he still hated to think of it, hated to think of his face over Maria's, his hands on her body. It made him sick. It made him want to kill him.

She sighed and sat up. Took his head in her long, brown hands and lay it onto her lap. "You. I love you."

"I love you too, Maria," he said, trying not to tear up. He missed hard drinking during times like this. But then again, he always thought it was going to protect him from his emotions, but really all it did was make him OK with showing them. It was the reason he'd started in the first place, because he was too emotional, because his emotions buried him, pushed him around, threw him into a black hole, left him for dead.

138

They had had some version of this conversation more times than Matthew could count. But eventually, they worked out a plan. Matthew was going to try to delay him for a few more weeks but if he couldn't, they were going to think about telling the cops.

Chris was still staring at him, Matthew sitting on the couch, rubbing his head, wishing he could be at the Railyards with Maria. "You're never going to let this go, are you?" Matthew finally said.

"That's my homie! That's my fucking man!" Chris said, stepping up to him and hitting him in the arm hard, and with affection. "Man, lately you been slacking. I thought maybe you just lost your taste for this life. That can happen. Shit can get boring, shit can get too good. But you're just bored homie. And this is gonna kick-start your heart, your soul. This is gonna make us OGs, this is gonna make us epic, Ishkeh."

Matthew nodded. And then he thought about what Maria had said.

"Chris, I got something for us. But you gotta delay for a little bit."

"Naw, homes, no way," Chris responded. "I got this set up! We gotta go in there, guns blazing and shit. I mean, the Zias are close to the MS13s man. And they bigger than us. The only thing we got going for us is the element of surprise."

"How's that?" Matthew asked.

"Oh, shit, that's the best part," Chris said, looking pleased as hell and shaking his head. "Math's got a connection. He was out doing a deal, and there was this little homie, man, this kid he knew from his block, and they got to talking. He's with the Zias 'cause his brother and cousins been in the Zias for as long as he could remember and ranked him in early, but see, he hates it. Starting talking shit about how 'cause he Pueblo and shit, they keep him a second-class citizen. So Math tells him that that's bullshit, and that if he wants to join the 505s, that's a gang that's Indian, and that he could rise in the ranks easy. The kid was interested, but course Math being Math, he's not gonna let him in for nothing, he sees an opportunity. He asks him where they keep all their shit, where they stash all their drugs and cash and shit, and the kid tells him that he'll tell him, and even let him in if he'll take him with him, protect him when he goes. So Math says shit yeah. So that's how this got all set up," he said, sitting down on the big, green couch and lighting a joint. "Shit this is beautiful."

Matthew didn't think it was beautiful at all. Matthew thought it meant death, at least for one of them. And then one way or another, that life he dreamed of with Maria was gone. It was funny. Death, to Matthew, had almost always meant nothing. Relief, really. As long as he could remember. But when he'd joined the 505s, he had felt a kind of righteousness to it, a kind of strange feeling of near religious necessity. He had found something terrible that could be tapped into. The nothingness he felt inside himself, for himself, became a thing that he could use to bring death to others, and there was something to that that fueled a desire to live. But now, it was different. He wanted the death to stop.

Matthew continued to try and delay Chris, telling him he'd found a guy who could get them a shitload of big, black shiny machine guns if they could only wait a few weeks, and though Chris didn't like the idea of waiting, he loved the idea of machine guns. Matthew knew he had him in the bag. The OGs came over almost every day, and Stanford and Math talked about it excitedly, like they were kids talking about Christmas. "This is going to make us," Chris kept saying to Matthew. Matthew would only nod.

"I don't want you to worry about shit," Chris was saying.

They were up late, smoking weed and talking, the dank green smell of it permeating the room. Chris was going on and on about the raid, about how they were gonna get all of those motherfuckers, about how they deserved it for thinking they were the shit.

"I mean, Mexicans are just Indians who don't think they're Indians, shit," he said, loading his pipe and tamping the weed down. "They need to learn. They think of us as like these lazy, homeless, untouchable fuckers who can't organize for shit, that can't do shit and it makes me so fucking psyched that we're going to mess them up.

And then maybe the MS13s will pay us some respect. I mean, they think Zias the shit, just because they're both Mexican."

Matthew felt that Chris was rambling at this point; he'd smoked three joints in a row, almost completely on his own. Matthew had only a hit or two, and only under relentless pressure. Lately the weed was only making him paranoid, making him think that Math was looking at him all the time, that he knew.

"I'm tired," Matthew said. What he really was, was thirsty. He wanted booze. He had a bottle tucked away for emergencies, and he figured he could just do two shots, just to help himself sleep.

"Yeah bro, you better get some serious fucking sleep, yo. We gonna be AK'n soon."

"Damn straight," Matthew said listlessly, and he walked over to Chris and they fist bumped, Chris throwing up a couple of signs sloppily, and Matthew walked over to his room. Chris had not said anything about Sharina not sleeping in Matthew's room anymore. Matthew figured that Chris thought it was none of his concern, or that they'd broken up, but Sharina was still in with the 505s, which was essentially true.

Matthew shut the door and sighed, walked over to his bed, and pulled the bottle of vodka out from under the big, plastic laundry basket he kept under it. He stuffed the basket with old clothes, and under that, the vodka. e didn't really need to hide it, but Maria didn't like it when he drank anything other than beer. He took a long drink from the tall, clear, expensive bottle and felt an indefinable sadness well up in him. He thought of his sister. He tried not to. Around the time that she had become a teenager, she had started hanging with boys. Boys who did drugs, boys who liked to fuck women and leave them. She was pregnant with her first at fourteen. Gone from the house at fifteen. But so was Matthew. As close as they'd been, they'd gone their separate ways—Matthew to the streets, his sister from one bad man to the next, just like their mother. He remembered when she was young how he would hold her, look into her little dark eyes and hold her bottle for her until

141

she could hold it herself with her tiny, soft brown hands. When she would cry, it would nearly break his heart. He would hold her and hold her, push her sweet, squirming, sweaty little body up and into his until she would stop crying and sleep.

The next morning, Matthew woke up to sounds of men talking in the living room.

"Ishkeh, yo," Chris said, as soon as he came out of his bedroom, "I got a surprise for you."

Matthew felt sick.

"We don't need your guns yo. Math had a connection and it came through this morning. We got all the AKs, machine guns we ever gonna need," he said, clapping Math on the back. "So get ready. We gonna do this right now."

Math looked at him, a strange expression in his eyes, and Matthew knew better than to argue. The Mathematician knew something. He didn't know what he knew, but he knew something. And there was no time for Maria to call the cops. And even if she did, he knew that they would want to know why she hadn't said something. His only hope was to let this go down, and try to minimize the damage. Make it so they lived, so that they could still make the shipment.

They got in their SUVs, Math in the back of the one that Matthew was driving. Math was silent the whole way, while Chris rhapsodized about this day, how it would go down in gangster history, about how their names would be emblazed in time, about how their names would be what people tagged shit with, instead of their own. The Mathematician just nodded like he was listening to a preacher, to a saint. The other homies were packed into another SUV, Damien driving, and they looked to Matthew, like the footage of the child soldiers he so often saw on TV, in other countries where children were made to serve the interests of their corrupt elders.

When they got closer to the house, Math texted his connection, told him to get ready, to unlock the door, asked if things were still go. They were. They parked a short block away from the house they'd been told held most of the Zia's stash. They were close enough that when they'd packed the big, black duffels they'd brought with drugs and guns and, if they were lucky, cash, they'd have a short walk back. But they were just far enough that hopefully, at this time in the morning, no one would realize the SUVs around the corner had anything to do with what was about to go down.

"Go," Chris said, and they were already ready by the time they were parked. They had guns and duffels in hands, and they marched quickly and quietly over to the house, Chris opening the door with one slam of his foot.

"What the—" a man, a boy really, said, who was sitting on the couch near the door. Their connection, the kid named Rafa, jumped up from the other end of the couch and faced the boy and with one hard punch to the front of his neck, the boy was down on his knees on the dingy gray carpet, choking, his hands at his throat.

"Get his fucking gun! Get to the other rooms and get guns in people's faces, now!" Chris yelled, and Matthew pulled the gun out of the back of the kid's pants. Rafa led the way, and the 505s marched determinedly toward doorways, kicking doors open. Matthew stayed in the living room with Chris, his gun at the kid's head, who was still choking.

505s came out of bedrooms with guns pointed at angry, resentful heads, men and boys were yelling insults in Spanish, and 505s were telling them to shut the fuck up.

"All of you! On your knees!" Chris said, and 505s kicked men until they were down.

"Where's your shit! Now!" Chris yelled. Matthew pointed his gun at one man's head. He looked weaker than the rest, tired.

"Man, I don't know. They're the ones who know that shit, and they won't tell you," the man said. He was only wearing boxers, and his hairy belly was poking out over them, making him look sad, middle aged.

"You're telling me you don't know shit," Matthew asked, and the guy nodded. "Seriously, I just sell for them, man."

"You know where some shit is," Chris said. "You're here. You're sleeping here. I tell you what. I'm going to shoot you, one way or another. But if you tell me where some cash is, some H, some guns, I won't shoot you somewhere where it counts, homes."

The guy began to whimper, beg. "I'm telling you man! I don't know! Ask them!" he said, and Matthew couldn't believe how weak he was. Not one of them would do this. The man was acting like he was some sort of hostage. He knew that after they left, he was dead. He didn't know how he'd gotten ranked-in in the first place.

"Puta de la Madre," one of the other guys said, and Chris looked over at him sharply. "You fucker. You're gonna pay for that," he said, and he looked at Matthew. Matthew swung the butt of his gun at the man's head, hard, and the man went down, blood began to soak into the carpet.

Math looked over at Rafa. "You know where the shit is?"

"Yeah, mostly. But we gotta work fast, yo. 'Cause we're making too much noise and the fucking cops are bound to come. And you would have wanted to ask this guy where the shit is," he said, walking up to the man who Matthew had knocked out.

"Thanks for telling me now, homes," Chris said. "OK, show Math where the shit is and I'll get the rest out of these two," he said, pointing with his gun at the other two Zias.

Matthew looked at them. They looked tough, OG. He didn't think they were going to get a goddamn thing out of them, and he knew that they'd better kill them before they left, or the retaliation would be something for the ages. One of the men was looking straight up at Chris, a sneer on his face, which was covered in tattoos of New Mexico, the Zia sign, spiderwebs, teardrops, women, so much ink that he hardly looked human anymore. And the fucker was leathery, inside and out. The other guy was a little younger, and almost as covered in ink, his eyes a strange, piercing green. A lot of old Nuevo Mexicanos had those eyes around here, wide, green. He was staring off at the window, almost as if he was daydreaming, as if he wasn't there.

144

Chris walked up to the first one and screamed in his face that he better tell him where his stash was, where the cash was, the H, or he'd kill him. The man continued to look up at him defiantly. "You ain't gonna do shit, homes. You full of words, but you just a little bitty baby. Fucking Indians think they're going to amount to shit. What? 'Cause you came to our house, took a little bit of our shit? We're going to wipe you out, like the conquistadores should have." The other guy began to laugh, and Matthew began to feel a rage inside himself, like he had when he'd shot that old man on the smash and grab, so long ago. He raised his gun, first to the leathery dude's head, and then to the other guy, shooting one, and then the other. They slumped to the floor, the blood spreading into the carpet, joining the first man's.

"What the fuck you do that for homes? Shit, we coulda got some information out of them," Chris said, turning to Matthew angrily.

"No, we wouldn't have. They weren't going to tell us a fucking thing. They're tough. And if we'd let them live, they would have talked. We don't want that." Matthew had killed. And he knew that if the cops found out, they wouldn't like that. He also didn't want these guys going around and spreading information. He figured that one way or another, if he had let them live, it would have gotten back to the cops what he had done. And he hated them. That too.

Chris looked at him incredulously. "Ishkeh, that's exactly what we want! We want people talking about the 505s! You heard what that fucking OG said? That Indians shoulda been wiped out in the first place, that—" Chris said, pacing, his hands up around his shaved head, his gun in his right hand, making it look like he was wearing some sort of strange iron headdress.

"No, you don't get it. We're nothing. The Zias, they're tight with the MS13s. It's blood man. We're not Mexicans. It doesn't matter that they're Indian too, it's not the way they think of it. If I didn't kill these fuckers, they'd go tell the MS13s that we're trouble, and they would have taken us out. Right now, we're nothing to them. But if we go taking out gangs that help them, taking their shit, we're competition, we're something to worry about."

Chris had stopped pacing and was staring at him. "No, no I can't believe that, we gotta dream big if—"

It was Matthew's turn to laugh. An expression of rage came over Chris's face, and he was about to explode when Math and Rafa came out with other homies, duffle bags in hands.

"Yo, we got a lot. Guns, H, around ten grand in cash."

They began to hear sirens. "Aw fuuuuck, let's go," Chris said. As they were leaving, Matthew could see the first guy Chris had hit stirring, moaning. Matthew raised his gun and shot him in the head, and he stopped moaning. He didn't feel anything. The only thing he thought as they were leaving was that he'd done those men a favor. They didn't have to live this life anymore, this stupid, angry, violent life.

THIRTEEN

"GET DOWN, YOU DUMB NIGGAS!"

They had been about to get in the SUV with a couple of homies on their way to a drop, when another huge, silver Escalade had come quietly creeping around the corner. Chris had been laughing, bragging at one of the homies about a stripper, one of his big, square feet halfway into the car, when the bullets began to fly. The drive-bys were constant now. The MS13s had gotten wind of what they'd done to the Zias, and the Zias and other gangs associated with the MS13s had made it their goal to wipe them off the face of the planet.

They hit the ground, and bullets flew. Matthew closed his eyes. When it was over and the noise had faded, he opened his eyes, and looked up. He was OK, and he could hear Chris cussing like mad, though he couldn't really understand what he was saying, but two of their homies were dead, and a pee wee, who had wanted to go along for the ride, was quietly wailing. He had been hit in the arm. He was eight.

A few days after the drive-by, Matthew could hear Chris on the phone.

"Nah man, don't worry!" he was saying. The men from their connection from Mexico were getting suspicious, scared. They had delayed the shipment, and Maria had told Matthew that she had told the cops, and the cops had said that they would just have to wait for the next one. But Matthew knew there might not be a next one, and if there wasn't, the deal would be off. And Matthew figured he would be the only thing left for them to come after.

Matthew suspected that the MS13s had put the word out into Mexico to stop them up. In many ways, the MS13s were Mexico. They had drug and prostitution rings everywhere, they were like ants, a huge army of red ants, building, massing, dying and rebuilding. And the 505s were now in the way. That was the thing with ants; it didn't matter how many of them you killed, there were always more. And Chris hadn't wanted to kill them, he had wanted to impress them.

"Nah, man you *know* we still the shit!"

Matthew sighed. He thought about his Shimásáni back on the reservation, about his uncles and aunties, about how they talked so quiet you could barely hear what they were saying. About their lives herding sheep and working for Peabody coal, working at the IHS, the school. About how some of them were drunks, were angry, were crazy, and he didn't blame them at all. This life, all of it, led to madness.

When the house was empty, Maria and he would lay together in his bed without talking, they would hold each other, and hope. When they did talk, Maria would tell him not to worry, that there would be another shipment, another chance. Matthew wanted her to be right. He hoped that if there wasn't, there might still be a way to be useful to the cops, that maybe they could tap the phone lines. Or maybe somehow they could just take some of the money and run away in the middle of the night. But that didn't seem likely. Without the cops to help them relocate, to protect them, Matthew figured they were finished. Especially now that they'd pissed the Zias off, and therefore the MS13s.

Sharina had left a few days after the raid. The 505s were in such a state of chaos, emergency, that she had finally been able to slip out. Matthew had woken up one day, and she was gone. He had walked over to the room she had been sleeping in, and all of her things, and Manuel's things, were gone. He had stood in the doorway thinking about her little brown hands, her gentle eyes. About how it had felt to hold Manuel in his arms, his warm, living, innocent body resting trustfully on his lap. He felt a distant kind of sorrow then, but what he mostly felt was relief. It was one thing he didn't have to think about, a thing he didn't have to worry about anymore. When he asked Maria about it, she told him that she was back at her old job, and that she didn't want anything to do with the 505s or gangbanging ever again. Matthew was glad. She was a small, good person. She deserved a small, good life. And he had never loved her. Maybe someday she would find a good man, a truly good man.

Chris came storming in one day not long after he'd come to understand that Sharina was gone, and Matthew could hear him all the way from his bedroom. The Zias were cutting them off at every turn at the behest of the MS13s, and Chris and his homies were retaliating, doing drive-bys to revenge on every drive-by, but there were fewer of them every day, and their reputation was growing weak. No one wanted to join. There was even a new Native gang who called itself Las Burques, and it was growing in reputation, taking a lot of its business to the pueblos, even to the Navajo reservation, where the hunger for H and meth were always present. Their connections back home were better. Chris had been disdainful about Natives who held onto the connections they had to their reservations. He didn't even like going to them. That was coming back to bite him in the ass. Matthew didn't have a problem with reservations or Natives from reservations. He just knew that he wasn't from one. He had grown up around so many Natives, around Native languages, culture, that the difference to him seemed minimal, abstract. He couldn't understand why it had always been such a thing with Chris. It was something he liked to talk about, how stupid skins from the Rez were, how much better urban Natives were. Matthew had always nodded. But in his heart, he had thought of his Shimásáni. Her good, small life. He had no desire to live on a reservation, but neither did he have any desire to disparage them. It was just another place Indians lived.

Matthew was finished with the few drop-offs for the day and Maria was out on an errand when Chris came stomping into his room.

"Yo, homes, we gotta sell the house."

"OK." Matthew had never liked it here anyway. He hated the suburbs, the false opulence, the glares he received every time he walked anywhere. He knew he'd never belonged here. And he'd known it wasn't going to last. They had already sold much of the furniture in the last week, Maria wailing as each piece went out the door, Matthew patting her back, Chris telling her that she should shut the fuck up before he punched her in the face, Maria screaming back at him that he should do it, that she didn't care anymore, and Chris pulling his fist back, and Matthew stopping it, again. He was tired of all of this. So tired.

"It's OK. I understand," Matthew said, drinking from a can of beer. "I never was really into this place anyway."

Chris was silent for a few minutes, and Matthew thought he would leave but after a while he spoke again. "I don't understand you bro. I thought you were into this. But you don't even seem to care."

"We'll be OK."

"Naw. Naw. I don't believe that shit. I believe you're weak. But I think you're choosing to be weak, because I seen you different. I've seen you come up like a man."

"Maybe I'm getting younger. Maybe I'm a boy now," Matthew answered petulantly. He looked out the window, the view nothing but another house just like theirs. Fake adobe. When they'd first moved there, he would often drive by their house because he simply couldn't distinguish it from the others.

Chris stared at him incredulously. "What. You just fucking with me now? Playing word games? This shit is serious. We're gonna have to move back to Albuquerque yo, and we can't operate there the way we could here."

Matthew sighed and rubbed at his tight black jeans. He was wearing his old clothes again, and he'd let his hair grow, and it felt good. "We're not using the space we have right now anyway. In fact, the best thing we could do is just start selling on the streets again, you and I. Wait until they trust us with another big shipment. Because that's where we're at."

"Naw. We'll build up again, I know it."

"I don't think so. I told you. We made ourselves competition. And the Zias are taking us out, and the MS13s are letting them because we got arrogant. We were never going to be bigger than what we were. We were lucky to be what we were."

"That's bullshit homes, and you know it! If we'd just done a couple more raids, just one on top of the other, taken the Zias out, the gangs that hate the MS13s would have respected us, and then the MS13s would have had to respect us, and we'd be where the Zias are now. We just didn't have time to recoup, and I just didn't know it was coming."

"No. I told you. We're not Mexicans. As far as the MS13 are concerned, we're just a bunch of stupid, drunk, lazy-ass Natives and you know it. And besides, the minute the Zias knew what we'd done, they were on us like flies on a body. There are too many of them, and you know what? The MS13s supplement them. It was over the minute we walked into that house."

"Naw. You just don't have any vision. I tried to give you vision, man, I tried to clean your ass up, but it wouldn't be cleaned up yo, it just permanently dirty. The fuck is wrong with you? I grew up with shit, but I'm not all some snotting all over myself motherfucker, I'm trying to raise up, to be something—"

Matthew stood up, anger filling him. He knew he shouldn't be saying any of this, that the best thing he could do would be to fill Chris with hope, so that maybe another shipment could be set up, but he just couldn't help it. "Something? You fucking stupid cunt. Something? Thugs is something? Men who use guns and drugs to get things? Who kill people? You know what, you're the stupid one. You can fool yourself all you want, but I know what I am. You? You're just a fucking arrogant child, thinking you're all the shit because you got a little money from being a good gangbanger." Matthew began laughing, trying to pull back from the overwhelming sadness, anger that was welling up, the strange, irrational feeling that he'd been betrayed somehow.

151

Chris drew breath, "You think you're any better, homes? That's a load of fucking shit if I ever heard it. You're a cold murderer, I seen it. Man, you shoot for fun. You don't just shoot for survival or money or power. I seen the look in your eyes, homes, pure fucking Diablo shit. I can see the joy homes, I see it. I saw that the first day when I spotted you stumbling around downtown. Yeah, I knew you was someone I could use because you were looking for a daddy, weren't you, but I could see that little devil in there, too, that thing you see on the Rez sometimes, those bad medicine men that do bad things. You like them, homes. Your soul bro, it empty."

Matthew felt sick, stunned. He felt inside out, off the ground, he felt like he was shooting toward some distant, dark planet that existed on the other side of the universe. He knew what Chris was talking about, his Shimásáni used to talk about those men in hushed tones, in Navajo, to other Navajo, talk about the bodies they would find sometimes. These were not things she liked to talk about, these men who were the dark shadows of the Road Men she went to, to be healed, to have ceremonies with. They were the men who pushed the last bits of their ability to feel outside of themselves by doing things like killing those that they loved, because they knew if they did things like this, there would be no boundaries, no borders, no way to ever be hurt again.

Matthew screamed and went for Chris's face. He was lanky, and Chris was short, but they were almost a match, Matthew's lean muscles pumping hard and fiercely against Chris's short, wide ones. They grunted, they sweated, and both of them thought of their guns, Chris's tucked, as always, neatly into the back of his pants, Matthew's sitting lonely and even slightly dusty on his dresser. They went for a while, but though Matthew was strong and though he twisted Chris around, over and over, pinning his arms so that he couldn't get to his gun, so that he could punch him in the face, Matthew had had a couple beers, and it made him clumsy, and Chris began to win. Chris got up, and Matthew slammed him against the wall, grunting hard and sweating even harder, the breath knocked out of Chris momentarily. But Chris was able to squirm out of his grip, and pull his gun out of his pants, and as Matthew came toward him, he pulled it out, cocked it and aimed it at his head. Matthew stopped.

Chris shook his head, panting, the sweat running down his huge bulldog-like face, his white wife-b soaked to the skin. He aimed at him and pursed his lips.

"Do it, you fucking coward!" Matthew yelled.

"That's just what you want homes, you fucked up death-wish Native. Fuck! The fuck is wrong with you!"

"Just shoot me, you fucking pussy. Come on. Get rid of me. Dump me off like you have everyone else," Matthew said, feeling sick. He stared at Chris, his lip trembling.

"I should fucking put you out of your misery, damn you're so fucking weak. Why I thought different, I don't even know. I wasted so much time on you, Ishkeh! I wasted resources on your drunk, sad ass," Chris said, keeping his eyes on Matthew, who was now leaning against the wall. Chris darted his eyes at the gun on the dresser. "And don't you even think about reaching for that gun, or I'll shoot you a few times where it won't make you die fast, let you bleed out, see how sorry you feel for yourself then."

Honestly, Matthew had forgotten about the gun. It had seemed so important a few minutes ago, but now it seemed like another distant, unimportant thing.

"Just shoot me," he said listlessly, and he walked toward Chris and into the gun. "We both know it has to end this way."

Something in the way that Matthew said this made Chris pause. That had never occurred to him, and he felt like there was something new, something he didn't know about underneath his words.

"You got something to tell me homes?"

Matthew thought about it. Telling him about Maria might make him shoot him. He was possessive about her, like she was a very expensive thing he had bought and paid for years ago.

"No," Matthew said. When it came down to it, he wanted to *live*. He wanted to be with Maria. He loved her so much. *He loved her so fucking much.*

Chris lowered the gun, shook his head. "Let's just sell this house, and get back to streets. We fucked up bro. We fucked up. I want us to be like we were."

Matthew sighed heavily and sat down on the bed. "It's never going to be like it was again Chris," he said.

"Naw. I don't believe that. I built this whole thing. I can build it again, learn from my mistakes. I can lay low and then get back up. You know, like a boxer." Here Chris smiled the smile that made him look like a little boy, the smile that always disarmed Matthew, made him feel a mixture of compassion and sadness for him.

"Sure, Chris. I've got to drop some H off at the Railyards. And I'll pack up when I get back. When we gotta be out?"

Chris sighed heavily, put the safety on his gun and tucked it back into his pants. "By the end of the week. We moving back into the old place. Shit, barely any homies left in it."

"I like that place," Matthew said.

"I fucking hate it," Chris said and they both stared at each other and laughed.

"Homes, wanna get high before you go?"

Matthew felt so tired, knew that the weed would only make him feel more tired, but he wanted to bond with Chris. Not because he had changed his mind about anything, or because he thought Chris was right. They were done, and the 505s were done too. But because he felt sorry for Chris, and because part of him wished things had never changed too. That they had gone on like they were, Maria being Chris's girl, Matthew alone, thinking of Chris like he did, a father, looking up to him like he could save him, like there was any saving of anybody in this life, or any other.

"Sure," Matthew said, and even though moments ago they were near killing each other, like boys wrestling in one of their homes, they were OK again, they were friends, they were going back in time if even for a moment.

Matthew followed Chris to the living room and sat down heavily on one of the leftover collapsible chairs, Chris in another.

154

The house was almost completely bereft of furniture, of things besides their clothing and beds. He realized that he was getting skinny again, really skinny. He had always been skinny and even when he'd gotten off the booze, he'd still been, but eating was of much less interest to him than it had been a few months ago, and he realized that his bones were hitting the plastic and making him uncomfortable. He sighed and looked over at where the big, beautiful green couch that Maria had picked out used to be. It was long gone. He thought briefly about Maria. He worried about her. Ever since the raid she seemed restless, worried, even though when they would talk about it, she would comfort him. Hold his head in her long, brown hands. But that thought soon drifted away as Chris sat down next to him, the smell of his drying sweat wafting over toward Matthew, reminding him of what had just happened, though even that seemed distant already.

Chris pulled his pipe out and stuffed some weed into the bowl and then pulled a small blue lighter out of the pocket of his pants and lit it, sucking in hard and then coughing just as deeply. He handed it over to Matthew, and Matthew took a hit, coughed. They passed it around until it was gone, and sat in a strange, masculine afterglow for as long as they could, not even turning on the TV, another leftover from the old house, after the giant flat screen had been carted away.

Matthew began to feel like he was dreaming awake, his thoughts turning back to Maria.

"Maria," he said, and Chris grunted.

"No. I mean," he said, blinking slowly and trying to focus. Chris smoked so much weed that it barely seemed to affect him—he could hit the pipe every twenty minutes and still hold a good conversation, even if that conversation was incredibly long-winded and full of ridiculous, outlandish assertions about how important he and the 505s were going to be. "I mean ... she's ... where is she? She went out for something like, hours ago."

"Fuck if I know. That goddamn bitch is a liability. Shoulda never hooked up with that fucking whore."

Matthew felt his anger building again, but he was just too tired to fight, he had done all of the fighting that he could.

"Why . . . do you love her then?" he asked. He had always wondered that. All they seemed to do was fight and get back together.

"I don't know. Started with her when I was so young. And like, now I don't know where she ends and I begin, yo," Chris said, and Matthew felt surprised to hear this. Chris was rarely thoughtful or profound and definitely not poetic. But this struck Matthew as true, pretty even. He nodded.

"But where is she?" he asked again, and then thought better of it. A niggling feeling started in his stomach. As much as he sometimes hated Chris now, he knew that if he found out about Maria and him, he'd be fucked up about it, and the last shred of camaraderie that they had would be completely gone and any chance of putting Chris in the line of fire would be over.

"Probably off scoring H, yo. Probably on that shit again. Dumb bitch hooks it when she can't get it from me. Have to find her and clean her ass up again eventually," Chris said. "Bitch thinks she's fooling me. Bitch is never fooling me, homes. Not this, Ishkeh. Naw. I know that bitch up and down, I know when she's been fucking around with someone, when she's on H. It's almost fucking funny when she thinks she's fooling me. Thinks she's smarter than me, dumb bitch."

Matthew wondered if Chris was fucking with *him*. He felt high. He felt like having another beer. He knew he had to go in less than twenty minutes. If he really knew, was he trying to tell him that he knew he'd been with Maria all this time? Was Chris playing with him, like a cat, enjoying his pain, his torture, before he made a final meal of him? He snuck a glance over at Chris, but Chris was staring into space, looking like his head was filled with nothing, absolutely nothing, and Matthew felt strange.

"Damn, now I'm hungry. You wanna order pizza?" Chris asked, coming out of his reverie.

"No. I mean, I can't. I gotta do a pick up. But leave some for me," he said, getting up and going over to his room.

"Cool homes," he heard Chris say as he shut the door. He sat down on the bed and thought about Chris, about whether he had been fucking with him. He shook his head. It couldn't be. That just wasn't Chris. That was the thing about Chris, he was direct. What he said was what he felt, he didn't hold anything back. He wasn't sneaky, one of the many reasons Matthew had always known they would never get beyond what they'd gotten to. A real OG had to be sneaky. Had to break the rules, fuck with people. Chris wasn't even sarcastic. They'd lost two of the OGs to prison, Stanford they hadn't seen in months. Matthew figured he'd gone back to his Rez, or was off hiding somewhere with family, waiting for everything to cool off, hoping Chris would take most of the heat. Rudolph was the only one left in Albuquerque, and he was like them now, doing drop-offs, trying to maintain the connections they had. He had been with the 505s since he was a teenager, part of the original gang, raised up by Mexican and Indian gangs in Albuquerque that didn't even exist anymore. When things had started to get rough, he'd told Chris and Matthew not to worry about it, that this kind of thing had happened before, and that it would happen again, and that all they had to do was lay low, sling on the streets themselves for a while, and that they could build it up. Matthew knew that Chris would always want more, more and more until it killed him. He thought about whether it was better to die by the gun, or by your own hand, from booze. He laughed quietly and then stopped. *No.* He and Maria could have a life together. He just had to lay low. Be patient. He picked his bag up and walked out into the living room, closed his door. Chris was texting, his short, stubby fingers flying elegantly over the phone, and Matthew knew he was at work, still trying to make it happen.

"Later," Matthew said, and Chris didn't even look up.

"Later homes," he said, and Matthew shut the door and walked over to his SUV. Those they'd kept. He knew Chris wanted them to be filled with homies, with brand-new Ishkehs, guns stuffed in their pants, ready for battle, ready to sell H. Chris had always refused to sell meth, said it was dirty, not worth it. But Matthew knew why he really didn't want to; Chris's mother had been a meth-head. It's why she had abandoned him. Chris couldn't stand it, though Matthew had never bothered to point out that, ultimately, heroin wasn't any different, that it was taking his girlfriend piece by piece, leaving nothing. Though he was sure Chris was wrong. He didn't know Maria as well as he thought he did. Matthew knew she was clean.

He started the car, and Cannibal Corpse began blasting from the speakers, and though it hurt his ears, he didn't turn the volume down, he waited to adjust. He needed something outside of himself to mirror the darkness, the hollowness that he felt inside. He looked at his phone, the flat blackness of it, and wondered about Maria. Wondered where she was. He kept one eye on the road and the other on his phone, and texted her, asking her where she was. As he sped into the increasing darkness toward Albuquerque, the lights of the city beginning to fill the night, he waited. But there was no response. He texted her again, told her he was doing a drop at the Railyards, told her he wanted to see her, that he missed her, that he was worried about her. But he had gotten all the way to the Railyards and parked, and still, there was nothing.

He walked into the building, the high ceilings making the sound of his footfalls echo eerily, the bums crouched in the corners not even stirring. At the other end he could see a light and hear voices murmuring into the near-darkness, and he knew it was the light coming from the cell phones of the men he was going to give money to for H, as per the usual. These buildings were beautiful, and old. He looked down at the tracks beneath his feet, and thought about the trains that had once occupied this space. How large they had been, how important. He walked toward the light, holding his own phone up toward his face, and thought about Maria, who had still not texted him back. He thought about her long, brown body, about when he would feel it next to his again. He walked toward the light, and wondered.

158

FOURTEEN

"YO, I'M TELLING YOU, WE GONNA GET OUR SHIT BACK TOGETHER, and get OG again!" Chris said, taking a hit.

Matthew smiled indulgently. He just wanted things to settle, be simple, like they were before they moved to Rio Rancho. He kind of liked slinging on the streets, talking to people, exchanging drugs for money in a man-hug or fake-shake, throwing signs up in the places where other gangs, friendly or rival, crossed his path, waiting at the Railyards with Rudolph, speaking the little Diné he knew and talking about his Shimásáni. But whenever he'd get time with Maria, to lay with her, pet her long dark hair, watch her sigh under his caresses, he knew what he really wanted, which was to be with her. And they were working their way up to maybe another shipment, and Maria had told him that the cops were interested. And there was hope again, hope for another life.

"We deserve this, baby," Maria kept saying. It was harder now to get alone time with her; there was less to do, and a smaller house, and she was gone as much as she could be because Chris was in a perpetually black and anxious mood and took it out on her by yelling at her, hitting her across the face with the back of his hand. Matthew hated this. But Maria kept telling him to be patient, to wait. That they would have their chance. Matthew began to feel excited, hopeful, uneasy all the time.

Rudolph, the last remaining OG, who was tattooed more than any other gangbanger that Matthew had ever seen, was sitting with them in the house, listening quietly to Chris go on about how they were going to restore their glory. They were splitting a six-pack of bud, though Rudolph didn't really drink much.

Rudolph liked to talk about life when he was a child in Albuquerque, about how he'd come here with his parents in the fifties, about how they often were turned away at restaurants, how they'd go home for ceremonies, how he and Myron and Stanford and a fourth guy, the one in prison for life, the one only known to Matthew as Béésh, had started the 505s up with the help of a few random mafia guys who had been part of a relocation program that had moved them to Albuquerque. They had learned how to do it from being part of other gangs. The 505s, he said, had been a way of protecting other Navajos in the beginning, of finding a way to make money when they couldn't get jobs, or lost their relocation jobs, of protecting themselves from Mexican gangs like the MS13s by becoming useful to them— or their rivals.

His hands were beautiful, Matthew thought, like his Shimásáni's. The way he spoke made Matthew think about the poetry he'd learned in school. There was just something about the way his Navajo made English that made Matthew's mind picture things almost instantly when he spoke about them, sometimes in English, sometimes in Diné, as they passed a bottle of vodka back and forth between them beneath the orange steel ceiling of the Railyards, the junkies eventually coming by to shake, and they would give them enough to stop shaking. It was hard these days for Matthew to curb his drinking, and sometimes he would give in, and the next day, his hands would be shaking too. "You gotta kill that demon," Rudolph would say, pointing with his lips to the bottle, and Matthew would nod. "I've cut down," he would say, and Rudolph would go silent.

"You need to chill out, Ishkeh," Rudolph was saying, his beer resting on his belly. Chris was unhappy all the time. Rudolph would tell him that he needed to learn how to lay low, that they had gotten arrogant. He told him that with Myron in jail and Stanford missing, they needed to accept what they were.

160

"Naw son, naw!" Chris said, and Rudolph frowned and went quiet, looked down at his phone. Matthew said nothing. Matthew and Chris rarely talked, and Matthew found a kind of peace in that. Chris was not his savior, his father, his brother. Chris was only someone who wanted more than he could ever have. Matthew had been happy to be used, that was the role he had played as long as he could remember. But he wasn't stupid. And he wasn't naive. As much as he wanted things to be like they were, there was something he understood about life that Chris didn't; that people were born into something, and it was the same something they almost always died into. There was nothing else, except moments of brief, unexpected joy.

After Rudolph left, Matthew went and sat on his bed with the lights off, sipping on a bottle and trying to convince himself to not get too fucked up. He was about to hit the streets. The door opened. It was Maria. She smiled at him gently and locked the door behind her before she made her way to him. Maria and he still had time to be alone, at the Railyards sometimes, when they knew Chris was going to be away, but she was gone so much now, and sometimes for days at a time, that he felt lucky and glad when he did see her, when they had a moment together.

He looked at her and wondered. She looked strange, nearly eerily beautiful. She had that ethereal quality to her like when she was high, and it was at those times, sad as it made him to see her like that, it was as if she was made of light. He pushed that thought away. No. There was too much at stake now, and she loved him, and she wanted them to get out. There was going to be a shipment, and Maria told him that the cops said they were going to get wired, and they were going to get out, go somewhere. She said the cops had talked about Washington. About Seattle. He liked this idea, liked the idea of sitting in a small apartment somewhere in a little bed, Maria's long brown body at his side, listening to the rain hitting the roof. She slipped into his bed, and he pulled his arm into a curve so she could fall into it like a pillow and they lay there silently, peacefully. He wondered if she and Chris still had sex. He hoped not. He couldn't bear the thought.

Matthew ran his hands down her arms, appreciating her soft brown skin. Maria sighed. He leaned into her, curling like a baby, and she pet his head, ran her hands through his hair, which had grown out halfway to his shoulders.

"I like your hair," she said.

"I like yours," he answered, and she laughed softly.

"I always thought it was stupid that Chris wanted everyone to have a shaved head. He hates the Mexican gangbangers so much, but he's always copying them. Stupid," she said, repeating herself.

They were silent for a moment, petting one another, and Matthew thought about how wonderful this felt, with her. This magic in her skin.

"How long do you think Chris will be gone for?" he asked.

"I'm sure a few hours. He's out west on a drop-off. Even if you and me weren't gonna get wired up and get that bastard caught, there's no way this could continue without another shipment."

"Yeah," Matthew said, "we're nearly dry."

"Matthew began to remove her clothes, kiss her. He stopped. "You guys don't—"

"What? Fuck? No."

Matthew felt reassured. "We should be quick though. I don't want to fuck this up by letting him catch us, not now, when we're finally so close to getting out."

"Like he'd care," she said.

This struck Matthew as strange. Chris was possessive, and Maria always said that she didn't love him. But he dismissed it, and they came at the same time, and it was quiet, and deep, and good. They lay together after, Matthew lighting a cigarette and passing it to Maria, the slight sting in his throat reassuring.

"It was weird that Math didn't want to live here," Maria said.

"Fuck that guy," Matthew said, "he's just like Chris."

"Yeah. Well, not exactly. He's smarter. And more fucked up. The way he treats the dogs," she said, shuddering and sitting up. She tapped her cigarette on the small yellow glass ashtray on the end table by the bed.

Matthew felt a small surge of jealousy. "Let's not talk about him."

Maria was silent then, and a few minutes later, Matthew could tell she'd fallen asleep. He watched Maria sleep, and she seemed peaceful, like a child. He thought again about the fact that someday she would die, and he hated the thought of it. He accepted his own death, but hers was painful to contemplate. He couldn't wait until they were far away from the 505s, from Chris, from all of this, somewhere green, lush. That's the way he pictured Seattle. But he worried too that somehow they would fuck it up. That eventually, he would have to start drinking hard again, and she would get on H again. That was why they loved each other so much, the fact that they were the same in this way. Matthew pictured spiders, big, black spiders living in their hearts, eating away at them. He pictured a big pair of pliers trying to pluck them out. He worried that as soon as the spiders were taken, that they would die, that they had been born with those spiders, that they had put their roots in them, like in that movie *Alien*, and that if they tried to remove them, it would be like trying to remove themselves. They were the spiders. Matthew drifted, fell asleep. Dreamed of death and spiders. Maria woke him.

"You were jerking. And talking," she said, and he blinked rapidly, trying to move the images away, out. They were like remembering that you'd eaten darkness. And you didn't even know why.

"Sorry," he said, sitting up.

She sat up too.

"What time is it?" he asked, and then reached for his phone. "Oh, man. I gotta go." He pulled his T-shirt on, and after locating his white sneakers—one nearly under the bed and the other under a pile of clothes in the corner—pushed his feet into them. Maria watched him and sighed.

"What?" he asked.

"I don't—"

"Just tell me."

She ran her hands through her hair, which was looking like it hadn't been washed in a few days, though it was still beautiful, long and black with hues of red peeking through here and there. Sometimes it would catch the light, and Matthew would wonder at it.

"I don't want to bring Math up again, but…" she said, folding her legs under her and looking out the window and then back at him. She frowned, waiting to see what he would say.

"But…"

"But I don't trust him. He's up to something."

"Fuck."

"Yeah. And I don't want him fucking things up for us," she said, lighting another cigarette.

"What do you know?"

"That he's gone a lot. That he got money he shouldn't. I mean, like, look at those new glasses he just appeared with the other day. And I know people that he knows, people that connect you to large shipments of H."

"You think he's with the Zias? He gonna rat us out or something? Ruin the next shipment?"

Maria sighed deeply, pulled her legs out from underneath her and inhaled. "I don't know. All I'm saying is there's a reason, and … not just me, that he decided not to live in this house. I think he's setting his own shit up, and that if Chris finds out, shit is gonna go down. That's all I'm saying."

Matthew sighed. This could not happen. Not if they wanted to get what they needed from the cops. It would mess everything up. "Why does shit always have to go wrong?" he asked rhetorically, and Maria laughed, took another drag, the smoke curling around her head.

" 'Cause humans are in charge of shit," she said.

Matthew laughed. "Well, they shouldn't be."

164

"I know baby," she said, putting her cigarette in the ashtray and standing up. She pulled her pants on, her red T-shirt, her sandals.

He opened the door, looked out. No one was around. Not that they had many people left. Only two other homies, Damien, who had survived, and another they had somehow managed to recruit.

Maria pulled him back in and kissed him, deeply, and he put his arms around her and felt good.

"I wish this wasn't our life," he said. "I wish we were already in another life."

She looked into his eyes and smiled, "I wish we were birds."

"Yeah. And we'd go around shitting on people's heads," he said, and she laughed.

"Romantic," she said.

They walked out together, Matthew not asking her about where she was going, Maria waving as she got into her car, an old black Honda that Chris had gotten for her years ago, that for some reason, with all of her love of fancy things, she had never gotten rid of.

"I'll see you soon," he said, but she was already closing the door. He closed his. Thought about Math. He knew what he had to do. He had to find him, find out what he was up to. As much as a part of him wanted Math and Chris to take each other out, Matthew also knew that if shit went down between them now, his chance for making that next shipment was over. The first thing he was going to do was his drop-off at the Railyards. Then call Math.

At the Railyards, after he'd done the drop-off, he stood around, drinking, thinking about all of the times he and Maria had laid in here, talked, had sex, read to one another, laughed. He thought about her impressions of Chris, how at first he'd felt badly about even watching her do them, and then how after a while, he'd joined in. He shook his head, wiped his mouth, and looked at his phone. He dialed Math. It went almost immediately to voicemail. He dialed again, same thing. Took a breath, cracked a beer open, just one, and finished it in one long glug. He threw the can into the darkness and listened to the tin clink on something as he walked out. He got in his car. He knew where Math lived.

As he drove, he thought about why Math pissed him off so much. A lot of it was because he was so much like Chris. And the thing was, he hated Chris, but there was a way in which he still had some kind of affection leftover for him. He still wanted to believe Chris had loved him, was only a guy who dreamed big, who wanted to be important, wanted everyone he'd grown up with to see him as a hero. He was a guy who'd grown up with Biggie and Tupac blasting on the TV. So maybe hating Math was a way of hating the part of Chris that had made him feel betrayed, unloved. Also, he wanted to stop any more chaos, as the 505s were barely hanging on by a thread as it was. He knew that if Math was up to what Maria thought he was up to, when Chris found out, it would be trouble, and that shipment would not happen. Goddamnit, if he could just get to that shipment, he knew everything would be OK. He sighed heavily. He also hated him for sleeping with Maria. And he knew why he'd done it. Because he wanted whatever Chris had. And then there was the way he treated the dogs. Matthew had seen him kicking them, a look of pleasure in his eyes when he did it. Matthew had told him to stop, and though he had, he could tell that as soon as he was out of sight, Math would do it again. And the dog fights. Those were wrong. Math told Chris he did them for money, and it was true that it brought in extra cash, but Matthew knew he did it because he liked to watch innocent things get hurt, die. He shook his head. He was coming up on the last turn.

He pulled up with his lights dimmed and parked not far from Math's house. He rolled his windows down. He could see the lights on, and there was music blasting. Some kind of new rap that Matthew didn't know. He laid low for a while, resisted the urge to pull another beer out of the back of his SUV. He wanted to stay as focused as he could. After a while, a couple of guys came out, Math following. Matthew narrowed his eyes at Math's new big, black chunky glasses. They looked expensive. Like one of those rap star brands. Matthew slunk down low and listened. They had turned the music down.

"Yo, so you know where you can get this shit now, right? You get it from me, direct."

"Damn straight, homes," one of the guys was saying. He was a tall dude. Looked like he might be part black.

"I'm telling you," he said, "those white kids are begging for H. Just begging for it. And you got the good shit."

"That's right I do. I've got my own connections now. Fuck the 505s. I knew that was going to happen. I prepared."

They exchanged elaborate handshakes, threw up some signs, and the guy Matthew thought might be part black and his friend, a skinny Mexican guy, got in their car, a beater of a Pontiac, and drove off. Matthew couldn't believe it had been so easy. Maria had been right about that fucker. She'd known all along. That gave him pause, how clearly she'd known, but then he thought about how smart Maria was, how observant, and he felt a surge of love for her.

Matthew knew what to do. He laid low for a little while longer, making sure that Math wasn't doing any more deals. He also wanted to make sure Math was alone. He got out, walked up, knocked.

Math opened the door, looking surprised. "What's up homes?" he asked, and Matthew pushed past him quickly and into the house.

"Surprised—" Math said, but Matthew shut the door in one motion and swung with the next. Math hit the floor.

"What the fuck," he said, and Matthew kicked him, hard. That was the thing about Matthew. He was wiry, but he'd always been strong and quick.

"Shut up! You know what the fuck!"

"Naw, man, I don't know what's up! What the fuck is going on here?" he said, wiping blood from his mouth. Matthew pulled his leg back and Math simultaneously curled into himself while trying to scoot away.

"You tell the fucking truth or I'm going to fucking kill you," Matthew said quietly.

"Damn. Someone's been telling lies about me, homes, I swear—" he said, and Matthew kicked again, hard. Math groaned.

"Now are you ready to tell me the truth, you lying little fucker?"

"OK. What...?"

Matthew pulled his fist back. "Tell me that you're starting shit on the side."

"OK, OK, damn, don't hit me again," Math said, crawling over to the red futon and pulling himself up on it. "Damnit, I'll tell you everything, just don't hit me again."

Matthew was silent. He watched Math with his arms crossed over his chest expectantly.

"You mind if I light a cigarette?" Math asked, and Matthew shrugged.

Math got his pack from the end table, groaning as he reached for it. He started to pull a lighter out of his pocket, when Matthew yelled at him to stop. Math paused. Matthew pulled his gun out of the back of his pants and aimed it right at Math's head. "If that's not a lighter, I'll put you out before you can even pull yours out."

Math laughed softly. "Damn, it's a lighter."

Matthew kept his piece pointed at Math's head. Math slowly pulled a little green lighter out of his pocket and lit his cigarette. Matthew put his piece back in his pants. "Just remember how fast I can pull that out," Matthew said, and Math nodded.

"You shouldn't hate me, bro. You know Chris is fucking crazy. I had to do something to start shit on my own before Chris brought everything down, which he did."

"Bullshit. You just want to be king," Matthew said.

"Yeah, well your problem is that you don't," Math said, inhaling. He had a bitter, calculating look on his face. "I mean, what the fuck did that fucker ever do for you?"

"Never mind that. You're going to make this shit even crazier when Chris discovers what you're up to. Why didn't you just bring your new connections over to the 505s?"

"Because we got a bad rap now. No one wants to deal with us. The MS13s and the Zias and gangs you ain't never heard of are out there making sure of that. The 505s are going down and you know it.

And Chris. Fuck," he said, shaking his head and then taking another drag and ashing, "he's not going to make it through the year. He was already an arrogant fucker and crazy with his shit, but now, man, the Zias want to take him out in front of God, yo, they want to show the MS13s they're bad ass. And me? I was just trying to separate myself, trying to survive. You should be doing the same."

Matthew contemplated this. It was true, everything he was saying was true. But when it came down to it, Math was dangerous. More dangerous than Chris, because he had no sense of loyalty.

"When we ranked you in, that meant something," Matthew said. "It's supposed to be 505s till you die. What the fuck kind of man are you?"

Math shook his head again. "The kind of man that survives. Look, I'll cut you in, if that's what you want."

"No," Matthew said.

Math began to look nervous then. He knew that the smartest thing to do would be to kill him.

"Maria tell you this shit?" Math asked, putting his cigarette out.

"Yeah," Matthew said.

Math snorted. "Bitch isn't stupid."

Matthew was silent, he watched the Mathematician, who wiped more blood off his mouth.

"The thing is, bro, you're loyal to the wrong people. Chris, shit, he'd as soon as watch you die as save you. It's all about how much use you are to him. And Maria? Don't you get that that bitch is a user? She and me, well, we were fucking long after you told us to quit. Shit, she told me to cut her in on this shit too. I'm guessing she ratted me out because she thought that . . . shit, I don't know, she had something to gain. Like I said, she's not stupid. She plays everyone."

Matthew felt shock build through him. "That's a fucking lie," he said. "You fucking liar. You're just saying that to save your own ass."

"Think what you want bro, but I'm telling you, Chris is going down. And you know what? I know you two been fucking. But you

169

better remember something: no matter what that bitch says, she loves Chris. Bitch will always go back to him. She'll make fun of him, she'll betray him, she'll fuck everyone close to him, but it's only to get his attention. Don't you know women like that? There are always women like that. I was only fucking her so I could get information about Chris's connections out of her. I knew from the get-go that this shit was not gonna fly forever."

Matthew didn't know what to think. He didn't want to believe him. But she did make fun of Chris with him. . . .

"I don't know man, I just don't know . . ." Matthew said, feeling weak.

"Look bro, if you want out of the 505s, just lay low. Don't do shit. You got a place with me, but I ain't gonna rat on you to nobody if you don't want it. I don't know what else you'll do after this shit, but shit, if you want out . . ."

Matthew thought for a moment. He knew what he was saying about Maria was a lie. And the rest, it didn't matter as long as he didn't do shit until the next shipment. He just had to make it to that. Then he and Maria would finally be free.

"I'm not going to kill you. For now. But you need to make sure Chris doesn't find out about this. I don't want any more shit, do you hear?"

"Fine, bro, fine. That's cool. But you better watch out for Maria. I'm telling you, the only man she's ever gonna go back to is Chris. And I know you love her. Shit, it's obvious. The only reason Chris doesn't know is because he's such an arrogant fucker. And because he knows Maria will put up with anything from him. Shit, that bitch would die for him. She almost has. I don't know what she told you, but—"

"Stop," Matthew said. He felt sick. "Just stop. I don't want to know."

Math stopped. "Bro, loving women like that, it's a weakness. You can't do that. I've been letting Maria think she's been playing me but the whole time, I've been playing her. But you, shit. You actually love her," Math said, shaking his head. He looked genuinely sad for Matthew, but Matthew didn't believe he felt sad for anyone.

"Just keep your shit out of our shit," Matthew said. "Though I don't know how you're going to do that. One way or another, it's going to come down to you and Chris, and you know it."

Math looked out the window and then back at him. "Maybe. And again, maybe you should think about why you're so loyal to that fucker. He doesn't think much of you."

"Shut up," Matthew said. He didn't want Math to know any more than he already did. That he wasn't loyal to Chris or the 505s. He just needed things to move forward like they had to, just until he got his.

"OK, bro, but you know I'm right," Math said.

"You're lucky I don't shoot you right here and now is what's right," Matthew said. "That's what I was planning on doing."

Math looked up at him, his expression clear and calculating. "Why don't you then?"

"Because shooting you now would cause more trouble than it's worth," he said.

"I'll stay the fuck outta your way, Ishkeh. I don't want to cause no trouble," Math said.

Matthew laughed, lit a cigarette. "You know what?" he said, taking a long drag and then ashing on the floor. Math watched the ashes float down and then looked back at Matthew. "It doesn't matter. Just don't start any shit any faster than you have to."

Math looked at him, a funny expression on his face, and Matthew walked over to the door, swung it open, and left without another word. He got into his car and looked at his phone, after checking things out around him. Math could have fuckers around. There were texts from Maria, asking if he'd gone and checked on Math. He laughed. She knew him, she really did. He thought about what Math had said about Maria. He knew how he felt about her, and he wondered if Math wasn't just trying to drive a further wedge, get him to join up with him. Matthew was a good gangbanger, loyal, tough. He knew the ropes, and without Chris fucking everything up, they could serve the MS13s, and the Zias would have to leave them alone. That is, if he weren't aligned with the cops. But he didn't regret that. It was the key to finally getting out of this, to being with Maria. He assumed that Math was hooking up with Las Burques, that new Native gang. He thought about it, thought about what it would be like to hook up with a new gang, leave Chris behind. But that was the thing, he had never wanted to gangbang, and he hated drugs. There was a part of him that could do it, that cold, nothing part that allowed him to do anything, that had no limits whatsoever. But he felt like if it was between a life of taking other lives and taking his own, he'd take his own. That was more honest at least. And now there was hope for something else. He had only been a gangbanger because he'd loved Chris, and he'd kept going eventually because he loved Maria, and because he couldn't imagine doing anything else. But if Maria didn't love him, if she still loved Chris, there was no point, no meaning to any of it. But he knew that wasn't true. That Math just wanted to hurt him, wanted him to have nothing left so that he'd join up with him. He thought again about that little apartment in Seattle, that little bed that would be their haven, their heaven; the rain on the rooftop. His heart lifted. He felt joy.

FIFTEEN

"YOU KNOW WHAT YO, I GOT SOME MAD SUSPICIONS ABOUT MATH, know what I'm saying?" Chris was pacing around the house, angry, his gun in his hand. They had lost one of their homies in a drive-by yesterday, and they were hanging onto their last connection by a thread—the connection that they had for the shipment. All they really had left was Math and Damien. Matthew had been sure that their connection was going to dry up, but Chris had managed to behave, and since he was good at what he did, they were giving them one last chance. But Chris had been texting Math for hours, with no response, and he was angry.

Matthew was pissed, and he was nervous. Math had promised to keep it all on the down-low for as long as he could. He was fucking it all up. Matthew knew that if he'd shot the Mathematician, that that would be one less 505 to do business, one more reason for Chris to go apeshit, and then Chris would have to wonder what had happened, though Matthew assumed he'd just think it was one of the Zias.

"Fuck, I trusted that fucker!" Chris said, walking over to the ashtray and picking up a blunt and lighting it.

"Let's say you're right," Matthew said. "Here's the thing Chris, the 505s are going down. We barely can keep a grip on what we got. Even Rudolph is saying this could be the end, and he was one of the first." Matthew was sitting on the couch, trying to think of a way to keep Chris calm, to fix all of this.

"Naw, naw, man, Rudolph, man, he don't know," Chris said.

"He does."

"He don't have vision like I do, dreams like I do," Chris said. He took a long hit, held it in, exhaled, and then immediately followed it with another, coughing afterward like someone with emphysema. Chris had been hitting the weed and the cigarettes hard these days. He generally spent his time stoned, but these days, he was nearly following one hit with another, all day. He was getting sloppy.

"Chris, look . . . I think I got a solution," Matthew said.

"Yo, me too. I was thinking we could bring this shit to LA, I mean, yo, there are shit tons of Natives out there, we could settle into a neighborhood, make good with the locals, shit, there are more Apaches out there, you'd like it. And over time, we could get some little homies, then raise 'em up to homies, and we'd be OGs out there."

Matthew closed his eyes and then put his head in his hands.

"Chris. The MS13s are even bigger out there. For fuck's sake all the gangbanging shit here comes from LA. We'd be dead in a week. I can't believe we're not dead *now*."

Chris looked at Matthew, and Matthew felt a wave of tired irritation move through him. The guy just wouldn't give up. No matter how fucking crazy whatever he had going on in his head was, he wouldn't give up. He thought it meant that he was perseverant, that he would win. But Matthew knew he just wanted to be right. He'd seen Chris argue with OGs, with people they needed to connect with, just because he liked to look smart, important, even when he didn't know what the fuck he was talking about. It was part of what had cost them.

Chris sat down on the couch heavily. "Alright homes, what's your great plan?"

"It's not a great plan. And you won't like it," Matthew said. "And it might get us killed. But I think it's the only thing left, if you want to keep doing this crazy shit."

Chris looked over at him, his expression one of curiosity and suspicion.

"Go on," he said.

"Look. One day, the Zias are gonna kill you and I both."

"Naw—" Chris started, and Matthew interrupted.

"Just let me finish, Chris. Then you can tell me how wrong I am."

Chris sat back, a grumpy expression on his face.

"One day *soon*," Matthew said. "But if we just do this one shipment, and then, like, go quiet for a while, after—"

"What?" Chris yelled, and jumped straight up from the couch as if he'd heard a gunshot, which was happening more and more outside of their house, as the Zias had clearly figured out where they lived, knew there were hardly any of them left. Matthew was sure that Math was responsible for that, Math or one of their customers, hoping to get a freebee. Matthew was always looking over his shoulder.

"Are you . . . what the *fuck*, Ishkeh?"

"It's the only way, Chris. Come on. Even you can see that. If we just get this one shipment, we can sell, then just stay quiet as fuck. Live on that money. Live real cheap. *Then* maybe later we can build back up." Matthew knew he had to give him some hope, some feeling that it could all be built up again.

Chris looked at Matthew and began shaking his head. "Dammit, I'm not giving my dreams up, Ishkeh. I'll lay low after this shipment. But only because after that, I'ma hit this shit harder than ever. And if you ain't with that, you can fuck the fuck off," Chris said, storming off, and going to his room. Matthew could hear his door slam, Tupac blasting moments later.

Matthew went over to his room, shut the door, fell onto the bed. He was tired. He pulled his phone out of his pocket, nothing from Maria. He hadn't heard from her in a few hours, and this made him nervous. He thought about what Math had said about her and pushed it away.

He heard the music lower in Chris's room, and then Chris's voice. He was obviously on the phone. Matthew figured that he was trying to keep that one connection alive. The thing was, they had always been good at moving H. And the last connection they had was the rival gang of the MS13s from Mexico that they'd been working with for a while, the one that Chris had started up with in prison.

Right around the time the girls had begun flying in from Mexico, they had started their own gang in Mexico and in the States. And they liked Chris. They saw him as like themselves. The problem was that between their fighting the MS13s and Chris's problems with them and the Zias, it was harder and harder to get drugs across and distributed. When Chris had decided to hit the Zias, they had been forced to pull back. Matthew wondered if the idea to hit the Zias had originated with this rival gang. Chris was arrogant as hell, but Matthew had wondered why he'd been so tremendously tenacious about it, when he knew the Zias were so intimately connected to the MS13s, who he knew were dangerous. And what were the 505s to this rival gang but a tiny group of men that could be used and then easily replaced? Matthew was sure that if this were the case, it was Chris's ego that they had knew to pump. But then it had all backfired.

Matthew sighed. He had to get out on the streets, hit the leftover little homies up with some H to slang for them, do some drop-offs. He slunk down onto the bed and into the covers, and he slept. He had an hour.

He woke up to Chris knocking furiously. He had forgotten he'd locked the door. A habit acquired when he started sleeping with Maria. He sat up, felt bleary. He had a headache, he was thirsty.

"Open the fuck up homes, I got us something to do!" Chris was yelling.

"Just a minute, goddamnit," Matthew said. "Crazy fucker." He swung his legs over and walked, still feeling like hell, like his legs were made of lead.

"What the fuck has gotten into you?" Matthew asked as he opened the door.

"Damn, Ishkeh, I been knocking for forever!" Chris said, walking in and immediately pacing. "Look. I got confirmation. Our boy Math has been setting himself up with the Zias, and we're going to take him out."

"What?" Matthew said. "No, I don't think so . . ." he said, trying to hide the nervousness in his voice. He knew that was true. And he

176

knew it was all about to go to shit. It was going to be the final shit storm. Because Chris wouldn't quit until he found Math, until he shot him, if Math, or one of the Zias, didn't shoot him first.

"Look, I don't know. I mean, who told you that? Some fucker who's trying to get you killed, I bet. I wouldn't believe a word. Let's just let shit ride until we get this last shipment," Matthew said, walking out of his room and over to the kitchen sink, which was piled with dishes. Matthew sighed. He and the homies always did the dishes, cleaned. Chris didn't do shit. Acted like he was above it. He got a glass from the pile, cleaned it and filled it with water from the tap. He drank it down, and then another, and another, until he felt almost human. Chris had followed him and had been talking the whole time Matthew had been drinking. Matthew began to do the dishes, his back to Chris, simultaneously trying to listen and think.

"No homes, you don't even get it. I heard it from Damien." Matthew sighed, his shoulders heaving. Damien was loyal as hell to Chris, would do, and had done, anything for him, drive-bys, smash and grabs. Shit, the kid had taken a knife for Chris once, in the middle of a fight with some Zias. Had let Chris leave him behind on one of those smash and grabs, though he didn't know Chris had left him behind on purpose. Matthew had never felt the need to inform him of the truth. Matthew knew this was it.

"OK, Chris," he said. He knew there was no way, no fucking way that Chris was going to let this one go. That his only hope was that if he helped Chris take Math out that maybe, maybe the cops wouldn't find out, and that once that fucking shipment came in, he and Maria could finally get away from all of this.

"Let's go," Matthew said, and Chris began to yell with joy.

"I figure we should start with that little fucker's house, case it, see if there's anyone in there. If there is, let's wait. Or if he goes somewhere, let's see if he's alone, or at least if he's mainly alone, like if he's only got one other fucker with him, we can handle it. I'm telling you, we just need to take him out. If we take him out, maybe we'll get some respect back, show those fucking Zias what happens when one of our own betrays us. Because if we don't we'll look like pussies. And besides, fuck that fucker! He deserves to go down. That's shit. You need to be loyal no matter what. That's the deal, we rank you in, you're with us. Dumb fucker. They probably would have taken him out themselves eventually, there ain't no way they respect that shit."

"Right," Matthew said. He walked back over to his room, looked at everything in it. It was nothing, really. It wasn't him. He wasn't his clothing, his bed. He wasn't this room, this house. He thought for minute that he would miss it anyway. And then he laughed. He wouldn't miss anything. If he got away with this, that shipment was coming in two days. In two days, he and Maria could blink out of this existence. He thought of his Shimásáni, of the ceremony she had had for him, when she first saw how sad he was, when she first saw that he was drinking, right before she died. He had loved her so much. And she had loved him too, even though he looked like the man who had left her daughter. She had even asked him to move in with her once, told him that she could take care of him. That he could work for Peabody coal, live a quiet life. That she would find him a wife, and that he could be happy. He had shook his head, her small, beautiful brown hand on his face, his tears hitting her fingers. "I understand, grandson," she had said in English. He felt sorry for disappointing her, and he knew that he had. That she would have never wanted this, this life for him. He thought about how he had gotten here, and he didn't really know how. It seemed like it had all happened without his control, although that wasn't entirely true. But he had never known how not to be taken by the tide, his mother an ocean, the alcohol an ocean, the 505s the last ocean. He sighed and looked at his phone. Nothing but texts from some little homies and from the guy he was supposed to drop for. He pulled his piece up from his end table and put it in the back of his pants. He was ready.

"Chris," he said, walking out of his room, "I've got some shit to do first."

"Man, no, we gotta hit this fucker now," Chris said.

Matthew knew that it was stupid to care, but though he was ready, he also felt like he wanted to do the normal, daily things that he always did first. He wasn't sure why. And it's not like these things were taking out the trash or dropping the kids at school. But they were his life, his normal. And he needed a few more hours in this life. To say goodbye to it, if that's what was going to happen. He hoped not, but he had to prepare for the worst.

"Chris, if we want to continue slanging after, we have to do the regular shit, and you know it. Chill out. Math will be there. And it's early. It's better to do this kind of shit in the dark."

Chris nodded. "OK, homes. Let's do this. I'm hungry too. Let's stop at the Frontier."

Matthew nodded. It seemed appropriate that one of his last meals here might be at the Frontier. "I'm hungry too," he lied. "I've got to meet some little homies and drop off some H first."

"Thas cool," Chris said. But Matthew could tell he was all riled up. He was ready to go and make Math dead.

They walked out, got into Matthew's SUV and took off. It was a nice day, and Matthew thought about a day like this in Farmington, long ago, when his mother had been in a good mood and had taken him and his sister to the fair. They had been young, Matthew twelve and his sister eight. And Matthew was so excited. His mother had been sober for a while and without a man for a while, and Matthew had hope. She had been going to her job regularly and had cleaned up the house and was on the phone with her friends a lot, talking about how good it was for her to be alone, how much she didn't realize that she didn't need a man. The lights of the fair were beautiful and strange, and his mother bought them cotton candy, which turned their tongues and lips a bright pink, Matthew and his sister laughing and pointing at each other. They had gone on the bumper cars, laughing and screaming and bumping into each other, over and over until the cars stopped nearly midmotion. His sister had begged to go again, and they had. His mother had bought them roasted corn, and Matthew thought he'd never tasted anything so good. He felt wonderful, it was like his heart was flying. They had gotten on the merry-go-round, his sister loving the beautifully painted horses, when his mother spotted a man she knew. Matthew's heart sank. It was over. Their good times were over. He watched as the man, a man who'd known her last boyfriend, convinced her to get on a horse with him, watched as the man touched her, his mother laughing and playfully slapping his hands away but just barely, watched as the man held a flask over to her, watched as she drank and drank and listened to the man go on and on about what a jerk her last boyfriend had been, how he would never treat a woman like that, never, his scarred and tattooed hands lifting the flask to his mother's lips again and again, his mother looking into the man's eyes. After that ride, the man walked with them, buying his mother a beer, and another, his mother eventually telling Matthew to take his sister on a few rides while she had adult time. He hung his head and did what he was told. *Here you go son*, the man said, handing Matthew a roll of blue tickets, and his mother looked like he'd handed him a gold bar. Matthew had taken his sister on rides, had won her a stuffed panda, had comforted her when she vomited after a ride, had waited for hours at the front of the fair when it closed down. When he realized that his mother wasn't going to show, he began walking home, he and his sister dirty and tired, his sister crying nearly constantly until she wore herself out and couldn't anymore, two hours later arriving home to an empty, and luckily unlocked, apartment. Sometimes, even during the time his mother had been without a man, especially when she was without a man, Matthew would hear her crying. He would open her door just a crack and peek in. She could see her holding a picture, the drawer of the end table pulled out. Later, when his mother had gone, he had snuck into her room and opened the drawer. He had found a picture of a man, a man who looked like Matthew, only even taller. He knew this man had to be his father.

Matthew looked over at Chris, who was silent and yet deeply alert in the passenger seat. He had always thought that Chris was like his father, his older brother. But he realized that he was more like his sister, and that he was like Chris's older brother. He was the responsible one, the reasonable one. He should have been like so many women had to be, the one controlling things behind the scene. This was the first time that he had recognized this, but it was too late.

"I just can't believe that fucker thought he was going to get away with this," Chris said, and Matthew nodded. They were at the corner where they were supposed to meet the little homies. Matthew pulled to a stop. Looked around. He didn't see any trouble.

A couple of kids on bikes came around the corner about ten minutes later, and Matthew recognized the little homies that they used to scout, guard, and, lately, to sell for them. They were both around eight, maybe ten years old at the most. Matthew stepped out of the car.

"What's up, Ishkehs," he said as they skidded to a halt.

They were both some combination of Mexican and Native, though of course, that was always a little difficult to tell, considering that Mexicans were almost always some combination of Mexican and Native in the first place. But he was pretty sure the taller one was Nav, and he gave both of them the handshake he'd taught them a few months back, which seemed to please them greatly. He looked around and told them that they had to remember to do that too, and to throw up some of the signs he'd taught them but carefully, that he didn't want any dead little homies. They nodded earnestly, and Matthew thought about how young they were. He sighed. He knew that if it hadn't been him, it probably would have been one of the Zias, or some other little Burque gang that would have made them into what they were already, but still, he felt bad. They didn't deserve this life. He wondered if he should say something but then thought better of it. It wouldn't make any sense to them and would only piss off Chris, who had the window down and was looking around as if Math would step out of the shadows any moment. And once the 505s were over, there would just be another gang ready to swallow them up.

He shook hands with the taller one again, this time going in for a side-man-hug so that he could covertly hand him some H, and withdrew. He watched them bike around the corner, tough and little, and he wondered how long they would make it. He imagined them older, tattooed, doing drive-bys and smash and grabs, and he shook his head. Maybe something would get them out. Some after-school program, some relative. He doubted that though.

He got back in the car. On his way to the Railyards, Chris began talking about what they were going to do when they took Math out. Matthew only nodded. The sun was bright this time of year, as they were heading into midsummer, and he knew it would be a while before it went down. Chris seemed excited, and as he talked about their future, the future of the 505s, how the Zias and therefore the MS13s would respect them enough after this to stay out of their way, Matthew began to think that Chris could be right; after all, the rival gang that they had hooked up with was making strides in Mexico. They were losing, but not by much. The leader of the MS13s had been taken out by one of them, and that leader had been the cohesive force, the reason the MS13s had been feared so intensely. He had been ruthless, merciless, torturing people and taking out children for fun. Without him, the gang was at least partially falling apart, and rival gangs, like theirs, were coming in. Matthew doubted it meant anything really in the long term. What it came down to was another gang eventually taking their place. Maybe that would be the gang they were dealing with. But Matthew also knew that the MS13s were still strong, and that there were a lot of them, and a lot of Zias. A lot of Zias who were, right now, Math's new best friends. Because that was the thing: the Burques knew how to make friends with people on the Rez and the Mexican gangs. Chris had never been good at that.

He stopped at the Railyards, and they got out after looking around. It was clear. They walked into the old, strangely beautiful, abandoned building. There were, as usual, bums wrapped in blankets, most of them scattered around, sleeping. One of them, an old Indian guy whose tribe Matthew had trouble identifying because he was so old, so scarred and so fucked up from the booze, was awake. He watched them.

182

"You..." he said, and Matthew and Chris turned around.

"What you want, you drunk ol' fuck?" Chris asked, and the man began to laugh.

"You think you're better than me. You're not! You're not!" he said, drinking from a bottle of what Matthew could see was Windex. There were several empty bottles of Windex—and one bottle of vodka—the kind that Matthew used to drink, all around him in a circle.

"Shit yeah, I'm better than you," Chris said, turning around and rolling his eyes.

The man began to laugh again, and they had walked on, when he spoke. "You're not any better than me. You're going to die, soon!"

Matthew turned around, and Chris held onto his arm. "Ignore that old fucker," Chris said, but Matthew turned anyway.

"Not you. Him," he said, pointing a desiccated finger at Chris. Matthew shuddered, the hair on the back of his neck standing up, and turned around, walking to the other end of the building to wait. He and Chris, mainly Chris, talked as they waited, trying to drown out the sounds of the old man, who was by now singing a traditional song in a language Matthew didn't recognize at all. That was the thing about Albuquerque, mainly Pueblo and Navajo ended up there, but often, because of the Native arts scene, or because for some reason they had a relative here, people of other tribes drifted and then stayed in Albuquerque. Matthew remembered one time Chris had been away for a few days, and he and Maria had decided to wander around Old Town. A man who was probably in his early fifties approached them, asked them for a cigarette, and when Matthew had handed him one, had begun talking about how he'd graduated from the Institute of American Indian Arts years ago. He talked about how he'd done sculpture, about the friends he'd made there. *All gone now, though*, he said, and Matthew didn't know if he meant they were dead, or back home, or if their lives were simply so distant from his that they might as well be gone. Matthew remembered thinking about school. About that school. He had liked to draw when he was younger. But he didn't anymore.

The junkies showed, and they exchanged drugs for money and talked about the next time they'd meet up. Matthew said to send him a text, and they nodded, anxious to shoot up. Matthew and Chris left them in the middle of that process, Chris talking about how sick it was to watch a junkie shoot up as soon as they'd cleared the building.

"OK, now shit gets real," Chris said, and Matthew steeled himself, tried to stop his stomach from dropping, his heart from sinking. There was no way out of this. The sun was beginning to set as he pulled up at Math's place, about a block away, behind another big SUV.

They watched his place for a while, and after about an hour, a couple of guys came out. Not Math though. They looked at each other.

"Text him, yo," Chris said. "Tell him you've got to talk to him."

Matthew nodded. This actually might work, and for reasons that Chris didn't even understand. Math would probably think that Matthew wanted in with the Zias. The thing was, that he might wonder if this was some kind of ploy and tell him he was alone, when he was going to be anything but alone. Matthew had pulled his phone out of his pocket when Math walked out the front door. And he wasn't alone. Walking right behind him was Maria. Matthew felt a darkness inside of himself that he could not name.

"What the fuck!" Chris hissed and it was everything Matthew could do not to break down, go crazy. "Man ... the fuck is going on?" he said. "That fucking ... bitch! I don't, fucking ... I'ma kill that bitch! I'ma kill her!" Chris said. Matthew was silent with horror.

They watched as both of them got into Math's car together and after they took off, Chris screamed at him to follow. Though he felt nearly blind with pain, he was so used to following Chris's orders that he did as he was told.

"I've been loyal to that bitch for years, even when she was all fucked up, I took care of her! Fuck her! Fuck her!" Chris said, slamming his fist into the dash.

They drove for thirty minutes, going east, until they hit another abandoned building. There were a number of them here in various states of decay, surrounded by metal that seemed as if it were melting back into the earth. The building they'd stopped at looked like it had housed some sort of large machinery at some point in relatively recent history. It was old and kind of beautiful in a way, with long lines of red rust running down the metal facade. Matthew parked in the shadows. Both of them were quiet now, though Matthew could feel the energy coming out of Chris in silent, angry waves. He felt like dying. They watched as Math and Maria met up with some Zias. They talked, exchanged a large, old leather briefcase for another large plastic briefcase, and then the Zias took off. Maria and Math began walking toward their car.

"Drive," Chris said, and Matthew did.

Math and Maria looked up at the headlights coming toward them and halted as Matthew pulled to a stop right in front of them. They got out of the car, both of them pulling their pieces out of the back of their pants as they did. So did Math.

"The fuck Maria?" Chris said.

Maria looked at Matthew briefly, pain in her eyes, then over at Chris. "Don't get all stupid, Chris. He just has H. It's nothing more than that." Matthew felt more shock build through him. She was on H again? How had not noticed that? Though it made him feel slightly better, the idea that she was on H, maybe she could get help, maybe that was the only reason she was with Math . . .

"You think I'm real stupid, don't you, you fucking bitch?" he said, moving toward her.

"Stop," Math said, pointing his gun at Chris. "We can all walk away from this."

Chris began to laugh. "Walk away? Bitch, you betrayed me. So did she. You have to pay."

"We're all gonna pay if you don't let this shit go. In fact, I can get you into the Burques. They help the Zias out. Who help the MS13s out. All you gotta do is stop being such a cocky motherfucker. Know your place," Math said, and Chris looked like he was going to jump on Math, tear at his eyes.

"You like being some Mexican's bitch? The fuck is wrong with you?" Chris said.

"Better than being your bitch, Chris. Damn, you can't help but fuck everything up. The 505s been around for how long? Now it's down to one old Navajo fucker, one sad-ass homie, this guy," Math said, nodding in Matthew's direction, "and you."

"Ain't you capable of loyalty? Fuck," Chris said.

Math began to laugh. "Loyalty? You value loyalty so fucking much?"

"Yeah, I do. It's what holds a gang together, for life, man, that's what you promised! You ain't shit."

"Then your Ishkeh there ain't shit either, homes," he said, nodding to Matthew again.

"It's true," he said, and Maria tried to shut him up.

"What's true?" Chris said.

"He's been fucking your girl, too," Math said, a smug expression on his face.

Chris turned to Matthew with a look of pure confusion. "Homes, no. He's just trying to start shit with you and me, right bro?"

"No," Matthew said. "I love her. I love her."

Chris was silent for a moment. Then he raised his gun and pointed it at Maria.

"Don't you do that," Math said, and raised his gun and pointed it at Chris.

"Everyone stop!" Maria said.

"Shut up you fucking whore!" Chris said, and Maria began to cry.

"I only did it to get your attention! You don't care about me, you don't care who I fuck! You just going around fucking whoever you want!"

Matthew felt sick. Math had been right. She had never loved him. Never.

"Because I'm your man! It's different for me! You supposed to be loyal!" Chris said, and Maria began to cry harder.

"Just put the gun down, and we'll all go home," Math said, and Matthew was silent.

"No way, motherfucker!" Chris said, "I'm taking you all out!"

In that moment, life slowed down for Matthew. He thought about everything, his Shimásáni and her hands, Chris giving him a bath like he was his own child, whispering that it was going to be OK, sitting on a blanket in the Railyards with Maria while the both of them laughed, the fact that he had heard through a relative in town a few months ago that his mother had died and that his sister was next, about the bright light that he saw sometimes right before he fell asleep, the one that filled him with fear and wonder and that made him jerk awake. Of the old man at the Railyards who'd told Chris that he was going to die, of all of the momentary hope and joy that he had ever had, and he raised his gun. He shot. He closed his eyes.

SIXTEEN

MATTHEW STUMBLED PAST THE WALGREENS, THE MAYAN THEATER, and the Hornet, where he always stood outside asking the strangely dressed white people for spare change as they came out, past the funky little stores that were popping up more and more on Broadway, swimming unsettlingly in his periphery, unseeing, drunk, and finally, violently sick in a narrow black trash can.

"Dear *God*," a woman said somewhere vaguely off to his left, but it didn't really bother him. He was used to it. He held onto either side of the can for dear life, dizzy, sweating, his eyes closed. He felt like everything was buzzing around him, like he was in a tunnel of high-pitched white noise that would soon, thank God, finally blink out, taking him with it.

After he was completely done, he opened his eyes and blinked a couple of times. The buzzing had subsided a little, and he wasn't sure if this was a good or bad thing. He was about to pull his head out of the can and move on, but once his vision had cleared, he saw that something was glittering insistently at the bottom of the can. He smiled and peered more closely. He loved beautiful things. He cocked his head, hitting the side of the can. For the most part, real or otherwise, Matthew had come to the point in his life where he accepted pretty much anything that he saw or experienced. This time, however, he couldn't believe what he was seeing. It was a beautiful, blue, pulsating light and as he looked closer, inching farther and farther in, he could see there was a woman at the center with long, dark hair and big, black eyes. Maria.

He started crying, just a little, and Maria shook her head reassuringly and smiled. She opened her long brown arms, and his heart leapt up sharply and into his throat, like a big, black bird that had flown into his mouth when he wasn't looking, and was working its way down. He opened his arms. Then something terrible happened. Maria and the blue light disappeared, and suddenly the trashcan was a giant mouth, opening and trying to swallow him. He screamed and tried to push his way out.

"Help!" he screamed. "Help!"

Finally, he felt someone pulling at his feet, and the mouth puckered and spit him out onto the sidewalk. He looked up to see who had rescued him. It was Maria. She was back, thank God, though how she had gotten from the bottom of the trashcan to the sidewalk was a mystery. He blinked and saw that she was wearing a uniform. He furrowed his brow.

"Maria . . . I didn't know you were joining the military?"

Laughter, and he blinked again and felt sad. So sad.

"Maria, please don't laugh at me. I love you. Why did you do it, Maria . . ." he said, moaning, and then, just as suddenly, she was gone, and in her place, two police officers. One of them was George.

"Oh," he said, disappointed. And then, "Did you see that?"

"See what?" George asked, a funny, sad smile on his face.

"That trashcan . . . it tried to eat me."

"OK, Matthew," George said, crossing his arms.

"Really, man, that trashcan's dangerous. Especially here."

George shook his head. "What you been drinking, Matthew?"

Matthew looked up at George incredulously. "Why you saying that?"

"Because you just told me that a trashcan tried to eat you."

Matthew sat down hard on the sidewalk and thought about that for a while, and about Maria, though he worked to push thoughts of her away. It's true that that had been the first trashcan that had ever tried to eat him, but it was also true that that trashcan had definitely tried to eat him. He didn't know what to say, and he was feeling faintly nauseous again. He knew that if he needed to puke, that wouldn't be a good thing, considering that if he did, he would definitely be on his way to detox and secondarily, that the only place to puke was the trashcan, and that trashcan was carnivorous.

"Here's the thing. We want to help you, Matthew, and I think if we can get you into detox for a while, that might be good for you," George said, and Matthew struggled to get up and failed.

"No, man, I'm cool. You don't need to take me there. I'm cool. I was kidding about that trashcan. I was kidding."

"I'm sure you were, but listen, you're scaring people. And we can help, get you a meal, some new clothes," he said, looking down at Matthew's vomit-stained shirt and pants, both of them lifted from a trashcan not that far from the one they were all currently standing around.

"No, man, I hate detox. I can't drink there," Matthew said, shaking his head.

"Well, that's kind of the point, Matthew," he said, and he bent down and tried to help Matthew up, his large, black, muscular hands closing around Matthew's thin brown ones. The other officer, who Matthew didn't recognize, went to help. Matthew shook them off and fell back onto the sidewalk.

"Come on Matthew, let us help," George said.

"No," Matthew said, sitting on the ground like a petulant two-year-old.

"Matthew, you know that no matter what, you're getting in that car, right?"

Matthew looked stonily in the direction of one of the boutiques. It had several different Styrofoam heads in the window, all of them holding a different, unnaturally colored wig. One was pink. Another yellow.

"Matthew?"

"What," he said, wondering what George would look like with the pink wig on. He started laughing uproariously and rolling around on the sidewalk, people scattering left and right to avoid being rolled into.

George turned to his partner, a young Russian guy who'd come recently from New York. "Looks like he drank something bad. Windex, something like that."

Peter looked down at Matthew, his steely blue eyes never wavering.

"Matthew?" George said, looking down at him, but Matthew was gone, his eyes closed, and his mouth pulled into a half smile.

In Matthew's mind, he was getting his first tattoo, the sound of the machine like the sound in his head, the artist a young Mexican man covered in tattoos too complicated to separate into individual images. He was looking up into Chris's eyes like a child, Chris looking down at him with love, his muscular, many times over tattooed arms crossed over his crisp white wife-beater.

"It's gonna be amazing," Chris said.

"You think?" Matthew said, and George looked back into the seat where Matthew lay. They had managed to pick him up, he was only 125 smelly pounds after all, and lift him gently, like a sleeping baby, into the back of the car.

"Yeah," Chris said, and Matthew smiled.

"I'm glad I'm here for your first one," Chris said.

"Yeah, me too," Matthew said and looked over at his arm, where the machine was still running ink into his skin.

WHEN MATTHEW WOKE, IT WAS LIGHT OUTSIDE, AND HE WAS shaking.

He sat up, closed his eyes and rubbed at them, hard. He stood and walked over to the front of the tiny cell and peered out. He could see a guard.

"Hey," he said, and the guard looked up.

"Could I get a cigarette?"

The guard shook his head and said nothing.

"Please? I'll daaaaance for you," Matthew said lifting one eyebrow. He began to shuffle his feet in a sort of sloppy and hilarious tap dance, his gaze on the guard the whole time. The guard looked at him for a while, his mouth a tight, small line. Finally though, he smiled. He sighed, walked over, and handed him a Marlboro Red. Matthew stopped dancing, put it in his mouth, and leaned close as he could get so that the guard could light it.

"Thanks, man," he said. "I know I'm a regular Justin Timberlake but frankly, it's time to retire. Can't handle all the female attention." The guard rolled his eyes. He was young, Matthew thought. And he sort of looked like Opie, with his red hair and freckles.

"Hey, any idea when I'm getting out?" Matthew asked. He was shaking pretty hard. And he felt bad. Real bad. It was getting worse.

The guard turned around and said, "First you gotta see the counselor, *Justin*."

"Aw, fuck, I forgot about that," Matthew said.

"And you promised me a dance," the guard said, smiling a little. Mathew shuffled his feet for a moment and bowed.

"You know, I bet Britney feels sorry for dumping me for that greasy-haired white trash dude and is gonna bail me out," Matthew said.

"I'm sure that's true bro. Can't break true love," he said, and Matthew laughed and made his way back to the bed. He sat down heavily onto the narrow, uncomfortable little cot that was chained to the wall and leaned back and finished his cigarette, which helped. He stubbed the cigarette out on the windowsill once he was finished with it, and it lay among all of the other cigarettes stubs and dead flies.

I gotta get a drink. Just one. Just one, and I'll be OK.

He looked down at his hands and held them while they shook.

Time passed like he was in a tunnel. He kept looking out the window, his eyes finally adjusting to the light, his brain feeling fried and empty. He couldn't believe how long it was taking, had no idea how long it was in actual time. He looked down at his hands. It seemed like they were shaking more.

I'll tell her whatever she wants to hear. I've got to get outta here. I've got to get a drink, I don't care how I get it. One drink. One fucking drink. . . . I gotta be much more careful with what I drink when I get desperate. I'm starting to lose it, and I can't afford to be locked up in here another night. I wish Maria was here. . . .

Matthew knew that was impossible though. He knew that he would never see Maria again, Maria with her long brown hands and long brown legs and sharp, lovely mouth, and this only made him feel sad and empty. He lay down on the cot and slept, curling into as tiny a shape as possible.

Matthew began to dream, though the dream was more of a memory. One that Matthew could never drink himself hard enough away from. In it, Chris was staring at him that way he'd stared at him the last time Matthew had ever seen him, the pain in those eyes something that Matthew had never really seen before with Chris. With Chris, it had always been about anger, about control. There was no sadness. That was something that had drawn Matthew to Chris in the first place, because Matthew had always felt almost nothing beyond sadness, though he knew how to make other people laugh. He began to wake up, mercifully, when the dream began to shift toward Maria.

When he opened his eyes he could see the guard unlocking the cell, letting a counselor in. She walked in and sat down. He sat up and smiled shyly. This one looked Mexican, and that surprised him. Here, in Denver, they were usually white women. Though they were often Mexican in Albuquerque and had been mostly Indian in Farmington.

The counselor sat down on the little tin folding chair the guard had placed in the cell for her and opened a folder. She began flipping through the pages before looking up at him. He looked at her through half-opened eyes. She had long curly hair, tied back, and a terrible, cheap suit. He liked her.

When she was done, she smiled.

"Hi Matthew," she said, extending her hand. "I'm Esperanza."

"Hope," Matthew said, and she looked at him and smiled.

"Yes, that's right," she said. "Do you speak Spanish?" she asked, looking down again at his folder.

"Only when I'm singing love songs."

She laughed a little, and then looked at him silently for a moment, her eyes taking him in, wondering.

"Do you have a cigarette?" he asked.

"Sure," she said, and sighed, and pulled a pack of Virginia Slims out of her old, cracked briefcase.

"Sorry, they're girlie cigarettes. Hope that doesn't bother you," she said, and smiled sheepishly. Her expression held pity, and Matthew accepted this.

"I'm preeeetty girly," he said, taking one and then the lighter she offered. She laughed again.

"Thanks," he said sincerely, lighting his cigarette and then handing the lighter back to her.

"Don't guess you have a beer on you too?"

"Oh, sure, I've got a gin and tonic in my briefcase."

He laughed weakly and took a long drag off of the cigarette. She looked down at his hands, which were shaking hard, and that embarrassed him.

"So, it says in your paperwork that you used to be in a gang in Albuquerque," she said, looking at him quizzically.

"Ha. Yeah," he said.

"That . . . surprises me," she said.

Matthew laughed and took another drag. "Me too."

She laughed and pulled a cigarette out for herself and lit it. She exhaled a long plume of smoke. Matthew could see that her fingernails were bitten down.

"How early did you start drinking?"

"Pretty young. I mean, my mom drank. I guess I get it from her. And then the men that my mother . . . went with, they drank. All they did was drink."

"Hmmm. Well, have you ever quit for a long time?"

"Yeah. Well, not completely quit, no, but I started drinking a lot less when I was living in Albuquerque. Where I had friends. But I'm a lot less fun sober. Not as good a dancer. Just ask the guard. He's seen me work."

"I'm sure," she said, smiling. "So you drank less when you were in..." she said, looking down at the paperwork again. "The 505s."

"Yeah," Matthew said, looking down at his old black sneakers. He thought he remembered George saying something about getting some new clothes before he'd completely blacked out. He was hoping for at least some new shoes. His toes had been peeking out of these for some time, and winter was coming.

"You drank less while in the 505s?" she asked, her brow furrowing.

"Yeah. I ... didn't need to as much then. And I smoked a lot of weed. And I was ... happy. Sometimes. Well, at least, I was happier than I'd ever been." Matthew looked back up at her "I don't really like to talk about it. Not unless you really do have that gin and tonic in your purse."

"OK," she said. He knew what she was thinking. That he looked more like someone's grandfather than an ex-gang member.

"Do you abuse other substances besides alcohol?"

"Not unless you count Windex," he said and laughed cynically.

"I see," she said, frowning.

"Like I said, I used to smoke weed back in Albuquerque, and I would party with a little coke or speed from time to time, and I did drink. But now, all I do is drink, and a lot more than back then. Though before that, I was headed in the same direction I am now."

"What direction is that?" she asked.

He was silent for a moment, smoking. He turned and looked out the window, then back at her, and he smiled and looked back down at his shoes.

She closed her eyes, briefly, and Matthew thought that maybe when she opened them, he would disappear.

"Matthew, I want to give you my card. The address for the shelter is on it. It's at 1130 Park Avenue on Lawrence Street. They can hook

196

you up with a bed, and with an AA group too." She handed the card over, and he took it, both of them knowing that he would probably throw it away as soon as he left the cell.

"You know," she said, "you kind of look like my brother."

"How did he turn out?"

"Not so good," she said, and Matthew could see she was sad. Sad for her brother, sad for him. He was sure she was wondering how long he would live, which winter would kill him, if she would even know. He wondered about her brother, if her brother was alive. If he had been a junkie or a drunk like him.

"It was good meeting you," she said. "And good luck. You know, with your dancing career," she said.

"Thanks," he said. "I'm allll about *Dancing with the Stars* these days."

SEVENTEEN

BACK ON THE STREETS, THE CARD SHOVED INTO HIS BACK POCKET, not thrown away but definitely forgotten, Matthew walked quickly back to his old haunt on Broadway. If he set up there for a while and was really lucky, he would get enough for something, even if it was just a bottle of Windex. He was hoping, though, to be able to drink booze. Windex and things like that was what put him in detox, because it made him hallucinate and act funny ... and think about Maria. And it definitely *did not* improve his dancing. Though lately the hallucinations had been happening so much that Matthew had come to view them as part of his life. He had come to view a lot of things as just part of his life.

He'd been to the shelter, but they wanted him to stay sober, and he couldn't do that. Besides, he did actually have a home of sorts. There was a large abandoned warehouse farther along on Broadway. He and a handful of alkie bums lived there, sharing food and booze when they could. They weren't like his gang friends in Albuquerque, but he liked them, and basically felt like they could be trusted, mainly because none of them had anything left to lose.

There was a little corner liquor store, and he would go in as often as he could, buying the cheapest drink available, which was usually vodka. When he could, he'd get grain alcohol. That lasted for a while, even for him. Though of course when it was cheap enough, and he had the money, he'd get a case of the cheapest beer and take it back to the warehouse to split between all of the guys. He had won over a lot of

199

hearts doing that. That kind of thing was an indulgence, however. It wasn't worth its weight in drunkenness. Sometimes it was just about getting a little Boone's or Thunderbird to keep the shakes away. Most nights, it was him and whoever was at the warehouse passing whatever people had brought back around until everybody passed out. Occasionally, the booze lasted until the next morning, but usually it didn't, which was the only real reason besides food, which wasn't a big priority, that any of them left the warehouse.

Sometimes he slept outside wherever he passed out, like in the old days in Farmington. That was risky, though, because, with the exception of a few nice guys like George, the cops in Denver were tough. He'd even heard that they'd gathered a bunch of bums up one time, stuck them on a bus, and dropped them off in New Mexico.

Whenever he slept outside, he feared that he would wake to an angry group of men. As much as he didn't fear death, he did fear dying that way. That's what'd happened to his friend, Spike, or so he heard. One day Spike was there on his corner, his cardboard sign reading, "Hell, why lie? I need a beer," and the next day, he was gone. He asked around and the rumor was that there was a group of white kids from DU who had decided to start a group that would go around and beat any homeless person they saw to death. Especially if they were brown. Matthew didn't know if it was true, but he knew that there were people out there who would kill the homeless like that, or at least beat them up really badly, and nobody really cared. Matthew figured people were probably grateful when one of them died, whatever the cause was.

He sat down near The Hornet, waiting to see if anyone would come out. After about fifteen minutes a couple, talking happily and holding hands, appeared in the doorway. Matthew hoped that they would have some spare change, some change they would be willing to give to him. They looked young and that was sometimes good. Single women were the nicest though. They were softer and not usually as rude. He could tell they often felt sad for him even when they felt a little afraid, although their expressions betrayed their disgust for him, and this always made him feel bad.

The couple were walking past him when the guy, a tall blond, spotted him and turned in his direction. Matthew hadn't even opened his mouth.

"Hey, man. Do you want my leftovers?" the guy asked. He was incredibly skinny, almost as skinny as Matthew, almost as skinny as his girlfriend, and both of them were wearing what seemed like impossibly tight pants.

"Sure," he said, taking the Styrofoam box. "Thanks . . . any spare change? I'll dance for it," he said, beginning to shuffle. Sometimes people found this charming, and it would make them laugh and hand change over. People who lived around here called him the Dancing Mexican. Of course, he never bothered to correct them. Sometimes Matthew could tell they just felt bad for him, and embarrassed, and that's why they handed their change over. Other times people would just shake their heads and walk on, or say *No!* really loudly.

The guy looked pissed for second because he had after all, just given him something, and Matthew thought he'd fucked it up, but the guy relaxed, shoved his hand into the pocket of his impossibly tight orange jeans, and pulled out a small handful of mostly old, blackened pennies and handed it over, his girlfriend smiling awkwardly and then looking down at her phone.

"Thanks," Matthew said, and the couple wandered off. That was the thing about the ones who gave you food. It's not that Matthew didn't want food, though it was more than secondary to booze, it was that after they gave you food, they felt like they'd done enough, and didn't want to give you money.

Matthew opened his palm and sifted through the change with his fingers. Suddenly, and with great excitement, he remembered that he had shoved a couple of dollars in his back pocket right before he had been picked up by the police. He'd been all fucked up on the Windex he'd had to drink when an old woman had shoved a couple of dollars into his cup. He stood up, put his hand in the back pocket of his old, gray-black jeans, and hoped. He could feel the papery dollars between his fingers, and his heart soared.

If I can just get a couple more dollars, I'll be set for the night. I have food, and I if I can get some booze, I'll go back to the warehouse and just chill. And probably one of the other guys will have some booze and food.

Matthew sighed with almost sexual longing and hunkered back down in his corner. There was a spot near the Hornet that he liked. It was nothing special, just a place under the awning, but far enough away from the restaurant so that the waiters didn't feel obligated to chase him away, as long as he didn't stay too long. He looked over at the trashcan that had been the reason for his brief incarceration the day before and sighed. He looked down at his hands, which were really beginning to shake in earnest. He looked up at the sun and thought again of Chris. Pushed that away.

THE NEXT MORNING, MATTHEW WOKE UP IN THE WAREHOUSE. He blinked and sighed and felt like going back to sleep. After a couple more hours, he woke again, and saw that only Frank was still there, his arms tucked into his arms, the lower half of his body wrapped around an old, gray blanket. The guys had drunk the small amount of vodka that had been left when Matthew had passed out, and had already gone back into the city to beg. He wasn't feeling very good. The shakes were back, and knew that he'd have to go out soon too.

"God," he said, sitting up and stretching. He looked down at the tattered copy of Dante's *Inferno*. He picked it up and opened it and read through a passage he'd underlined heavily and then set it down, sighing. He figured it was sometime past noon. He stood up, stretched, and walked over to the room where he kept a couple of gallons of water, a bucket, and a rag. Matthew took his clothes off and poured water and a little liquid soap into the bucket. He took the rag, dipped it into the bucket and soaped himself down. He rinsed with the rag and then threw the dirty water out the window, where there was an old abandoned lot. Often, what drove him to the shelter was the desire for a really good shower. It was there that he was able to wash his clothes as well.

He walked back into the room where Frank was still sleeping, his mouth wide open and making gentle snoring sounds—his head cocked back, and his eyes staring sightlessly at the ceiling.

Once, after waking up, he'd gone to the other room to rinse, came back, and realized that one of the guys was dead. He didn't know what to do, was afraid if he told the police about the body, they'd try to lock the building up, and they wouldn't have any place to live. He had gone to where he knew one of the other guys liked to panhandle, and told him about it. The guy had nodded and said, "Wait until tonight." When he'd gotten home, the other guys were waiting. They bundled him up in his old blue blanket that smelled inexplicably of tar and, under cover of night, took him to an unlocked dumpster that was outside of a business that wasn't too far away. Matthew remembered hefting his sad, bony body up and into the dumpster. The smell of death had been overpowering. They all stunk of the whisky they'd drank, and he remembered walking away, feeling empty and like he was abandoning him somehow, alone in that dumpster in the darkness on the edge of Denver, like they had buried him alive.

Matthew looked over at Frank, who was suddenly still and silent. But then Frank's chest began rising up and then down, and after a few seconds, he began snoring again. Matthew sighed with relief. He walked out the door and started toward Broadway.

Around noon, the streets were busy with people out getting lunch, shopping. They were fancy, hip, and they had money. But that's why Matthew liked it. He liked to people-watch and this was a good place for that. There were gay couples holding hands, and Matthew liked that. He hadn't grown up in a place where that kind of thing was allowed. There were people with brightly colored hair, red like a fire truck and blue like the sky, and Matthew liked that too. The people were like peacocks, like brightly colored birds on a plain. He especially loved to see the tall, joyful drag queens walking down the street, the angry teenagers in black that reminded him so much of himself at that age, cigarettes in their long thin hands, tiny knives tucked into their tight black jeans.

He sighed and leaned into the doorway of the Skylark, which was ideal because it didn't open until four. Usually, he went up and down Broadway and ducked into the alley to drink. The thing was, if he just stayed in one spot for too long, eventually one of the store owners would try to chase him away, and sometimes they'd call the cops. Bums weren't good for business.

"Change?" he asked quietly from the corners, dancing.

Most people ignored him or quietly smiled and said *Sorry* and the thing was, he couldn't blame them. He hated it when other bums would sit next to people, try to tell them stories, real or not, trying to get money out of them. Matthew felt like he just drank, that's all, there was no story to it. And besides, after everything that had happened in Albuquerque, he was just so tired. It had hurt too much. Matthew felt like he was born in pain, and the only thing that dulled it had been booze, and for a while the love he'd had for Chris. And especially for Maria ... oh God, even thinking about her now, what had happened, hurt so much. But now he had booze again, and eventually it would rock him to sleep forever.

"Change?" he asked a man coming out of a store that was full of little odds and ends, things like little green metallic baskets full of soaps shaped like fruit.

"Get a *job*," the man said angrily, and Matthew backed quietly away into the shadows. Usually these guys were pretty innocuous, they would just say shitty things and move on, but sometimes they would hit, and that could mean down time, or an infection. Or just days and days of pain. Sometimes George, the nice cop, would pick him up and take him to the hospital, but that was hard for Matthew, because he was so far along as an alcoholic that things would get really bad for him in there. The DTs would come on, and Matthew wasn't exactly the healthiest guy in the first place, so as much as he was waiting to die, he didn't need that to happen tomorrow, in a painful way, shaking apart in a hospital bed. He was hoping to float off, surrounded by his guys in the warehouse. Though sometimes, he wished a nice nurse would come along, one that could just give him lots and lots of morphine until he went away.

"Hey! It's the Dancing Mexican!" a dude who regularly gave him change said, dropping a few pennies and a quarter in his cup.

"*Síiii*," Matthew said, in an exaggerated Mexican-restaurant accent, shuffling a bit.

"Yeah, yeah, dude, *si*!" the guy said.

A few hours passed, and Matthew did his rounds, up and down Broadway, standing in front of the Skylark, the shakes beginning to get bad. He went into the alleyway around six to count his change. Only a few dollars. He began to worry, to wonder if he was in for a night of pain. He wouldn't go back to the warehouse until he had something. That wasn't fair to the other guys, he had to pull his weight. He shuffled slowly onto Broadway again and walked over to the liquor store. He stood outside of it, looking into the doorway longingly, when a man came out with a big paper bag and turned to him.

"Knock yourself out bro. Been there," he said, handing Matthew the paper bag. Matthew stared at him, at this tall, skinny *real* Mexican man with tattoos running down his arms like rain, a couple of teardrops tattooed near his eyes. Matthew recognized his tattoos. They were gang tats, like his, even though they were obviously from very different gangs, from different areas. And Matthew had a couple of teardrops tattooed around his eyes as well.

"Thank you," Matthew whispered, and the guy nodded and walked on. Matthew opened the bag like he was five, and it was Christmas. It was a giant bottle of vodka, and Matthew nearly started crying with relief. One more day. One more night where he wouldn't have to feel the shakes, where he could share with his guys, where he could try not to think about Chris and Maria. But maybe he could remember them without feeling sad this time. Maria. She had fucked it up for him and Chris, but he wasn't angry at her. He understood her. He had more in common with her in a way than he had ever had with Chris. She was also born with a need that she didn't bother to try to understand, a need that encompassed everything, a need that was stronger than love for people. He thought of his favorite passage in the *Inferno*, the one he had memorized long ago.

> Through me you pass into the city of woe:
> Through me you pass into eternal pain:
> Through me among the people lost for aye.
>
> Justice the founder of my fabric mov'd:
> To rear me was the task of power divine,
> Supremest wisdom, and primeval love.
>
> Before me things create were none, save things
> Eternal, and eternal I endure.
> All hope abandon ye who enter here.

EIGHTEEN

"MATTHEW. MATTHEW, GET UP," GEORGE SAID. MATTHEW GROANED and looked around. He had passed out somewhere downtown again, and he had either been doing crazy shit during a blackout or was just something that the locals didn't want around. At least it was George that had responded and not some other cop. He was always nice to him.

"Fuck," Matthew said.

George looked down at him, his bright, silver badge reflecting sun directly into Matthew's eyes.

"Oh God," Matthew said, "the light. Get it away."

"I'm thinking if you're not too fucked up to get back to wherever you go, I want to offer you breakfast. On me," George said. "After all, you don't smell too bad."

"Gee, *thanks*," Matthew said. "OK." He scrambled up and stumbled, George holding his arm out, and Matthew taking it gingerly, like an old man. He felt like an old man.

They walked along until they got to George's cruiser, and Matthew stopped, digging his heels in. "I'm not getting in your police car man. You'll just drive me to detox and I don't want to go there."

George sighed heavily. "No. I promise I'm just going to take you to the Denver Diner. I'd suggest walking but I don't want to ruin your rep."

Matthew looked over at George suspiciously and then laughed. "Yeah. My rep. It's pretty hard to keep that up when people call you 'the Dancing Mexican,'" he said, coughing hard. He bent over, and coughed for a long time, George handing him some tissues. Matthew coughed into them. When he was done, he noticed the blood. That had been happening a lot lately. When he thought about his insides, he thought about this old, shitty Ford that had sat in the parking lot of their apartment for years. Matthew liked to play on it, and though it had gotten him a case of tetanus once, he never quit. When he had gotten tetanus, it was a teacher at school who had taken him into IHS, when she realized that the gash on his arm looked infected. His mother had never noticed. He remembered scrambling up and getting on top of the old truck, pretending he was some sort of king looking out over a jungle. He loved to imagine it: the jungle, it's greenness, tigers prowling, monkeys hooting in the trees. One day, while his mother was raging drunkenly inside the house over the latest man, he had gone out into parking lot and instead of climbing on top of the truck, he had lifted the hood. It was completely empty, and that emptiness had made him feel a keen, piercing loneliness. The feeling had never left him. He pushed the tissues into his pocket and thanked George.

"OK. If you promise you're not taking me to detox," Matthew said.

"I'll even let you sit up front," George said.

"That'll really ruin my rep," George said, but he got in after George opened the door for him. He smiled at Matthew through the glass, and Matthew smiled back. There was all kinds of stuff up front, all kinds of technical stuff; a walkie-talkie, which was squawking, a computer affixed to the dash.

George got in.

"Thanks for opening the door for me. Romantic," Matthew said, and George rolled his eyes and spoke into the walkie-talkie.

"It's fancy in here," Matthew said.

"Just don't touch anything," George said and put the car into drive. Matthew looked out the window, the sound of the walkie-talkie a kind of quiet backdrop. They moved down Broadway, took a right and then another right onto Lincoln, the stores looking as hip as the people who were going into them and though Matthew always felt an inescapable separateness from these people as they passed him on the street, sometimes handing him change, sometimes ignoring him, sometimes yelling at him to get a job, from this perspective, he felt friendlier toward them, less separate.

They turned onto Speer, and then Colfax, the Denver Diner coming into view. Matthew always thought it looked really friendly. Whenever he had a little money, he'd go in. They usually didn't bother him. Unless he'd had to drink something really bad or he'd just had far far too much, he was a quiet drunk.

They were seated, and Matthew looked out the window. It suddenly occurred to him that George might want to talk and this made Matthew squirm.

"How you doing Matthew?" George asked, and then drank his water.

"Still a drunk," Matthew said, feeling clever and rebellious. It was funny, when he was with the 505s, he was the quiet one, the one who came with unexpected violence. And sometimes he was funny. But now, he liked to be sarcastic all the time, and he was never violent. He guessed that he was just bitter and old. Matthew was twenty-four.

"Very funny Matthew," George said, crossing his long, dark arms and smirking.

"I'm really funny," Matthew said.

The waitress came and looking at the odd pair, couldn't help but squint quizzically for a moment, but being a woman who had seen much, much stranger in her day, handed the two menus and asked them if they wanted anything to drink.

Matthew laughed and then asked for a cup of coffee.

"Me too," George said.

They were quiet. The coffee came, and Matthew began to feel a little bit better, even though the urge to drink began to edge up on him. He knew he didn't have long before he'd have to go. He didn't like having the shakes in front of regular people. It was embarrassing.

"I talked with that social worker that saw you the last time," George said.

"Tell her yes," Matthew responded.

"Yes what?"

"I'm single."

"You're full of them today, aren't you, Matthew?"

"I think she likes my tattoos. Likes the rough dudes," Matthew said, rubbing his hand up his arm and then smiling at George. Everything was different up here, the gangs more Mexican, though there were Natives he'd seen with gang tats intermixed with the Mexican gangs. Sometimes he'd see them shuffling around the city but he would try to avoid them. Too many memories. And his tattoos marked him. If they saw them and recognized them, who knows what they would do.

"I'm sure you're right, Matthew. But she wanted to talk about the 505s. About the fact that you used to be in a gang, and how that's affected you. There's a new program, you know, for ex-gang members. They give you a place to stay, food, they've even got counselors," George said. "Get you all right in the head."

Matthew laughed. "But I'd have to be sober."

"Well, that's the thing. This is different. You'd have to go into counseling, and they'd try to work you to sobriety but no, you could go in as you are. That's why she was so anxious to find me. She knew I'd taken you in, hoped I knew where you might be."

"But I don't want to get sober."

"Why not?" George asked, but before Matthew could say anything, their food had arrived. Matthew found his stomach rising in unexpected hunger. He'd ordered a grilled cheese and fries, which was his favorite.

They ate in silence for some time, and George didn't say anything until they were done.

"Just think about it," George said. "It doesn't have to be like this. And if you're worried about the cops picking you up once you get more visible if you did things while you were in a gang, well, they have lawyers who can often cut deals. Really good ones." He picked the check up and walked over to the register. Matthew sighed and got up, slowly.

"Where to?" George asked, after opening the door for Matthew and then getting in himself.

"Back where you found me."

When George dropped him off, he handed Matthew a card, and Matthew thanked him for the meal. He watched the car pull away and walked over to the trashcan, the same one that he thought had tried to eat him. He started to throw the card in and stopped. Looked at it, put it in his pocket, and headed for the liquor store.

He felt strange, milky. There was a tightness in his stomach that he wasn't used to, something he remembered from his childhood. He felt sick. The bottles in front of him were swimming, and he wasn't even drunk yet. He needed to be drunk. He went over to the shelf where all of the vodka was kept, ran his eyes low, and picked the cheapest, biggest bottle he could afford. George had slipped a five in with the card, knowing full well what Matthew would spend it on, but also knowing that if Matthew could spend it on real booze, he wouldn't have to drink Windex or something like it. He pulled the bottle off the shelf, his cracked brown hands closing around the neck of it reassuringly, and went up to the counter. The cashier was young, Middle Eastern. Matthew smiled furtively, and the guy smiled back in a quick, perfunctory line, handing Matthew his bottle back in a paper sack.

Matthew decided to take a few drinks first, in the alley, and resist the temptation to drink it all now. If he could steady himself, he could do a little work on the streets first and have enough for the next day maybe. He walked into an alleyway behind The Mayan and opened the sack. Christmas. He twisted the knob off and drank thirstily until the shaking of his hands ceased. He took a few more drinks, regretfully placed the bottle back in the sack, and put it in his greasy black backpack.

Out again on the streets, he begged, and he danced, ignoring the insults and smiling at the folks who put a few pennies, or maybe a dollar even, in his cup. A couple of people who knew him came by and yelled, "The Dancing Mexican!" and gave him a quarter, a dollar, a few dimes. Around four o'clock he felt like he had enough, and he wanted to get back to the warehouse and relax and drink, and see what some of the other guys might have pulled in for the day.

Walking back, he thought about George. He wondered why George was so nice to him. He had always figured it had something to do with the fact that Matthew was brown and George black, some sort of ethnic camaraderie. Or maybe it was because he felt sorry for Matthew on account of the fact that he was so pathetic. But it had never occurred to Matthew that it might be because he thought Matthew had potential, could be something else. The only other person who'd thought that had been Chris, and look how that had turned out. In addition to the fact that Chris had just been using Matthew to build what he thought was his empire.

"Empire," Matthew whispered to himself and laughed. He didn't like to think about Chris, but sometimes he couldn't help it, something would trigger it. He moved through the streets, the image of Chris floating through his head, and he had to duck into an alleyway and have a few hard swigs before continuing on. He thought about the time that he and Chris had been sitting around on the couch, waiting for Maria, before all of the shit had really come down. It had been a few weeks after he'd gotten clean, and they were sharing a joint. It really had helped him, at least at first, to quell the urge to drink. And he liked the way it made everything funny, instead of sad, like the booze could.

Chris had been making fun of Rudolph because he was almost completely silent most of the time that they met up, except to occasionally repeat whatever had last been said while nodding fervently.

They had died laughing for almost an hour, Chris nodding and nodding, that tuned-out pseudo-serious expression on his face so close to the OG's that Matthew laughed so hard he ended up on the floor. He remembered thinking that he hadn't felt that deeply good since he was a child. Actually, he had felt better. Matthew sighed and let the vodka make its way through his system. Chris *had* made him feel that way, he had to admit that. Chris had made him less afraid to feel. For most of his life, he didn't have the opportunity for joy, and even feeling happy made him feel sad, dark so quickly, that he tried his best not to feel at all. The only time that he felt good had been with his sister. Though sometimes his mother would get jealous of them and rip them apart, putting his sister in the closet for hours while she begged to be let out, Matthew crying in the living room, his mother threatening to slap him if he didn't stop, which he didn't. So she would slap him across the face, making him cry harder, her hand hovering over him, his cries turning to quiet whimpers.

He thought about this, too, and frowned. He pushed it away, but that only let thoughts of Chris come back in. And then worse, thoughts of Maria. He blamed George. He was a nice guy, but he was always trying to open Matthew up, crack his ribs open and get in. Matthew couldn't afford that. It was too dangerous.

Back at the warehouse, he was alone. That was fine too. He figured he would settle in, drink some vodka, start a fire. Read from the *Inferno*. He had held onto that. They had set something up in the middle of the warehouse for when it was cold, and it was starting to get there. The winters were the hardest. Many of them died during the winter, and often, the only way they knew was through some other homeless guy. They died with their faces down in an alleyway, they died in the homeless shelters, they died because they had been beaten to death by a group of white, university kids.

Matthew made a fire and sat by it, drinking. That was the good thing about booze, it was always there. It made being alone OK, it made living without a TV or real friends OK too. He watched the fire and drank.

In Farmington, he'd go into the library to read with his old library card, and one of his obsessions had been constellations. He'd sat in the library, looking them over, trying to memorize the different constellations, their stories, their origins. He knew a few old Navajo ones from his grandmother. He thought he'd seen the Pleiades when he first started looking up, but then realized that that was a winter constellation. He didn't know exactly what he was looking at, but it was pretty. He thought for a minute, his long, black eyes narrowing. Something his Shimásáni had said long ago when he and his mom were visiting her on the Rez ... yes, he could see it now. It was Náhookòs Bi'ááf. A woman. A nice woman, just like his Shimásáni. Matthew sighed and took a pull from the bottle of vodka. He lay back down. He remembered.

NINETEEN

MATTHEW OPENED HIS EYES. CHRIS AND MARIA WERE ON THE ground, and Math was holding his shoulder.

"Fuck," Math said.

"What—?" Matthew said, looking around, wondering why he was still alive, and unhurt.

Maria was dead. He had shot her.

Matthew looked over at Maria and the tears started. Now he would never know if she had ever really loved him.

Chris was still alive. Matthew whipped his own phone out of his pocket. "I'm calling 911," he said.

Math pointed his gun at Matthew. "Don't you touch that, bro," he said. "She's dead. And he's almost dead. And nothing's going to stop that."

"You don't know that," Matthew said hysterically. "He could live!"

"No he won't. What's done is done here, and it's for the best. I'm glad you shot that bitch in her black fucking heart. And Chris? He was aiming for *you* before you shot her. And I woulda been next. But he was too slow, Ishkeh."

Matthew looked at his gun lying on the ground where he had dropped it.

"You're better off without them anyway, and you know it."

Chris was wheezing painfully now, blood sputtering out of his mouth with every labored breath, his shirt soaked with it.

"Let's go. Before someone discovers this mess and the cops come. You can ride back with me, or you can die with these fuckers here, your choice."

Matthew thought about dying. He didn't want to live without Maria. He didn't. He looked at his gun. He picked it up.

Matthew stared at Maria, an expression of rage and pain frozen on her face. He walked over to her and lifted her bag. He sifted through it. It was there. His copy of the *Inferno*. He looked into her eyes as he stood back up. There was no peace there. Chris exhaled noisily and then stopped breathing altogether. Matthew followed Math to the car, picking Chris's gun up along the way and tucking it into the back of his pants. He had nothing to give the cops now. But it didn't matter anymore. Nothing did without Maria.

In the car, Matthew began to cry, and though he thought Math would be like his mother and hit him, tell him to shut up, instead he stayed quiet. Matthew sobbed. He didn't understand Math. He was cold as they came—look at the way he treated the dogs, the people they went to collect on. But he was being kind to him now. People were strange. He would never understand them. They pulled up to Matthew's house, now empty. Matthew knew that he would have to tell Rudolph and Damien something, but all he could think of was the bottle of vodka he had stashed in his room. How he wanted to bury himself in it, pass out, try not to shoot himself, think of reasons why not to try not to shoot himself. Right now, he couldn't think of any.

Math looked at him as he shut the door, a mix of sadness and determination on his face. "Look, Ishkeh ... this is the way it was always gonna go down. Maria, she was a fuck up. Angry. She was always switching sides. That bitch only loved Chris, and even then, not really. Only because he got to her when she was really young. And you know damn well Chris was gonna die. Fucker was arrogant, I told you that."

"We ... were going to get out together," Matthew said.

"What?"

"We were talking to the cops."

216

Math was silent for a while, and Matthew wondered if he wasn't going to kill him now. He had told him this hoping that he would.

"Ishkeh . . . you ever talk to the cops yourself?"

It was Matthew's turn to go silent. "What do you mean?"

Math sighed. "Ishkeh, you ever meet with the cops yourself, or Maria just *tell you* all about her supposed meetings with the cops?"

Matthew's mind began to reel. "No . . ."

"I been trying to *tell you*. That bitch was only about herself."

Matthew felt sick. He turned toward home.

"And call me. Really, I could use you," Math said, and Matthew turned around but, barely, nodded again and turned back to the house and shuffled forward until he was at the door.

Matthew closed the door and stood there for a moment, wondering if he was alone. He heard nothing. In his room, he fell onto his bed, hard. Reached around under his pillow for the bottle. It was almost empty.

"Fuck," he said to himself. He got back up. He didn't know what to think. She had . . . been with Math, but, maybe . . . he didn't know. He just didn't know.

After a quick trip to the liquor store, he was back in his bed, the house blissfully silent. He wondered if he'd hear from Damien at all—news spread fast in this town. He thought perhaps that he was already knocking on Math's door, ready to join the Burques. He had always seemed so crazy-loyal but the 505s were done now. There was nothing left. Not really.

He turned around and stared up at the ceiling. The image of Chris's face, his mouth sputtering blood onto his T-shirt came to him, Maria by his side, blood spreading underneath her onto the dirt in a big, black puddle. He squeezed his eyes shut but the images wouldn't dissipate. They only became sharper. He began crying again, and he brought the bottle to his lips and drank, hating himself, how weak he was. He kept drinking, and then he began to look at his phone, at all of the texts from Chris and from Maria. He couldn't believe that he wouldn't ever get another one from either of them again.

Never another, *where u at, Ishkeh?* from Chris, or a short, sharp *hey* from Maria. He wondered if their bodies had been discovered yet. He thought about Maria's mother, how sad it was that she had followed her into death. He thought about Sharina then, realizing that he hadn't in a long, long time. He wondered how she would feel. As far as he knew, she and Maria had stopped talking not long after she moved out. But they had been best friends since childhood. He was sure they would all blame Chris, and that Sharina would feel lucky for getting out when she did. And Chris. He wondered who would attend his funeral. He had so few friends left and hadn't talked to any of his family in years and years. Though he'd grown up with gangs all around him, his arrogance had driven his family from him.

He passed out with the image of Maria's face in front of him.

A banging on his bedroom door woke him. He was still drunk. He put his hands over his face and moaned. The banging continued. He shuffled to the door, expecting Maria or Chris, and then remembered. He hadn't realized he'd locked it.

He opened the door, and it was Damien, looking lost and confused.

"Is it true?" he asked.

Matthew nodded. "Come into the living room with me."

Damien followed, pulling his pants up on his skinny, tall body as he went. He sat down heavily on the couch and looked imploringly at Matthew. Matthew had brought the bottle of vodka he'd just bought, and handed it to Damien, who took a long swig and handed it back. Matthew felt sorry for Damien. He'd grown up in this neighborhood, had been helping the gangs since he was old enough to stand, to serve as look-out. He was fifteen years old.

"Chris is dead? Maria's dead?"

"Yes," Matthew said.

"What the fuck! We gotta hit whoever did it back, we—"

Matthew began shaking his head, and Damien looked at him incredulously. "No? I don't understand, bro, I just don't. Whoever they are, they deserve to die!"

Matthew took a long drink of vodka, even though he was still drunk as hell. "The 505s are over. That was already happening. But this is the nail in the coffin, Ishkeh. You need to accept it and move on."

Damien shook his head. "No, man, I mean, ain't you being premature? I mean, didn't Rudolph tell us that all we need to do is lay low for a while, and—"

"Rudolph is old, he's tired. He's probably just going to live with his little nieces and nephews and retire from this shit. You know he's got a bank account with lots of cash in it, right? The only reason he was still in it is because he was one of the first. All of his friends are in jail or disappeared, all because of gangbanging. I don't see him trying again. And there are the Zias and the Burques—"

"Fuck the Zias, man! Fuck the Burques! Those fuckers killed off all of the 505s! And you know damn well it was one of them, and I told you, they deserve to die! Fuck it, I'll get in the car with you right now, take a bunch of those fuckers out, and then we'll see if they want to try more shit with us!"

Matthew sighed. "It wasn't the Zias. Well, it was, sort of."

Damien looked confused. "What the fuck you talking about man? Not the Zias? Then it was some MS13 motherfuckers, and I don't care if I die tonight, I want blood. Blood for blood." Matthew sighed again and handed him the vodka.

"Drink," he said, and Damien drank.

"If I tell you who it was, you'll go out and try to kill him. And there's been enough blood for one night. And you won't be able to kill him. He'll kill you. And then it would be like I killed you. And I don't want to be responsible for that. And the 505s are over," Matthew said, leaning back on the couch.

Damien jumped up and walked over to him, looked down at him with an expression of fury on his face. "What the fuck is wrong with you? I thought you were a thug, the real fucking deal, down for the 505s, man! You and Chris were on your fucking way! And now you're gonna let the fucker who shot your best friend down go?"

Matthew began laughing.

"You gonna laugh at me! What the fuck, Ishkeh! What the *fuck*!" Damien yelled, and began pacing. "I'm just gonna find out on my own if you don't tell me, I'm gonna get my blood no matter what. So you might as well tell me, man."

Matthew shook his head. "Look, I'm not laughing at you. I promise, I'm not laughing at you *at all*. I'm laughing because Chris—man, he had me convinced too. He fires you up. Or . . . well, he did fire you up," Matthew said, thinking of his face again, the blood, the glazed expression in his eyes that seemed to come so suddenly as he died. Matthew began to cry. "You think I'm not sad? I'm not torn to shit over this? I loved Chris! But I don't want any more death, and you're a kid man, you're just a kid."

Damien stopped pacing and looked at Matthew with hurt in his short, almond eyes. "I'm not a kid! I'm a grown-ass man! I've killed men! I've been to jail. Well, I been to juvie, which you know damn well is the same thing. I've smashed and grabbed and fucked women twice my age, more! I'm a man," he said, his lip trembling. "I'm a fucking man . . ."

Matthew looked at Damien, and though he didn't see himself, he saw a part of himself, that part that just wanted something else, something he could believe in, give himself over to. He could understand that. Maria, she had made him feel that more than anything else. He also understood that he was looking at someone who would be dead before he hit twenty years old. He was determined to live this life, this life filled with blood-pumping violence, excitement, drugs. And yet he wasn't smart like Math. Math was calculating. Math would survive to be an OG. Math would put money away, and Math would use any poor fucker that came across his path. But Math wouldn't end up like Chris. Math didn't care about how people saw him, he cared about the money. This kid, this beautiful kid with his long, black eyelashes, though, he was like a sacrificial lamb.

"You are a man. I'm not saying that. But you're young, Ishkeh."

"So fucking what!" Damien said.

"OK, sit down. Sit down and let me tell you what I think you should do. And you can say *fuck that yo* right after. But know that I'm not going to help you kill anyone tonight, or ever. And that I'm done with the 505s. That Rudolph is *done*. And that no matter how bad you want this to be the case, the 505s are fucking done."

"But!" Damien said.

"Just sit down!" Matthew yelled and because Damien was a boy who was used to taking orders from men, he did.

Matthew was silent for a minute. He wanted Damien to chill the fuck out, as much as that was possible.

"The man who killed Chris ... and Maria," he said. "He was someone that Chris trusted, it's true. It was bullshit, what he did."

"Then why aren't we out there putting that fucker out!" Damien yelled, bolting up from the couch again.

"Stop!" Matthew said. "You said you'd let me finish! Have some respect, Ishkeh."

Damien pulled his lips into a tight, angry, contained line, and sat down again.

"I want you to know something. I thought I was gonna die tonight. I *knew* that what I was getting into would kill me. I didn't know if it would kill Chris, and I sure as hell didn't think it would kill Maria. But I was going to die, and I was at peace with that. I was at peace with dying for Chris, with him. You gotta understand one thing: I love ... loved Chris, he—" and here he started to cry. He pulled the bottle up again, realizing that before the night was through, he would have to get another. He waited until his sorrow was under control.

"He cleaned me up. I was on my way to dying from this shit," he said, lifting the bottle. "And now I'm back on that path. But Chris found me. He got me almost sober. He was like a father to me. But that's the thing with Chris: he uses people ... did use people, I mean..." Matthew said, trailing off.

Damien crossed his arms over his chest, screwed his lips into a tighter line.

"He doesn't—didn't love you. No one can love anyone, not really, when you're gangbanging for years, man. It's too rough a life. Chris got to where he did by finding a way to make guys love *him*, to get their loyalty. And then he'd shove them into the line of fire. Damien, I'm telling you: you don't know how many guys have come before you, before me. The only reason I'm not dead is because I came into this thing with nothing to lose. I got a darkness, and it made me good at this. But Chris was arrogant. And I began to see that. I *told* him not to try to fuck with the Zias. I knew they were in deep with the MS13s, and I knew that once we hit them like we did, they would take us down. But he wouldn't fucking listen. And that's why he's dead."

Damien was quiet, his arms crossed, and his mouth in that hard, little line.

"You finished, bro?" he asked finally.

"Yes."

"And you ain't gonna tell me who did this?"

"No. But what I will tell you, though, is that you should get the fuck out of this shit; if you want, I'm sure there's a place for you in the Burques. If that's what you really want, how you're determined to live your life. Me? I'm gonna drink the rest of this, and then I'm gonna drink another bottle. And another. And when the rent for this place is due, I'm not gonna be able to pay it. So there won't be any place for you to stay. So whatever you gonna do, you better decide soon."

Damien shook his head. "You changed man. I looked up to you."

Matthew shrugged, drank.

Damien got up, went to his room. When he got back, he had his bag in his hands.

He stood over Matthew with an angry, nearly weepy expression on his face. "I should fucking kill you. Put you out of your fucking misery."

"Why don't you," Matthew said flatly.

Slowly, Damien pulled his piece out of his bag and lifted it to where it was level to Matthew's head.

222

Matthew looked at him, feeling drunk as fuck and full of darkness, pain, exhaustion. He said nothing.

Damien's hand trembled, then his lip did. Tears ran down his face, and Matthew thought about the time he and Chris had been like this. That seemed like it happened a million years ago, in another universe.

"I should fucking do it!" Damien said.

"Then why don't you? I'm already dead," Matthew said, lifting the bottle of vodka and drinking. "I told you I thought I was going to die tonight."

Damien began to sweat, visibly, the sweat mixing with his tears, his eyes and Matthew's locked. Matthew genuinely didn't care if he shot him, he just hoped that if he did, he would go fast. He was tired of pain.

"If you're going to do it, shoot me in the head," Matthew said. "Here." He pointed to the part of his temple where the bullet had the best chance of going clean through, and hitting him where he needed to be hit to die.

"You're ... you're like the sheep," Damien said.

"The sheep?"

"Yeah. My grandma raised them. On the Rez."

Matthew laughed.

"What's so fucking funny?" Damien asked, still sweating, though he'd stopped crying.

"I'm always surrounded by Navajos," Matthew said, sinking farther back into the couch. He felt sleepy.

Damien laughed, a short, tight laugh. "Welcome to Albuquerque, fool."

"Yeah."

"But you are. Like the sheep I mean, bro. When it was time to slaughter them, they knew. They knew they were going to die. It was part of life, part of my grandmother's life. And it's funny when I think about it now, 'cause I've killed men, but I hated it. I hated watching those sheep scream, knowing they were going to die. I got sick the first time, and all of my cousins who lived on the Rez made fun of me, called me billyganna."

"I'm not screaming," Matthew said.

"But you are. Just not out loud," Damien said, lowering the gun. "You been screaming inside since I met you, Ishkeh. I thought at first that darkness was power. But now I see you just meant to be slaughtered. But fuck it. I can't do it. I can't slaughter a fucking sheep."

Matthew looked at him, said nothing.

"Don't expect to see me again," Damien said, placing his gun into his bag.

Matthew sat in the living room for a while then, turning the TV on and watching the images float by on the screen, none of them making any kind of linear sense. He thought about a show he'd caught once, about that artist who threw colors on his canvas from above. He'd liked that, but there was an emptiness to it too. Some kind of sadness he couldn't put his finger on. Something chaotic that he understood. He drank again, his hand still gripping the bottle at his side as he began to drift into sleep, the blue light of the television casting a shadow on his wide, angular face.

TWENTY

THE NEXT MORNING, MATTHEW WOKE UP LATE. HE COULD SEE THE clouds moving through the broken slates in the warehouse ceiling. There was a guy sleeping next to him that he didn't recognize and a few guys that he did. He figured that he'd passed out before they'd come in. The bottle next to him was empty, and he felt gray. He'd thought and dreamed about Chris, he knew that. And about Maria. Maria. He wondered if she'd ever loved him. He loved her still. It had been with Maria that his love of Chris had faded, turned sour. He wondered if she'd done that on purpose and why. He had really believed her when she said she'd loved him, when she'd said she hated Chris. He still had no idea if she'd really gone to the cops or not. But that was the thing about love, it turned to hate so easily. It was the kind of fire that burned brightly for some people, no matter what.

He sat up, rubbed his greasy face. He felt shitty, but not shaky yet. He thought about coffee. About the coffee they'd had at the house in Albuquerque. It had been so nice to get up, out of a bed, go to a kitchen and start coffee. Sit in a kitchen at a table and drink it slowly and silently. He wondered what had happened to that house, that coffee maker. He remembered he and Chris had picked it up at a Starbucks. Chris had loved Starbucks. He bought mugs there, got his drinks there. He loved the fancy drinks. The lattés, the Frappuccinos. There was nothing funnier than watching stocky, tattooed tough-ass Chris drink a giant caramel Frappuccino, complete with whipped cream and caramel sauce. That was the thing about Albuquerque though, everyone had tattoos. Lots of them. He'd never felt weird there. He always felt like he belonged. Denver was strange. There were Indians everywhere, and in fact, there were all kinds of tribes, more than there had been in Albuquerque, but it was as if the city pretended that they weren't there at all, and though there were certainly people with tattoos, with shaved heads, with long hair, it was different. There was a tension that wasn't the same. He couldn't really understand why, and he knew that he would never go back to Albuquerque, but it wasn't the same, and he missed the Southwest. He missed Chris. And Maria. Of course, Maria....

He sighed heavily and wondered if he was capable of getting out, finding some coffee, an old muffin in a dumpster somewhere, or on the top of the trash in a trashcan. It was amazing what people threw away. Most times, he didn't need people to give him their leftovers, though he liked going into a restaurant when he had the money. Most times he found what he needed in the dumpsters, though he had to be careful, because the owners didn't like bums rooting around in the trash and would sometimes call the cops.

He wasn't particularly hungry though, and though he was tired, he felt strangely restless. These days, he felt shitty in body, but he was at peace mentally. It was all that talk of getting help George had done, that's why he felt so strange. George had made him feel like he could do something different, be something different. But what? He was born to be a drunk, that's how he had always thought of it. If it hadn't been for Chris, he would already probably be dead by now, and there was a part of him that desperately wished that he was. He couldn't imagine another life, another him. It just wasn't in him, that kind of direction, imagination. Fucked up as Chris had been, he had had those things. He had been able to scoop people out of their lives and say march, go, do this, be this for me. In another life, Chris would have been a CEO of a company, a senator, a dictator. And though he thought it had been a different thing with Maria, it really hadn't been. She had also been a reason to live. A person who told him what to be, who to be, what to do. Though when he thought about what he had done to her—the sorrow, it was too much. He thought about the neighborhoods not fifteen minutes from where he was sitting. The people in those houses lying on their soft beds, angry at their wives or husbands, turning the channels and thinking about the people they had once loved, or thought they did, their children screaming in the background. He shuddered. At least he'd never gotten anyone pregnant, not as far as he knew. He couldn't imagine being responsible for a child, and though he had dreamed of one with Maria, when he thought of it now, the very idea of being a parent seemed insurmountable. He wasn't even responsible for himself. Chris had been responsible for him for a while, had been his dad. He'd been a shitty dad, but a dad nonetheless. He pulled the card George had handed him out of his pocket. Stared at it for a moment, turned it over and back again. *Lifeline*, it said on the front and underneath: Gang Rehabilitation. On the back was a phone number and an address. It was on Colfax. He laughed. Of course it was, that way the fuck ups didn't have to go far from where they already lived. He looked over at the fire pit. The fire was out. He thought about tossing the card onto the pit, letting it burn that evening. The idea of sobering up, training for a job, talking to counselors about the 505s, Chris, Maria. Living in a house. Sleeping in a bed again. It seemed like something from another world. He would like to have coffee in the morning though. He shoved the card back into his pocket.

Matthew sighed and decided to just get himself together, go to one of the dumpsters. He washed up the best that he could, knowing that the stink of alcohol sweating off of him meant that his washing wouldn't do him much good, but still glad for the ritual of it, and walked out and onto Broadway.

Matthew went over to his favorite big green dumpster, the one outside of The Hornet. For some reason there always seemed to be a lot of leftover food in there, and they didn't lock it. Lots of restaurants locked their dumpsters, so that the bums wouldn't eat from them, or so that random people wouldn't overfill them. The great thing, too, about the dumpster outside The Hornet was that usually the stuff on top was pretty good. Matthew looked around for anyone who might want to stop him from scrounging around in the dumpster, then opened it up and immediately saw half of a hamburger and fries right on top of some cardboard. He pulled it out, closed the lid of the dumpster and sat under a telephone poll and feasted. It wasn't even really that old. Maybe an hour. He ate, listening to the noise on the streets, the buzz and chatter of the people living their lives around him. When he was done, he sat a while longer, knowing that he had to get on the streets, get some change for booze.

He was getting up when he heard a car drive into the lot and park. The lot was fairly busy, as there was a bank and a Walgreens in front, so cars came in and out all day. Matthew had heard a number of them while he'd been eating his burger. A group of men, boys really, started piling out of the doors of a large, black SUV, and they were talking loudly, laughing and hitting each other. One of them hit another hard on the ass. "Faggot!" the guy said affectionately. Matthew watched them. They were probably around his age, but they looked much younger. The smell of money emanated from them, their sharp, masculine cologne coming off in waves, their shirts bearing strange, postmodern statements and images that seemed to relate to sex or sports in some way that Matthew couldn't quite understand.

One of them spotted him as they were rounding the corner and pointed. "Look at that fucking Mexican fucker," he said and the others stopped laughing and joking and looked. The guy who was pointing was a short guy with dark hair and a thick, white neck. "Fucking drain on the fucking country. Smells like shit I bet."

"Wetback," another one of them said. They stopped.

There were about four of them, and Matthew knew that he was in trouble. He began to scramble away, moving as fast as his tired, aching body could take him. It was daytime, and that was good. Usually bums got beat to fuck at night.

"Where you going, you Mexican fucker? You move this fast when you came over to *my* fucking country?"

Matthew was almost around the corner to the relative safety of Broadway. They hadn't started running, and he figured they just wanted to impress each other. Or so he hoped.

On Broadway, he stopped. Turned around. They were behind him, but he was now surrounded by a sea of people. He smiled.

"You fucking piece of shit," the thick-necked one said.

"Yeah. You think you can like, be in this country, and like, take all of our jobs, and we're not supposed to do anything about it? Like, my dad worked hard for his money, you fucking bum. Go back to Mexico," a tall, blond kid said to him. He looked like he couldn't be more than twenty. He still had acne.

Matthew began walking away, and they watched him. He knew they were, because he could feel them at his back. He was about ten feet away when something sharp and undeniable rose up in him. He turned around. "I'm fucking Native American you stupid, ignorant fuckers! Get out of *my* country!" he said, his face red, angry, his fists stiff at his sides. They began to advance, but just then, a cop car appeared, it's blue light circling. Someone must have called.

The group of boys stopped in their tracks. Matthew heaved a sigh. He was about to turn around and keep walking when the thick-necked one yelled, "You'll pay, you fucking *wetback*." He began high-fiving his friends, and they laughed, the sound of it sinister, hateful.

Matthew shook his head. He didn't understand people like this. He needed a cigarette, badly. There was one bum that someone had nicknamed "Smokes," that usually had them, and would give them out for a dime. Matthew put his hands in his pockets, and came out with a few pennies, a nickel. He counted. It was enough. He began walking angrily, with as much purpose as his body could muster toward where he knew Smokes hung out.

On his way, he asked for spare change, a couple of people sighing and placing a few pennies, a quarter in his cup. "Thank you," he said every time, trying to meet the eyes of the people that gave without looking threatening, without looking like he was even really there.

"Hey Smokes," he said. Smoke's leathery white face was full of long, pleasant lines. He liked to hang on Broadway and Fifth.

"How's it hanging, Matthew?" Smokes asked. "Need a smoke?"

"Yeah. I really do," he said, sighing.

Smokes looked at Matthew sympathetically, cocking his head and smiling. "You look like you really do need a smoke," he said, digging into his pocket and coming up with a Pall Mall. He handed it over to Matthew. "This one's on the house."

"Thanks man," Matthew said. Matthew leaned in as Smokes pulled a little pink lighter out of his other pocket and lit Matthew's cigarette. Matthew inhaled, closing his eyes.

"Oh man, that's better," he said, coughing a little. "Cuuuuute lighter, by the way."

"Fuck you man, it was free. Saw this little pink fucker just sitting in the middle of the sidewalk. Someone must have dropped it. It's full of gas."

"I would have picked it up too," Matthew said, "and given it to you."

Smokes rolled his eyes affectionately, and they smoked in silence for a while, Matthew beginning to calm.

"So, why the need for a cig?" Smokes asked. He was a leathery, stinky old dude, but he was a good leathery, stinky old dude. He was always nice to everyone. Matthew wasn't the first guy he'd given a smoke to on the house. And unlike many of the guys Matthew knew on the streets, he wasn't an alcoholic or a junkie, unless you counted cigarettes. He'd lost his job about a decade before and decided that he liked living on the streets. Once Matthew had been talking to him, and a young, well-dressed man of about twenty-five came up and hugged him, called him dad. Matthew had been surprised. The man asked him how he was doing, and they talked, and at the end of the conversation, he gave Smokes a twenty and told him he loved him. When he'd walked away, Matthew had asked Smokes why he didn't stay with his son. If he wouldn't let him. *Nah,* Smokes said, *living in a house just ain't for me. I did that. Losing my job was the best thing ever happen to me. Made me free.* Matthew had thought about this for a long time. He didn't feel free. But he couldn't say he felt imprisoned either. Exactly. He had never had a strong will to live, and ever since the shit with the 505s, his desire to disappear completely in alcohol, and then death, had increased exponentially. But he had never thought about it in terms of freedom. He still wasn't entirely sure what he thought about that.

He told Smokes what had happened to him, about the group of boys. What he'd said. Smokes listened patiently. When Matthew finished with his story, Smokes said, "Some people are just assholes. Man, you know I been beat up a few times. Always by a group of young guys. One time with a bat. Man, I don't know how I survived that."

Matthew remembered. He'd noticed that Smokes hadn't been on the corner for a couple of weeks. He began to assume that Smokes was dead, and he had been sad. Though there was general camaraderie on the streets, Smokes was special. He was sweet. Kind. Patient. He listened, and he helped if he could. He kept a couple of tiny bottles of vodka in his pockets, and though everyone knew he did, they only asked when they really needed it, when they were so drunk-sick it was unbearable.

"Be careful out there," Smokes said. "Don't get yourself killed, man. I like having you around."

Matthew smiled at him, and Smokes held his hand up and said, "Up high." Smokes liked to give high-fives, and though Matthew always felt weird about it, sort of like when your dad wanted to bond with you in public, he always gave Smokes a high-five back. Smokes laughed and then coughed, deeply. He always laughed. Matthew felt good walking away. The sun was out, there was a little breeze, and he had escaped hell another day. He begged.

TWENTY-ONE

MATTHEW STUMBLED AROUND THE STREETS OF ALBUQUERQUE, feeling like he had been in a time machine. So much had changed. Nothing had changed. Had he even been in the 505s? Known a man named Chris who had become his father? Loved a woman named Maria? Seen and been a part of so much death? Sometimes he would sit in an alleyway and cry for hours, his arms crossed tightly over his chest. He would cry for his sister, mainly, and he had to admit, for himself. He wanted to be held. He felt lonely. Tormented. Ugly. Somehow he'd managed to get through life with the 505s without any large scars on his face, though there were a few on his body that looked almost like Sundance scars. He wished sometimes that they were. Sometimes he would touch them, run his fingers in their grooves.

He had almost nothing. The piles of money the 505s had acquired in their heyday had gone down and down and down, as Chris tried to salvage what was left of the 505s and couldn't, and spent the money on trying to keep the suppliers they had, trying to get new suppliers, and when he couldn't, on strippers and weed to console himself. The furniture they had was all thrift, and the bling that Chris had worn had been sold long ago to the pawn shops that littered the city.

Matthew knew what to do. He knew to go home. To the streets, where he belonged. Though he knew he'd have to leave Albuquerque eventually. The morning after he talked with Damien, he stepped out of the house with his black backpack on his back, some clothing, a few toiletries and his last big bottle of vodka and 250 bucks. He knew where to sleep at night and where to panhandle. He walked over to the part of Central where Chris had first found him and hunkered down, put his cup out and waited for spare change. He knew his money wouldn't last long. But after a few weeks, when he realized that he didn't know any of the other bums anymore, and he watched the people go by, many of them starting to look, in his inebriated state, like Chris and Maria and Sharina, and like the boys he'd watched die, the boys he'd killed, he began to grow depressed. He began to need more and more to feel drunk, and that's when he started to turn to anything cheap to get there. And that's when the black hole came back, and began to swallow him.

One morning he woke up by a dumpster, and though his head felt like it was splitting in two, he knew one thing: he had to get out of Albuquerque. Now. He had lost his sense of time again, what days were what. He didn't know how long he'd been on the streets, but he wanted to die somewhere else, somewhere the memories of who he'd been and loved weren't so intense. Every day he'd pass someplace that he'd eaten with Chris, and he slept in the place where they'd done their drops, where he had been with Maria. The city was thick with ghosts. He began asking around, asking the bums he saw every day, the ones who were friendly, if they knew of anyone going up to Denver but of course no one knew anyone with a car. He realized he was going to have to hitch, and that would be dangerous and difficult. He certainly wouldn't pick himself up, that's for sure.

The day before he left, he was panhandling along Central, working up the nerve to hitch, when Damien about walked right past him and stopped. Matthew had said nothing, hoping that he wouldn't recognize him.

"Matthew!"

"Hey, Ishkeh," Matthew said, and Damien pulled him up by his hand and hugged him.

"You stink!" Damien said, but kindly, teasingly, and Matthew wondered why he was being nice. He worried for a minute that he

234

was working with the cops, but then he thought about how little he cared, and he laughed.

"You with the Burques now? You take my advice?" Matthew asked.

"No. No. I . . . well, I cleaned up."

"What? Thought you were going to shoot my face off for not being true," Matthew said.

"Yeah, I know," Damien said, sighing. "I drove around all night, ready to kill someone. I drove around like that for a long time. When I finally calmed down, I drove to my sister's house. She's not with any gangs. Always rejected that shit. She was the only person I knew to go to. And she told me that I could stay with her, but only if I was going to quit slanging, quit gang shit. At first I was like, just going to tell her whatever she wanted to hear, then figure out what I was going to do. But then . . . she had this friend. This sounds stupid but . . . well, her friend works with this program. They work with gangs and kids who been in gangs, guys in prison. They help them to do slam. You know, like, poetry and shit," Damien said, looking embarrassed but Matthew nodded. It was early in the day, and he wasn't too drunk yet. Sober enough to listen.

"I liked her. Well, shit, homes, honestly I kinda wanted to see if I could get some pussy at first, you know. But then she kept coming around. And bringing guys, you know, who used to be in gangs. And we'd talk. And rhyme. And it felt good. And now, yo . . . I do that. I'm doing construction. And I'm good. And I'm gonna get my GED. And they even gonna laser my tats off, for free." Damien looked at Matthew, shyly almost, and Matthew was reminded of how young Damien was.

"I'm proud of you," Matthew said. "This is good."

"You could come with me! My sister's in the car, over there. I'm just running in over here," he said, pointing with his lips to a storefront, "to do an errand. But I *know* she'd be cool with you coming back with us—we could find you a place to live! There's a program they got, you know for guys like us. Please. Matthew, you a good guy. Whatever shit's in you, I know, you're a good guy. And I owe you my life. If you'd told me who to hit, I'd be dead right now, bro, and we both know it."

Matthew stood smiling at Damien for a bit, his smile sweet, sad. "I can't, Ishkeh. I did something. Something I can't tell you. Something that means I deserve to die."

"Nah, Matthew—we all done shit that means we deserve to die. But that's shit, that's what I learned—there's so many of us. I can't tell you how much I've learned. And you would, too, learn that it ain't your fault, that you can do better. I swear, Ishkeh, come with me, please!"

Matthew began to cry. "I killed Maria. And I loved her. I loved her so much . . . And she said we were gonna go to the cops but Math thought she was lying when I told him that so I don't know . . . I loved her so much, and she didn't love me," he said, and Damien held him.

"It's OK, Matthew, you don't understand, there's shit, my sister, her friend has a lawyer, and he specializes in this kind of shit. He can help."

"Try to understand, I can't. I just can't. But you go write poems and get your GED, for me, OK?" Matthew said, and Damien looked at him with such sadness that Matthew could see himself reflected back, could see how good Damien was. He was filled with hope, with hozho.

Damien finally left him, but only after Matthew told him that he would think about it, would maybe call. Damien cried as he walked away, and so did Matthew.

Matthew stood on the exit for I-25 every day for a week and a half after that, holding out a sign that said that he needed change or a ride. He got a little change, but no one wanted to pick him up. He was about to give up when the window of a truck rolled down and a voice yelled, "You want a ride or what?"

"Yeah!" Matthew yelled.

"Get in quick then."

Matthew stepped up to the door, opened it, and launched himself up and onto the seat. The driver was Native.

"Damn bro, you need a shower," the guy said.

"I know," Matthew said.

"I'll buy you one at a stop. And some dinner. But if you gotta drink, I don't wanna know about it," he said. "Been sober for five years."

Matthew nodded and they went silent for the first few hours. Eventually, they stopped and as promised, the guy bought him a shower. When Matthew got out, the guy had a T-shirt in his hand, one with a wolf howling on the front that had clearly been bought minutes before. Matthew took it and smiled gratefully, followed him over to the diner. They ordered, and Matthew felt grateful for the large bottle of vodka he'd been able to afford that morning, before he'd taken his position by the highway. He had taken his shower and drank enough of it to steady his hands.

TWENTY-TWO

MATTHEW BEGAN HIS WALK BACK TO THE ABANDONED WARE-house. He thought about Smokes. How happy Smokes was. Matthew was resigned to his fate, but he wasn't happy. He felt like he'd been sad his whole life. Why? He'd always felt like he had to be, like he was born that way, born thirsty. But maybe that was just something he told himself because it was easier. He had almost stopped drinking once. Had loved people. But he had lost so much.

Matthew began to cry, people passing him. He was never the kind of man to worry about what people thought about him. He was a tall, homeless Native dude. People judged him the minute they saw his face. And what was another drunk, weeping Indian to anyone anyway, but another drunk, weeping Indian. He stopped and cried silently for a few minutes, feeling sorry for himself, angry at his mother, at Chris. But he couldn't be angry at Maria, even though she had almost certainly lied to him, betrayed him. He still loved her so much. It was like a burn at the back of his throat, a sting, a heaviness inside him that he would never be free of. He thought of her beautiful face. He shook his fists in frustration and people streamed around him, looking worried, but still moving around him in an endless stream. He cried and cried and hit his knees, hard.

"Damn you!" he said, but he didn't know who he was angry at, and he was so tired, so profoundly tired of that emotion, and of sadness. His sobs began to shudder to a stop. He took a long breath and decided that he couldn't be angry anymore, he couldn't be sad.

Not at himself or at Chris or his mother. They were human beings. He was a human being. No matter how drunk he was, no matter how smelly, or what he'd done, that was true, and no one could take that away from him.

"Indeh. Diné," he said softly. "I am a human being."

He pulled the card George had given him out of his pocket and looked at it, really looked at it for the first time. It was wrinkled and dirty and it looked like it had been in his pocket for months, even though it had only been in there for a few days. He thought about what they were offering. It was a good deal. And there was no reason he couldn't try. He was so tired, he couldn't even be tired anymore. And he had been trying to die as long as he could remember and suddenly he was tired even of that. He had always told himself that he was born tired of living. But maybe he just felt that way because of what he had been born into.

He stood up straight and continued toward home. He began to smile. His hands were shaking, and he felt like he was ninety years old, and he knew he looked and smelled bad. But he had a phone number, and he was a human being, he was finally a human being.

He looked at the people passing him, the white people, the black people, the Latinos who thought they were Spanish but who were usually Indian, and there was something beautiful about them, and they began to glow as the sun went down, and it felt like that thing that his grandmother was always talking about was coming into him, that Native American Church stuff, hozhoni, that she was always going on about. Whenever his Shimásáni would talk about it, his mother would roll her eyes and say that it was useless shit, superstition, and his grandmother would shake her head. Once, when his mother had left him with her for a week, Grandmother had arranged for a ceremony. He barely remembered anything but his grandmother's face, happy, and the feeling of joy that seemed to live in all of the people praying. He felt that now again, joy for the first time in longer than he could remember, and more than joy, a good, strong peace.

"There you are you fucker, we been looking for you," he heard behind him and his heart stilled. He began to walk faster, and he heard collective laughter. The collective laughter of a number of boys, laughter he recognized.

"You fucking wetback, you think you can outrun us? You can't run for shit," he heard, and he stopped. They were right. He turned around. Facing him were the boys that had harassed him earlier that day.

They walked closer, the boy who had been the ringleader heading the pack. Before they were a foot from him, Matthew could smell the alcohol on them. He was silent.

"We been looking for you all day," the boy said. Matthew could see dark shadows under his eyes.

"Aren't you going to say something, you fucking Mexican? Aren't you going to speak some, you know, fucking Spanish at me and call me a fucking whitey in your language or something?" The guy was practically listing, he was so drunk. His friends laughed.

"Yeah, like blanco or something," a boy behind him said.

Matthew was silent. And then they moved.

As Matthew died, he thought about that day in Albuquerque, where they always went to pick up drugs, where he had made love to Maria, where he and Chris had laughed. He thought about the bum who had looked at him and said that Chris was going to die. And he thought about the fact that he had thought that he was going to die that day, and later, about how Chris had died instead, just like the bum had said. He thought about his mother, and her face, how beautiful it was when she would sleep, when she would pass out in front of the television, stinking of beer, the light playing on her face, peaceful for such a short time. Maria's eyes had been like that, like his mother's. He remembered thinking that the first time he saw her sleeping. He thought about his Shimásáni, about her wonderful long brown arms, how safe and loved he had felt in them. About the beautiful woman he had seen at the bottom of the trashcan such a short time ago. He

241

thought about how Damien was *not* going to die, about how he was going to write poems about all of this. He wondered about his sister, and right as the light went out, he wondered about what it would have been like to go to the place the card had described, he wondered about what it would have been like to live, to truly live, and to want to. And he smiled.